GONE BY NIGHTFALL

Gone
by
Nightfall

DEE GARRETSON

Swoon READS

SWOON READS · NEW YORK

A Swoon Reads Book

An imprint of Feiwel and Friends and Macmillan Publishing Group, LLC
120 Broadway, New York, NY 10271

Our books may be purchased in bulk for promotional, educational, or business use. Please
contact your local bookseller or the Macmillan Corporate and Premium Sales Department at
(800) 221-7945 ext. 5442 or by email at MacmillanSpecialMarkets@macmillan.com.

Library of Congress Control Number: 2019940968
ISBN 978-1-250-24522-9 (hardcover) / ISBN 978-1-250-24523-6 (ebook)

Book design by Liz Dresner

First edition, 2020

10 9 8 7 6 5 4 3 2 1

swoonreads.com

To my nieces and nephews, Heidi, Matt, Mark, and Jessie
You've been an important part of my life.

Chapter One

I PULLED THE collar of my coat close around my face as I sneaked between the sleighs and automobiles parked in front of the grand duke's house, hoping I could get beyond the light of the braziers before our coachman spotted me. If Yermak saw me, he'd want to know why I was leaving the ball early and without my stepfather.

No one inside would miss me. The partygoers were too busy sharing the latest rumors swirling around the czar and the czarina. And even though I liked dancing, the choice of partners was limited to friends of my stepfather, or staff officers who had wrangled headquarters jobs for themselves to keep away from the fighting. For some reason those men felt the need to constantly remind one of their great wisdom and wit.

Sewing up a saber cut is not like embroidering a handkerchief, my dear Miss Mason! You should stay with your nursing instead of trying to become a doctor, though you should really attend to soldiers instead of working in that absurd hospital for women. I must say, you American girls find the strangest ways to occupy your time!

The captain who had made this pronouncement about my future was so pleased with himself that I wished I'd had a suture needle handy. I would have sewn the ends of his overly long mustache to his overly bushy eyebrows before he knew what was happening. I hoped by the time I returned, he'd have found another victim to bore.

The sounds of the orchestra faded as I walked away toward the square, picking up my pace as I moved into the darkened streets. The snow had tapered off, so I was at least able to see where to put my next step. I loved Petrograd during the day, when the sun shone on the beautiful buildings painted in a dazzling array of pastels, but at night the city changed. Then the silent buildings felt more like giant tombs, and I could never forget the story visitors were told: that the city was built on bones, the skeletons of a hundred thousand serfs who were forced to erect a city on a swamp, all to please the ego of a czar.

I breathed easier when I saw Znamenskaya Square ahead of me. Since it was nearly two a.m., the square was mostly empty, though there were a few groups huddled around small fires, refugees who had poured into the city from the war zones with nowhere to go and no money to procure a bed or even a warm spot on a floor.

When I reached the entrance to the hospital, I didn't see the dark shape standing outside the circle of light the streetlamp cast until I heard a soft voice that made me jump.

"Charlotte, I'm here," Raisa said as she moved into the light.

"You were holding so still I didn't see you." I put my hand on my chest. "I think my heart skipped a beat or two."

She laughed, a sound I hadn't heard from her for a long time. "Then my practice has paid off. Tell your brothers I've been working at staying still so I can be a better vanishing lady in your magic show. When we're able to practice again, I want to be ready."

"I'll tell them," I said, though it was a bit of a struggle for me to imagine a future that included amusing ourselves with our little family circus again.

She loosened the shawl that was draped around her head, shaking off the snow. "I want you to teach me the trick of pulling a rabbit out of a hat, too. I promised my sister I would show her that when I see her again."

"We'll have to recruit some new rabbits," I said. "Mr. Hatter and Miss Fluff have grown too big to fit in a hat. They spend all day lazing around their pen being spoiled now."

Raisa smiled, but then a shiver overtook her, and she wrapped her arms around herself. I noticed that her gloves had holes in them. I knew I wouldn't be able to get her to take mine, but next time I'd bring her another pair, some that had been my mother's. She wouldn't refuse those.

"Come into the hospital and get warm," I urged. "We can talk a little. It's been weeks." I'd missed her so much, and I didn't know when we'd be able to meet again.

"I wish I could, but I don't want anyone inside to see me."

"There is only a night nurse on duty. We can trust her. You'll be safe, I promise."

"You don't know that." She lowered her voice. "People are so desperate, they'll try to sell any information they have to the Okhrana for a few kopeks."

Even the mention of the Okhrana, the secret police everyone feared, sent a shiver down my back. I knew the nurses were on my side, but I understood why Raisa didn't trust people she didn't know. Her father had been betrayed by one of his own employees and sent to prison for speaking against the czar inside his own newspaper office.

Raisa pulled a chamois bag out of her pocket and gave it to me, the bottles inside clinking together. "It's only four. I was afraid to take more."

"Four is more than I'd hoped for! We ran out of the last of our laudanum yesterday, and we don't have anything else that helps with the patients' pain. Are you sure your uncle won't notice?"

"He won't. I changed the inventory numbers, and he's usually so drunk he can't remember what he has." She shuddered. "It's amazing he still has any patients left at all. I wouldn't let him near me if I was sick. The fumes from his breath would be enough to finish me off."

I hated that she had to live with that man. I knew she wasn't even allowed to practice her music anymore, because her uncle said the noise of the piano irritated him. "I wish you would come stay with us," I said. "You could find another job, or if you can't, the offer for you to be the twins' governess still stands. The two of them are too much for their poor nursemaid."

Even in the faint glow of the streetlights, I could see her face take on the fierce look she so often wore. "You know I don't take charity," she said. "And I would be a terrible governess. Besides, I have to stay in good graces with my uncle so he'll keep sending my mother and my sister money. He says he's sure they are wasting what he sends them, though I know from my mother's letters he's only giving them a pittance. I can't give them anything at all, so I can't make him angry."

If I believed in curses, I would have put a particularly potent one on the man. Just when I thought he couldn't get any worse, he found a way. "Have you heard any word about your father?" I asked.

"The guard who takes the bundles of food I bring him said he is all right, though his hands are swollen with rheumatism." She brushed at her face and I knew she was trying to get rid of a tear. Raisa hated crying. According to her, it served no purpose, so she didn't allow it. I pretended not to notice, because I knew she wouldn't want me to. Better to talk of something else.

"Where is your uncle getting the laudanum?" I asked. "It's dangerous for you to keep taking it. Maybe I can go directly to his source."

"He's got a friend at one of the embassies who has them brought into the country in the diplomatic bags. I don't know which embassy."

An embassy contact didn't do me any good. Even if Raisa could find out who it was, I doubted they'd admit to their black-market work unless I could offer far more money than I had to get in on it.

"I need to get back if I'm going to get any sleep tonight." Raisa reached into her pocket and pulled out a small book. "I brought this for you to give to Miles. It has some poems he might like."

I tried not to show my surprise at the gift. I had thought Raisa had gotten over her infatuation with my brother months ago. Raisa was so sure of everything that she couldn't comprehend Miles wouldn't return her regard. She didn't seem to realize he barely noticed her, and I didn't want to hurt her by pointing that out.

"How is he?" she asked. "He looked fine when I saw him, but I know that doesn't mean much."

"When did you see him?" He hadn't mentioned it to me.

"I . . . I ran into him on Nevsky."

"Oh," I said. That was an odd place for Miles to frequent. Nevsky Prospekt was Petrograd's main shopping street, and I couldn't imagine Miles actually shopping. He expected most things to appear before him as if by actual magic. "He's been better this winter than last, at least."

"I'm glad." She looked around before she spoke again, even though we were all alone. "When revolution comes and my father is let out, Miles can come work for the newspaper. He's such a good writer, and I'm sure his health will improve when he can do something he likes."

Raisa sounded so sure about revolution, but I didn't know what to believe. It felt like we were in limbo, where just one act could tip us one way or the other. If she and I had had more time, I would have asked her what rumors she'd heard about the political situation. Even stuck at her uncle's, she seemed to hear far more than I ever did.

"Thank you again for the medicine," I said, taking off one glove to get the bundle of rubles out of it.

As I handed the money to her, a voice called, "You there. What are you doing out here?"

I turned around, trying to block the view of whoever it was so Raisa could put the money away. At first the man's black uniform blended into the night so that his white face was like a specter hovering toward us. As he got closer to us, I realized he was a policeman, one of the regular force, not the secret one.

My heart sped up. I wished there were more people around, even though I doubted anyone would be brave enough to intervene if he decided he wanted to arrest us.

He came too close, towering over me. I forced myself to stand still, though the smell of him made me want to gag. He stank of bad teeth and pickled fish.

"What are you girls doing out here this late?" I knew he was trying to figure out where we ranked in the hierarchy of Petrograd society. If he noticed Raisa's threadbare coat, he might very well haul us in. A certain class of not-too-poor people often found themselves in holding cells, bargaining to be let out, under the threat that they'd be charged as nihilists agitating against the czar if they couldn't pay a small bribe. The police knew those people wouldn't go to anyone higher up to complain, so the officers could pocket the money themselves.

I didn't want him to notice the bag, either. The laudanum wasn't illegal, but if he saw the bottles, it would only lead to more questions.

The police were always on the lookout for any signs of black-market activities.

I needed a distraction to hide the bag. It would have been a good time to pull a rabbit out of my dress, but since I didn't have a bunny handy, I did the only thing I could think of.

I took a step back and then acted as if I'd lost my footing on the slippery snow, dropping the book and flailing my arms. The book fell down by my feet and I screeched as loudly as I could, pretending I was in incredible distress at having dropped it. The sound of the bottles knocking against one another was so faint compared to my other noises that even I couldn't hear it as I reached down to pick the book up, stuffing the bag in the top of one of my boots at the same time. The boots were the traditional Russian felt ones that were big enough for a dozen bottles.

I straightened up and brushed the snow off the book. "I don't think it's damaged," I said, hugging it to my chest. "But how clumsy of me."

"You didn't answer my question," the man said, his tone a bit more menacing. "Who are you?"

I stuck my nose in the air and tried to sound snobbish. "I'm Charlotte Mason, General Cherkassky's stepdaughter. My mother founded this hospital, and my friend and I are stopping in to check on a patient."

The man contemplated that as if weighing whether or not to believe me. "English?" he asked.

"No, American."

"Your Russian is very good for an American." I heard the suspicion in his voice.

"I've lived here a long time."

"I've heard that name . . ." His voice trailed off.

"Of course you have. General Cherkassky is a war hero," Raisa said.

"No." He stared at me. "Something in a report about a redheaded girl named Mason."

My breath stopped. It was extremely unlikely there were any other redheaded girls named Mason in Petrograd. I couldn't be on a police report. The only people who knew about my various black-market arrangements would never tell. He had to be bluffing, to try to scare me into paying him a bribe to forget he'd seen me. I clenched my teeth together, determined not to let him see my fear.

"You say this is a hospital?" The policeman looked up at the building. "It doesn't have a sign on it. It looks like a house to me."

"It's a small hospital," I said. "There's a plaque by the door. It was a house, but my mother turned it into a hospital." I decided I had to take some action to get rid of him. The longer he talked to us, the more likely we were to say the wrong thing.

"Good night," I said. "We need to get inside." I put my arm in Raisa's and pulled her up the steps, my shoulders tensing as I waited to hear if the policeman would call for us to stop.

He didn't, and when I pushed open the door, I felt the tension ease. I didn't look back to see what he was doing, and once I shut the door, I leaned against it in relief.

"I'll just tell the night nurse I'm here so she knows it's not a new patient," I said to Raisa, "and then we can go out the back door, but now that we're in, you can at least stay for a minute. The fire will be lit in the sitting room, and it will be warmer in there."

She nodded, so I took the bottles to the night nurse and gave them to her to log in. The nurses were used to me coming and going at all hours bringing various supplies, and we were in such desperate need that they never asked questions.

When I went into the sitting room, I got a look at Raisa in a stronger light and was shocked at how thin she'd gotten. Her cheeks seemed almost caved in, her neck too fragile to hold up her head.

"You can't save all your food for your father," I scolded. "You have to eat too! He wouldn't want you to starve yourself."

"I know. Don't lecture, please. Every time I take a bite, I think of how hungry he must be, and that spoils the food for me." She sighed and leaned her head back against the chair. "Two years ago, I never imagined how much I'd think about bread. Now I think about it every day, how to get it and how to hide it." Her fingers moved up and down on the arm of the chair as if she were playing the piano. "Back then if I thought about the future it was to imagine I'd be getting ready to perform my first public concert, and you would be in medical school, already on your way to making great discoveries."

I didn't really want to talk about the past. "We were silly school-girls back then. We should have known that plans don't always work out, especially when war changes everything."

"I think about those days," she said in a dreamy sort of voice, one I'd never heard from her before. "About how I didn't have anything to worry about except practicing enough so my teacher wouldn't get angry at me. And I think about how much I loved going to your house after school. Your mother was always so kind to me, asking me questions as if every detail of my life was so important to her."

Raisa closed her eyes as her fingers moved up and down again, like she was playing heavy chords faster and faster. Then in one quick movement she was back on her feet and back to herself. "Enough of all that. I want to talk about you."

"Me? Why? There's nothing to talk about."

She came over and sat down next to me. "Yes, there is. You shouldn't be doing this, putting yourself at risk to get medicine for the hospital. I know the hospital was important to your mother, but you need to think about you. Even though I don't want you to go, you have to get away from Russia. Pavel is dead, and you staying here won't bring him back. Go to America and visit your grandmother. She can't be as bad as you say she is. Or travel. Your stepfather would give you the money." She grabbed my hand, and when she spoke again, her voice was almost frantic. "Other people can manage the hospital and take care of your little sisters. Your mother would want you to go. She was always saying don't let the past hold you back."

I didn't understand why she was so upset. "Raisa, don't fret about me. You have enough to worry about."

She bit her lip, and I saw that her eyes were full of unshed tears. "I do worry about you. You don't have to have your life ruined because of the war. I'm afraid it's going to drag on and on, and everything is just going to get worse and worse."

I wanted to cover my ears and pretend I hadn't heard her. She of all people should have understood I'd never leave my family. "No, the hospital is important to me too, and I'm sticking to my plan." I wanted to remind her it was the plan she had encouraged me to make, back when we thought writing down our future would make it become a reality. "My mother's death isn't going to stop me from going to medical school. And the war isn't going to stop me either. Besides, I barely remember the United States. This is my home."

"You wouldn't have to go away forever. When do you have time to study with all you do? The entrance exam is brutal. And missing the last year of school is going to make it that much harder for you."

I should have known she would keep pressing me. Raisa was relentless when she got an idea in her head. I tried one more time. "I do study on my own at night when I get back from the hospital." I didn't say that most nights I only managed a few paragraphs in my

Greek or Latin textbook before I fell asleep. "And as soon as I manage to find a governess for the twins, I'll have more time to study."

I looked over at the clock on the table. "I have to get back. It's getting late," I said as I pulled my hand out of hers and stood up. This hadn't been the kind of talk I'd hoped we would have.

"You sound angry," Raisa said. "Don't be, please."

"I'm not angry. It's . . . it's just . . ."

"It's just you don't like to be told what you should do." She jumped up and hugged me. "I know you. I'll stop, but think about what I said. And give everyone my love."

We went out the back door, both of us acting as if we'd see each other soon. Raisa darted away, and I turned back to the grand duke's house, trying to concentrate on the task at hand. I had to get back into the party without anyone noticing I'd been gone.

Chapter Two

I DECIDED THAT if anyone saw me coming back in to the ball, I could say I'd felt a little faint and needed some air. I hoped no one would question that, even though the temperature outside was well below zero, the kind of air that took your breath away rather than gave it back to you.

The two footmen by the front door were polite enough to act as if they didn't notice I'd walked in shivering with cold and carrying a book I hadn't had when I left. I went into the little sitting room off the hall that had been set aside as the women's cloakroom and left my coat, my boots, and the book there and put my dance slippers back on. I'd be too noticeable if I wandered the party looking for my stepfather all bundled up.

Back out in the hall, the scent of the orchids was so strong it made my head ache. The grand duchess had gone overboard with the flowers, as if filling the house with a jungle of them could make the partygoers forget the bitter cold and the war raging not so far away. There were so many, she had to have ordered several heated railroad cars to bring bushels of them into the city from the southern greenhouses, taking up space that should have been used for food supplies.

I was about to go back to the ballroom when I heard the voice of the obnoxious captain I'd been forced to listen to earlier, so I darted behind a pillar wrapped in a garland of orchids. I listened as his voice moved away from me and toward the door, hopefully on his way out.

A little voice came from above me, startling me so much I bumped into the pillar, crushing several orchids and releasing yet more fragrance.

"Charlotte, why are you hiding?"

I looked up to see the grand duke's youngest granddaughter, Anna Andreevna, wearing her nightdress and peering through the railings of the staircase.

"Are you playing a game?" the girl asked. "Can I play too?"

I put my finger to my lips. "I am playing a game, but it's hard to hide in this dress. I'm waiting for a man to leave the party."

"Why?" She was five, the same age as my little sisters, so I should have known she'd want a reason.

"I don't like him very much."

Anna stood up. "You don't have a very good hiding place," she said in a loud whisper. "I always hide under a bed. Do you want me to show you a good spot upstairs?"

I was actually tempted. A nice quiet spot under a bed would mean I could sleep for a few hours undisturbed before I had to meet Ivan coming in from the country with food supplies for the hospital. Probably not the best idea to take a nap, though. "No, but thank you anyway. Next time I bring the twins over, you can show me."

I peeked around the pillar to see the captain going out the door.

"That's not the man who was looking for you before," Anna said.

"I don't think there is anyone else who would be looking for me."

"There was," she insisted. "The man asked the footmen and said your name and described you. They said they hadn't seen you. He had a mean face. I think you should hide from him, too."

Bless the footmen. I didn't know why they hadn't given me away, but I was thankful they hadn't. I had no idea why a different man would have been looking for me, and I couldn't really think of anyone I'd danced with who had a face Anna would call mean. And none of the men had been that interested in me besides the captain, who would have talked to a pillar if it had been wearing a dress. Even if I had wanted a suitor, which I didn't, I'd be unlikely to attract one. My red hair, freckles, and sturdy frame did not measure up to any standard of beauty in Russian society. And besides that, my mother's reputation preceded me.

Everyone assumed I would follow in the footsteps of my mother: an American actress labeled a gold digger for bewitching an elderly Russian count into marriage and adding her three unruly American children into the bargain. The mothers of marriageable sons were particularly wary of me after Pavel showed an interest, and when the war took him, they saw me as a continuing threat to the others. I couldn't exactly shout at them that I didn't want their sons, that I had other plans, which didn't involve marriage. Pavel had been a little like a dream out of nowhere, and I had no desire for anything like that to happen again, at least not for years and years.

Anna forgot to whisper. "Is the party almost over? Are there any chocolates left? The chocolate mice looked very good. Mama said I could have some if there were any left, but I'm afraid they'll all be gone." Her mouth turned down. "The musicians are allowed to eat after the guests leave, and they always eat everything. I promised I'd bring Nadia some if I could."

"Who is Nadia?" I asked. I thought it was probably the name of a doll and Anna Andreevna wanted the chocolate mice for herself. It was a scheme my sisters would try.

The girl twirled one of her braids. "Nadia is the new helper in the nursery. She's very nice. She doesn't pull my hair when she brushes it. She's never had chocolate mice."

The taste of a chocolate mouse from one of Petrograd's best chocolatiers was something everyone should experience. "We'll have to make sure she gets one," I told Anna. "I'll go look and bring a plate of them if there are any left." If there was enough, I could have one too. A bit of chocolate might tamp down the ache in my head. After that, I could go in search of my stepfather and try to get him away from the card table.

"Hurry!" Anna clutched the railing. "I don't hear the music anymore. The orchestra will be there any minute!"

The supper room was empty when I went in, but I knew that as soon as the musicians had finished packing up their instruments, they'd be here. Grabbing a plate, I scanned the tables. There had been no skimping on the choices. Even though the party was nearly over, platters full of smoked salmon, eel, and smelts interspersed with bowls of caviar still filled the tables. If I hadn't been aware of the severe food shortages crippling the city, I'd never have guessed it from the display of abundance.

I realized what had bothered me about the room when I'd been in it earlier in the evening. The artful displays of white roses and ferns cascading down the walls behind the tables were supposed to give the illusion of a series of waterfalls, but they more closely resembled the shrouds we used at the hospital to cover the dead. The fishy smells from the food mixed with the heavy scent of the roses and made my stomach do a little twist. I hurried to fill the plate so I could leave.

No chocolate mice remained on the dessert table, but there were plenty of bonbons. I selected a variety of flavors, piling the plate high. Even without adorable little eyes and ears and tails, the bonbons would taste just as good as the mice.

I was about to go back to Anna when I spotted one lone chocolate mouse that had fallen off a tray. It was missing a tail, but I thought Nadia wouldn't mind. I put it on the very top of the pile.

I heard the clicking of boots behind me. Someone else had entered the room, and the clicking meant someone in uniform, which meant a man.

Baron Eristov, one of the czar's closest military advisers and some sort of cousin to my stepfather, came up to the table and stood right next to me. I hadn't expected to see him at a party, not with the war going so badly. He should have been at the front. We'd lost so many men; every last soldier was needed there. The baron and I had never actually spoken beyond a long-ago introduction, so I assumed I could just give the man a polite nod as I left the room.

I nearly dropped the plate when he spoke. "There you are, Miss Mason. I've been looking for you. I was hoping for a chance to have a private talk with you."

His expression was grim, not the look you'd see on the face of someone who wanted a social chat. Some found the baron handsome, but he'd always repulsed me. Everything about his face was as if someone had drawn in his features with thin lines, except for his mouth. His lips were too big and too pale, like slugs that had been plucked from the ground. I closed my eyes for a second, willing another image into my head before the thought of slugs made my stomach twist again.

When I opened my eyes, he leaned in close and motioned to my plate. "I know Count Cherkassky's gambling debts are building up and his money is being wasted at that ridiculous hospital, but I didn't know he was putting his household on such lean rations that you must fill up at parties."

I felt the heat rise in my cheeks. I wanted to snap at his rudeness, but I suspected he was bringing up my stepfather's debts to make me react. I wasn't going to give him the satisfaction. I couldn't keep quiet about his slur on the hospital, though. "Women need medical care just as much as men, even with a war on," I said.

He made a snorting sound and then took hold of my elbow. "Shall we sit? I believe you'll want to hear what I have to say."

I was too curious to say no, so I let him guide me to one of the small tables set about the room. As soon as I sat down and put the plate on the table, he began to speak. "I'll get right to the point. Your stepfather doesn't need the aggravation of three nearly grown step-children, especially not ones such as yourselves and at such a time. You should leave Russia, you and your brothers."

Not ones such as yourselves. The contempt in those words was like an actual slap to my face.

I clasped my hands together so I wouldn't make throttling motions with my fingers. "I don't think you are the one to determine what my stepfather needs or doesn't need."

"And you are?" The snorting sound came again. "Not from what I've seen of your actions. You and your brothers are bringing down the reputation of the Cherkassky family by associating with the wrong sort of people."

"Which people?" I suspected I already knew the answer.

"The Tamm family and their disreputable theater." He paused as if he expected me to protest. When I said nothing, he continued. "I suppose it all seems rather daring, especially for a young girl, to attend their parties and meet the radicals who associate with them, but you need to stay away. All the talk of revolution will come to nothing, and in the meantime your connection with them is drawing too much attention."

"I've met no radicals at the Tamms'." Not exactly, anyway. I didn't add I had heard the same talk that was everywhere, the endless gossip about the precarious state of the monarchy. We all wanted change. As much as I loved Russia, there were some parts that were terrible. We wanted more freedoms for women, more elected officials who actually had some power, and a change in the laws that allowed the horrific oppression of Jewish people, so, yes, we talked of it, but if I said anything, it would make him more suspicious.

"Why are you worried about our reputation?" I asked. I had no intention of giving up visiting the Tamms, but I was curious as to why the baron was involving himself in our lives.

The man sneered. "I care nothing for *your* reputation, little girl. Your stepfather's gambling debts are a problem, but he is a loyal supporter of the czar. However, when you associate with radicals, you become of interest to the Okhrana, and therefore your stepfather draws their interest too. Given the past history of the family, that could be very dangerous."

Hearing mention of the Okhrana twice in one night made my palms start to sweat in my gloves. I didn't understand what he meant about the "past history." My stepfather had served in the army with great distinction as one of its top generals, and my mother had been completely uninterested in politics.

I heard someone come into the room. The baron leaned in even more and put his arm over the back of my chair. I forced myself not to cringe away from him. I knew he was trying to intimidate me.

When he spoke again, his voice was so low I knew he didn't want anyone else to hear. "I realize girls are not interested in politics, but the situation is very precarious right now," he said. "We must do everything we can to ensure stability if we are to win the war. Even though your stepfather is retired, he is still a notable figure, and unfortunately, he has enemies who have not forgotten the past. He must be seen to be unwavering in his support of the czar. If you care for him at all, you won't want to be a burden on him."

His eyes were so fixed on me, I felt my mouth go dry. Did he want me to reassure him that there were no treasonous thoughts allowed in our house? What if the baron was part of the secret police himself? I wouldn't put it past him to have some devious plan in mind to trap me. He could report any response I made.

"Thank you for your concern," I managed to choke out.

A group of men came in, talking in loud voices. I shifted away from the baron to get a look. It was the orchestra. They ignored us as they surrounded the food tables.

The baron reached into a pocket and pulled out a folded piece of paper. He set it on the table. "Look at the quote from the American and then show this to the Tamms. See what they say. Then burn it until there is nothing left but ash."

I picked up the paper and unfolded it. As soon as I understood what it was, I dropped it on the table, wanting to wipe my gloves on my dress as if the words had leaped off the paper and were stuck to me, screaming for everyone to read. Being in possession of a paper calling for the overthrow of the czar could get me arrested. Even sitting at a table next to such a paper could be grounds for arrest.

He pushed it toward me and smiled as if he was pleased with my reaction. "I suggest you read it all." I picked it up again. It was in Russian, but as I skimmed it, I saw what the baron had been referring to. One line stood out. *As the American Patrick Henry said in his country's successful bid for freedom, give me liberty or give me death!*

I recognized the name Patrick Henry. I was a bit shaky on American history because not much of it had been taught in the French and Russian schools I'd attended, but my brother Miles had many books on the American Revolution. He had gone through a phase where he'd describe in excruciating detail seemingly every day of the fight for liberty. We'd had to beg him to stop talking.

Did the baron think I knew who had written it because it quoted an American? That was absurd. There were thousands of Americans in Petrograd and hundreds who spoke Russian well enough to write such a thing.

"Remember, you never know who is spying on you," he said. "Don't trust anyone. And you should think about how much easier your life would be in America. You don't belong here." He stood up and nodded to me, then walked out of the room without another word.

As soon as he was gone, the full implication of his words hit me, almost taking away my breath. Even though I doubted the Tamms had anything to do with the flyer, if the Okhrana suspected them of revolutionary activities, my association with them turned the spotlight on me too, and that meant they might put spies on me as well. So far my black-market arrangements for the hospital were secret, but it would be harder to keep them that way if I was under scrutiny.

But why give me a note to show to the Tamms while warning me away from them? I couldn't decide if it would be safer to leave it where it lay or take it away with me. I rubbed my temples, feeling the ache come back. I needed to be away from this party so I could think.

I folded up the paper as small as I could and tried to put it into the top of my glove, but my hand was trembling so much I dropped it instead and it fell to the floor.

Before I could reach for it, another hand appeared and picked it up. I looked up to see a young man in the dazzling white dress uniform of the Imperial Horse Guard standing in front of me. His image wavered and the room grew hotter. I closed my eyes, and when I opened them again, I realized I was not seeing a ghost. Pavel would never come back, not even as a spirit, since he was buried a long way away in an unknown grave on a battlefield.

This young man was not nearly as tall as Pavel had been, though he had the same blondish hair and dark eyes. The line of his jaw wasn't quite as square, and there was something about him that made him look out of place in the uniform, though I couldn't pinpoint what that was.

He held out the paper. I snatched it out of his hand and squeezed my own tight around it as if it were going to somehow jump out and open by itself.

I saw a shudder pass through him, and I noticed he had a cane gripped in his other hand. His fingers were very long and white against the ebony of the cane, and he wore a gold ring with some sort of bird on it. It was only then that I noticed a bulky bandage around one of his knees.

"Where did you come from?" I blurted out.

"I've been sitting over there." He pointed behind me, and I twisted around to see a small table nearly hidden by some of the potted plants. He motioned to his leg. "Dancing does not agree with me at the moment."

The table wasn't close enough that he could have overheard the baron and me, which was a relief. Nevertheless, I wished this young man would go away.

"You managed to get a chocolate mouse," he said, motioning to my plate. "Lucky you. Those were my sister's favorites." His stared down at the plate of chocolates as if transfixed by them.

I didn't know what to do. I couldn't just snap my fingers to get his attention or get up and leave. "Would you like one?"

He gave a start and turned his gaze back to me; then his eyes flicked to the paper. So he'd seen the baron give it to me.

I felt the dampness in my palms again.

He shifted his weight, another shudder passing through him. When he spoke, I could tell it was taking some effort for him to get the words out. "I see you are acquainted with Baron Eristov. Have you heard the old saying 'Be friends with the wolf but keep one hand on the ax'? In the baron's case, I'd make that two hands, and I'd also make sure the ax was very sharp."

In another circumstance I might have been interested to hear what he knew about the baron. With a piece of treason in my hand, I didn't want to say anything that would encourage him to continue talking.

I stood and picked up the plate with my other hand. "I have to be going now."

"Wait, if you could give me just a moment," he said. "I wanted to meet you earlier, but I couldn't find anyone to do a proper introduction and I couldn't ask you to dance. I'd like to talk to you."

As I walked away, I called back over my shoulder, "I'm sorry, I really have to be going. Perhaps next time." I knew I was being very rude, but I didn't need to get to know any more handsome young soldiers who would disappear within weeks. I couldn't play the game of pretending everything was fine, writing them cheerful letters, waiting for them to return in triumph, and then have my heart ripped out and crushed when news came of their death. No more. One had been enough. And I didn't need any distractions. Keeping the hospital open while staying out of the hands of the Okhrana was more than enough to occupy me.

Chapter Three

WHEN I GOT back to the hall, Anna was waiting at the bottom of the staircase.

"I thought you weren't coming!" she said.

I handed her the plate and then tucked the paper into my glove, making sure it was pushed down far enough not to fall out. "I'm sorry. It took longer than I thought. There was only one chocolate mouse, but I'm sure Nadia will like the other chocolates. You'd better hurry up to bed before someone catches you."

"Thank you, Charlotte! Nadia will love these!" The little girl smiled and then headed up the stairs, carrying the plate carefully. I watched her, hoping Nadia actually got to eat the chocolates. If the governess found them, Anna would be scolded, and Nadia would get nothing.

A group of people came into the hall, heading for the cloakrooms. From the lack of sound coming from the ballroom, there couldn't be too many guests left. Before I could go in search of my stepfather, he appeared from a drawing room off the hall, leaning on one of his old friends, who was struggling to support him.

I rushed toward them. "What's wrong? Papa, are you ill?"

He nearly fell, almost bringing both of them down.

"He appears to have had a little too much to drink," his friend Prince Shulga said as he struggled to regain his footing. The prince was even older than my stepfather and not in good health.

I thought I hadn't heard him correctly at first. My stepfather never drank to excess.

"There you are, dear Lise." My stepfather smiled at me and then shook his head. "How do you stay so young-looking when I have gotten to be such an old man?" His expression changed to a frown, and a tear ran down his face.

A chill ran through me. Lise had been my mother's name. I looked nothing like her, and she'd been gone for over a year.

"Time to go home," the prince said. "Perhaps we old men should not drink so much nor stay at the card table so long."

"I'm not drunk," my stepfather replied, his words slurring. "Tell Sasha I'll pay him tomorrow. And tell the baron to send the young man over to the house tomorrow morning. No sense in waiting."

"Yes, yes, old friend. Come along now."

I hurried to get our coats but fumbled putting my own on. I couldn't concentrate on buttons. Papa hadn't recognized me. He couldn't be ill. We'd only just managed to find a way to go on after my mother's death.

I reminded myself that I was a nurse and I should pull myself together. I was not going to panic.

The prince and I helped him into his coat and then out to our sleigh, where the coachman, Yermak, lifted him inside. Thank goodness Yermak had the size and strength of a bear. He acted as if he were lifting a child. My stepfather leaned back and closed his eyes.

"Is the general ill?" Yermak whispered to me.

"I don't know," I said, covering my stepfather with a fur from the pile on the seat. "Let's get him home and we can decide if he needs a doctor."

My stepfather roused himself for a moment. "I've made arrangements . . ." A snore finished his sentence and he slumped back again. I wrapped the fur blanket more tightly around him. Maybe he was just overtired. He wouldn't admit he was growing old. We shouldn't have stayed so late. We shouldn't even have come to the party, but he had insisted, saying I needed to get away from the hospital more.

As we drove away, I studied his face as if it would reveal what ailed him. Were we actually a burden to him? He'd never acted as if we were. He'd never once suggested my brothers and I should leave. He'd been wonderful to us from the very first day we met. I wished I were already in medical school and had some training. My exposure to medicine consisted of taking care of my brothers and sisters when they were ill and my nursing training at the hospital, which was mostly for women who had gone through difficult childbirths.

He'd never mistaken me for my mother before. Even if it turned out to be the ill effects of drink, I decided I'd send for the doctor anyway.

My stepfather coughed and struggled to sit up straighter. "Lise, we should have a picnic tomorrow," he said, smiling at me. "The children can hunt for mushrooms in the forest."

I clenched my hands together and tried to keep my voice from wavering. "We'll see," I said. We definitely needed a doctor.

When we reached home, the butler and the footman put my stepfather to bed while Yermak went for the doctor. The doctor arrived, grumbling about the lateness of the hour. I told the man all about the confusion and the stumbling, mentioning possible causes, but the doctor didn't make any comment.

He made me wait outside in the hall while he examined Papa. When the doctor came out, he said, "Your stepfather is fine, but he's an old man who shouldn't be out gallivanting at all hours of the night. *I'm* an old man. I shouldn't be out on calls all hours of the night just to reassure nervous girls. You should have asked the house-keeper her opinion about his condition. She may not be trained as a nurse, but she's seen far more illness than you."

"She was asleep," I explained as I followed him down the stairs. "What about my stepfather calling me by my mother's name? Why would he do that?"

"I'm sure it was just a slip of the tongue. Send a note tomorrow if he isn't better, though I'm sure he will be."

Once he was out the door, I went back upstairs not as reassured as I hoped I'd be. I decided I'd still talk to Dr. Rushailo when I got to the hospital in the morning. My stepfather would never consent to having a female doctor examine him, but she would be able to help me determine if there was something else I should do.

I walked to my room as the familiar pang hit me, the one where I wished I could talk to my mother. Right before she died, she asked me to promise that I'd take care of everyone. I'd said I would, not thinking at the time what that meant. I hadn't even considered that I'd have to worry about my stepfather, and I'd just assumed that so many things took care of themselves, not realizing exactly how much my mother had done both with the hospital and at home. Every time I thought I had one problem solved, two more would appear. Dropping out of school had helped, though that hadn't worked out exactly the way I'd expected either.

I'd been so naive not to realize that a war would make getting food and medicine so difficult, and I'd certainly never expected to have to worry about the Okhrana.

I wished the baron had never given me that piece of paper. I took it out of my glove and put it inside my Greek book. No one would pick up the book except me, so it was a safe hiding place until I could show it to the Tamms.

Once I closed the book, I thought I'd be able to take my mind off the paper, but it was as if I could see the words through the pages. I grabbed the book and put it on the top shelf of the armoire, then shut the door on it and made myself go to bed. I pushed the paper out of my mind by making a list in my head of things I needed to do the next day. I got to ten before I fell asleep.

I woke up to someone shaking my arm.

"Wake up, Lottie! Wake up! You've been sleeping for hours and hours and hours!" I recognized my sister Nika's voice.

When I opened my eyes, I could tell from the weak light slanting through the window that I had in fact not been sleeping for hours and hours. Maybe three at the most. I closed them again.

I felt Nika move closer, and then she used her fingers to pry open one of my eyelids. "I know you are in there," she said. "Don't go back to sleep. Did you meet a husband last night?" I opened the other eye. She was inches from my face. If Nika was in my room, then her twin, Sophie, had to be there as well, and sure enough, when I looked at the end of the bed, I saw her.

"Polina says she has a potion you can use if you find one you want to catch," Sophie said. "You sneak it into his tea. Her babushka makes it out of boiled frog legs. She's going to teach me how to make it next time we go to the country. We'll get you a husband in no time. And maybe if he likes cats, he'll give you a kitten and we'll take care of it for you."

I ignored the part about the kitten. The twins were always begging for one, but Papa didn't like cats. No, it was more than that.

He had a strange horror of them. No cats for us. I reached out and tickled Nika. "Why do I want a husband?" I said over her laughter.

"So you'll have someone to give you presents. Like kittens. Polina says that's what husbands do. And they kiss your hands all the time." Nika looked down at her own hands. "I don't know why girls like that, though."

"Why are your hands orange?" I asked her.

Nika giggled and covered her mouth. I knew that gesture. It boded no good and made me realize something else was not right about her.

The early morning sunlight seemed to have added an odd orangish tint to both girls' blond curls. But it was an unnatural shade of orange, more like the color of the fruit.

I sat up, trying to keep my wits about me. If I made too much of a fuss about what they had done, they were sure to do it again. They delighted in being naughty.

Reaching out, I touched one of Nika's curls. "What a lovely shade! It looks like the orange from the paint box."

She nodded her head, grinning. "Sophie helped me dip my hair in orange paint water, and I dipped hers."

Of course they had. "Oh, I see. Where was Polina when this was happening?" Polina was their nursemaid. I didn't know why the poor girl hadn't quit long ago, but I was happy she had stuck it out so far. I'd have been pulling my hair out without her.

Nika wrapped a curl around her finger. "She was very tired last night, so we said we were tired too, but we really weren't."

"So after she fell asleep, you did this?" At least the paint was from a watercolor set. I assumed it would wash out. I didn't know how they'd managed to get the color so vivid. I probably didn't want to know.

They both nodded. An orange feather fell out of Sophie's hair. I noticed two more at the end of the bed. I picked up one of them. "Feathers, too?"

"Yes!" Nika jumped off the bed and ran around the room flapping her arms. "We're firebirds, but we need you to help us stick the feathers to us. Polina says we can't use paste unless she's there too."

I got out of bed and put on a wrap. "I suppose she didn't say the same about the paints."

They both shook their heads. "She never said anything about paints."

I sighed. No one could think of everything to tell the twins not to do.

Sophie climbed onto the bed and jumped up and down. "Once we have all the feathers stuck on, we'll be able to fly too!"

My heart skipped a beat. "No, no. That's not the way it works. People can't fly, even with feathers. Promise me you won't try. Promise!" I had a horrid vision of them leaping out a window without a second thought. Neither of the twins had any concept of second thoughts.

Nika gave a very loud sigh.

"Promise," I said again.

I saw Sophie give a slight nod of her head to Nika. "We promise," Nika said. "At least will you paste the feathers on us? We have a lot of them."

A lot. That could mean anything from ten to a thousand. How many pillows had given up their innards? "Show me."

It turned out there were less than a thousand but still a considerable number of feathers drying in the schoolroom. Polina was both mortified and angry the twins had tricked her. I left her to scold them about wasting good feather pillows.

Before I went downstairs, I checked to see if I had enough money to pay for the supplies coming in from the country. The hospital was very low on food, so I hoped Ivan, the man making the delivery, wouldn't be delayed or his sleigh stopped and searched.

I grabbed my Latin book and went downstairs, intending to get in a little studying while I waited for Ivan. Archer, Papa's English butler, was consulting with Osip, the footman, in the hallway.

"How is my stepfather this morning?" I asked Archer.

Archer gave me his usual look of disapproval, which on his skull-like features was not all that much different from his normal appearance, except for a tightening of his mouth and a furrowing of his almost nonexistent eyebrows. "He's fine, Miss Charlotte. He's already breakfasted and is working in the library on the memoir."

The memoir took up a large part of Papa's day, given that he intended to record every detail of every day of his military career. I was glad he had something to occupy him. If he ever finished the book, I had no idea how he'd spend his time.

I went into the breakfast room to get some tea, settling down in a spot where I could look out the window at the frozen Neva and the sky above the broad river. I never grew tired of the view; it was like my own ever-changing watercolor.

The street along the quay was crowded with sleighs, their bells jingling so loudly I could hear them through the window as I opened the textbook. When we'd first arrived in the city, back when it was still called St. Petersburg, I'd loved the sound of all the bells, and it made me believe my mother's words about our new home. She had tried hard to convince us we would be as happy there as we had been in Paris, where we'd lived after my father died and during my mother's disastrous second marriage.

It's like something out of a storybook, she'd told us. *Built by giants who wanted a beautiful city with buildings that looked like a pastry chef made them. And in the winter, it's a wonder of glittering snow and gold domes and air so crisp, you'll feel the most alive you've ever felt.*

She'd been right. I couldn't imagine living in any other city. I never wanted to live anywhere else. And once I became a doctor and opened a practice, other people would realize I meant to stay.

I opened my book and started memorizing verbs. I hadn't been at it for very long when I noticed the room getting darker. I looked out to see the sky turning to the color of an opal as the sun disappeared and snow began to fall. It fell heavier and heavier, floating down in big flakes. It reminded me of the times we had spent at Papa's dacha in the country, riding the horses, hiking through the birch woods, building fires to roast potatoes, and no matter what we did, we laughed, so much laughing.

I told myself we'd do that again, as soon as the war was over. I wasn't going to let it be just a memory. When the war was over, we could go back to the way things were before. Raisa's push for me to leave still stung. A person didn't have to be born in a place to make that place their home.

I spotted a man outside, standing on the quay, leaning against a lamppost. It wasn't so odd to see someone there, but it was odd that he wasn't looking out at the river. He was looking right at our house. All the stories I'd heard of people being watched by the secret police came rushing back to me, how people hadn't realized their everyday activities were being monitored until the police came pounding at the door.

We had our own watcher.

Chapter Four

I TOOK A few deep breaths, trying to stay calm. I knew the man outside was from the secret police. He had to be. There was no other reason someone would watch our house. The baron had made it sound like we didn't yet have the Okhrana interested in us, but he'd been wrong. If someone had put an observer on us, they weren't just sniffing around.

The front bell rang, and the sound of it made my hand jerk, knocking into the glass of tea and spilling some of it on the tablecloth. To hear the bell that early in the morning was odd, not only because we got very few callers, but because it was early for anyone to make a call. The watcher outside straightened up, his gaze focused on whoever stood on our front steps. I went out into the hall as the footman was taking the cloak of a person so covered in snow I couldn't make out much about him except that he was a man. I didn't think I made a noise, but the person turned in my direction as he handed over his gloves and shifted a cane from one hand to another. It was the soldier from the night before.

Since I'd been thinking about our times at the dacha, my first impression was that he looked like he'd just come from a hike in the birch woods. His hair and his eyelashes were frosted with snow, making his dark eyes stand out in his face. My breath caught. He looked even better than he had the night before, especially since he was no longer wearing the elaborate white dress uniform. The simple dark blue uniform that was the standard daytime wear of Horse Guard soldiers suited him much better.

I froze, staring at him, unable to think why he'd be standing in our entry hall. Surely he hadn't really wanted to speak to me so badly he'd come to the house.

Archer cleared his throat. I glanced over at him. He was looking at me with a puzzled expression on his face, probably because I'd been standing there like a statue.

I managed to choke out a few words. "Good morning,"

The young man nodded at me without smiling.

"Lieutenant Dmitri Antonovich Sokolov to see General Cherkassky," Archer announced. "I was just about to show him into the library."

"No need. I'm right here." My stepfather came into the hall. He sounded perfectly alert, and he was walking just fine. Maybe the spell he'd had the night before had just been from tiredness. "Welcome, welcome, Dmitri Antonovich!" he said. "I'm so pleased to meet you. And there you are too, Lottie. Perfect timing. This young man is to be your brothers' new temporary tutor." My stepfather beamed as if he'd just given me a present.

"Tutor?" I said. "What happened to Monsieur Girard?" Girard had only been hired the week before. I'd been so pleased to find him, convinced he'd be the perfect fit since he'd spent his whole career as a teacher.

"I thought I told you. He quit yesterday." Papa shook his head.

"Just packed his bags and walked out. Some nonsense about his nerves and about the house being cursed. I've never heard such foolishness from an educated man."

It took all my self-control not to yell for my brothers to appear that instant. A cursed house? I was sure the boys had pulled a devious prank on Monsieur Girard, and I was also sure I knew the identity of the ringleader. Miles.

"Very glad you are here, Dmitri Antonovich," Papa said. "Tutoring the boys while you recover will help us all out. We'll make sure you get plenty of rest so you can get back to your unit as soon as possible. I know the Horse Guard needs every man they can get. At some point, I do want to hear your impressions of conditions at the front."

"Yes, Excellency," Dmitri replied. He made the same motion he'd done the night before, shifting his weight, which caused another shudder to his whole body. I could see the pain on his face.

Papa beamed again. "No need to be so formal here, young man. I've been retired a long time now, and I promise I won't report you to your commanding officer. I told the boys yesterday I'd find someone right away and gave them quite a stern lecture that they need to settle down and concentrate on their studies. They should be ready and willing to work at your direction."

Which meant my stepfather had said a few words about studying and then one of the boys had asked a geography question, Papa's passion, so the talk would turn to that. The boys were experts at deflecting attention from discussions of their own behavior.

I didn't understand why a member of the Horse Guard would even want to be a tutor. They would consider such a job beneath them. Even before the war, being in the Horse Guard was a full-time occupation for those men who were meant to bring honor and glory to their families. Only the sons of the wealthy were allowed to join, and their families supplied the money to purchase horses and all the elaborate dress uniforms. It wasn't for those in need of funds, who had to take extra jobs to make ends meet.

The baron's words came back to me. *You never know who is spying on you. Don't trust anyone.* The man I'd seen outside watching the house was an obvious danger, but I was sure the Okhrana had more devious methods, such as sending in a stranger who was not really a tutor.

Or was I just being foolish? Would a member of the Horse Guard lower himself to spy for the secret police? Pavel would never have done anything like that. Even those who thought the Okhrana were necessary still held them in contempt for the way they turned on ordinary citizens. There had to be another explanation for his presence.

"My boy Stepan will be joining the Horse Guard when he's old enough," I heard Papa say. "He'll be delighted to meet you. Charlotte, perhaps you can introduce Dmitri Antonovich to your brothers. I have to go out or I'd do it myself. Dmitri, Charlotte will help you with anything you need. I don't know what we'd do without her. She's the eldest, you know, so she takes care of everything."

She takes care of everything. A voice in my head wanted to yell, *No! She doesn't want to take care of everything!* but I gritted my teeth instead. I'd always be Charlotte, the eldest, never just Charlotte.

I scrambled to think of another way to forestall bringing this person into our house. Whatever reason he had for being here, he wasn't what we needed. We needed someone older who would be able to get some work out of my brothers and who wouldn't be run off by them. "Papa, perhaps we should talk before you hire a new tutor. I'm sure Dmitri Antonovich is very qualified, but the boys need help in specific subjects." The young man didn't appear to be much older than me, so he didn't actually look all that qualified.

"Mathematics, I know, Lottie dear," my stepfather replied. "I'm told Dmitri Antonovich had the highest marks in mathematics on his university entrance exam, which he took three years early. It's a shame the war interfered with the young man's studies, but it's lucky for us."

I'd clearly lost that round. Time to try something else. "Their Greek is very poor too," I said. "And their Latin only marginally better."

Papa chuckled. "Lottie, I'm surprised. You aren't thinking very clearly this morning. You know Dmitri Antonovich would have had to pass both Latin and Greek to get into the university. I'm sure he's quite capable of teaching those subjects too. Aren't you trying to improve in those yourself? Perhaps you could sit in on their lessons." He turned to Dmitri. "Charlotte left school early when my wife was ill."

"I'd be happy for you to join us," the young man said to me as a flicker of a smile crossed his face.

I couldn't swear out loud, though I really wanted to. I hadn't expected my attempt to get rid of the tutor to be foiled so easily, and I did need help in Latin and Greek. Did I really want to accept it from this person, though?

I tried to picture myself sitting next to him reviewing Latin declensions while he watched me trying to come up with the right answer. He would be too distracting. I couldn't do it. The word *formosus*, "finely formed and beautiful," popped into my head for some reason. I hadn't even realized I knew that word, but suddenly I could remember all the cases: *formosi, formoso, formosum, formoso, formose.* Finely formed.

Dmitri Antonovich's smile disappeared and I noticed beads of perspiration forming on his forehead as he bit his lip. He was clearly in a great deal of pain. He'd never be able to tutor my brothers. They could wear down a healthy man in a few days. I realized I might not have to intervene at all. Dmitri Antonovich would be gone by nightfall.

The housekeeper came into the hall, and when Archer saw her, he made his common noise of disapproval, a sound between a cough and a snort. I knew he didn't like it when Zarja appeared in front of guests.

Zarja ignored him, as she so often did. "Lottie, there is someone to see you at the kitchen door." She emphasized the word *someone*. I knew who she meant. Ivan had arrived with the delivery.

"I'll be there soon," I said to her.

I didn't want my stepfather to ask any questions about who had come to see me, so I decided I'd do what he asked and show Dmitri Antonovich upstairs and then escape to the kitchen.

"This way," I said.

Dmitri followed me up, though he took each step slowly. I could tell his leg hurt him by the way he grimaced. At the second landing, he stopped, his breath coming in short gasps. "Just a moment, please," he said. We'd been speaking in Russian, but he switched to English. "I forgot to ask the general which language he prefers I use to teach your brothers," he added.

Dmitri's command of English didn't surprise me, because most educated Russians spoke some, but I was surprised that he'd feel comfortable enough with the language to teach in it. As if he read my mind, he said, "My brother and I had an English nursemaid when we were children, and my parents spoke the language as well."

"Either Russian or English is fine," I said. "The older boys' Russian is very good, and Stepan is fluent in English because he's been hearing it for years, but his French needs work." I didn't tell Dmitri my brothers had tried to fool previous tutors by making up words and claiming they were obscure English ones the tutors should learn.

He nodded, his breath slowing a bit. While we stood there, I felt I should say something about the previous night. "I'm sorry I was so rude to you at the grand duke's party." I felt a twinge of embarrassment that I'd actually thought he was interested in me.

"Don't mention it. I wanted to meet you before I came to the house this morning. I'm sorry I said what I did about the baron. It's not my business to intrude in strangers' friendships."

He said the word *friendship* with a little too much emphasis, as if implying that the baron and I were more than friends.

I certainly wasn't going to explain why I'd been talking to the baron. "Let me know when you're ready to continue."

He nodded and took the next step. As we moved on, he began to hum under his breath. I thought I recognized the tune, a Russian folk song. "Isn't that the sleigh song about the galloping horses?" I said.

"What?" he asked, stopping again.

"The song you were humming. It's a sleigh song, isn't it? The one that goes 'Fly, my horses, at the gallop / to my dear, you know the way! / Fly, my horses, fly at the gallop / to my dear one's house, you know the way.'"

Dmitri's face turned red. "I'm sorry," he said. "I didn't realize I was humming. A nurse suggested that in the hospital as a way to forget the pain. I've been doing it so much I don't even think about it. It's one I used to sing with my family when I was a child." He looked away from me, twisting the cane in his hand.

"Don't apologize. It's a good idea." I wished I had thought of it. It might help our patients too. "I like that song. We've sung it at my stepfather's dacha." Or rather, we *had* sung the song, when my mother was alive.

"Shall we go on?" I asked.

He nodded. By the time we reached the third floor, his face was wet with perspiration. He took a handkerchief out of his pocket and wiped it.

I wished I knew the extent of his injury. It felt wrong to be forcing him to do something that caused him such pain. "I'm sorry," I said. "My brothers are very . . . lively. This may not be the best post for you. Please don't think you have to stay if it's too difficult. I'm sure my stepfather would understand."

"I'm fine," he said through clenched teeth. "I just need another moment." He took a few breaths. "Perhaps in the meantime you can tell me about your brothers before I meet them. I wasn't told anything about them except that . . ." His voice trailed off.

"Let me guess. You were told they were wild and undisciplined."

He didn't respond, as if weighing what to say.

"I'm afraid it's true," I said. "Now would be a good time to change your mind."

"I'm not going to change my mind," he said. "Tell me about them."

We'd see how long his stubbornness would last once he spent a few hours with my brothers. "Well, there's Miles, who is seventeen. He's interested in history and politics and books and is determined to be a writer. He's quite brilliant but will only work on what he wants." I didn't go into detail about Miles's health. That would be obvious soon enough.

"Then there's Hap, which is what we call Harold. He's fifteen. He's not the best student, because he concentrates on his music and his art. He draws beautifully. And there's Stepan. He's eight and obsessed with animals, especially horses, but not much interested in other subjects."

Dmitri's face took on a puzzled expression. "Why isn't Miles going into the Horse Guard if he's the eldest? I thought General Cherkassky said Stepan had been put down for a place."

I'd practiced the explanation about us many times. People were always puzzled that Stepan didn't resemble any of us and that he and the twins didn't have the red hair of me, Miles, and Hap. "We have a very complicated family," I said. "Miles, Hap, and I are stepchildren to our stepfather. Our father was an American named Daniel Mason. Stepan is the son of our stepfather and his second wife, so he's our stepbrother and the actual eldest son of our stepfather. That's why he'll go into the Horse Guard instead of Miles. Our mother was Papa's third wife, and they had two children, my little sisters, or, to be precise, my half sisters, Sophie and Nika. They are five years old."

Dmitri wiped his forehead again. "Complicated is an understatement," he said. "I'm ready to move again. Please, let's continue."

I hoped he'd remember I'd given him a way out but that he'd chosen not to take it.

"This way to the lion's den," I said.

Chapter Five

AS WE APPROACHED the schoolroom, I could hear Miles's laughter, which quickly turned into a bout of coughing. I counted the seconds until he stopped. Only six. Not too concerning. If it went past fifteen seconds, it was a bad sign.

When I opened the door, warm air flowed out, because Hap was good at keeping the stove going. He knew it helped Miles feel better. Hap and Miles were standing in front of their worktable as we came in, but our entrance startled them so much that Miles stumbled backward and Hap spun around. I got a good look at the table.

What appeared to be Stepan's head was sitting on top of it. Dmitri made an odd sound in his throat, like he was trying to suppress a scream.

In my younger days, I would have played along with the boys and pretended to be horror-struck, maybe even screamed myself to see how Dmitri responded. But since I was supposed to be the responsible one, I refrained.

"Hi, Lottie!" Stepan's head called. "Look! I don't have a body anymore."

"Excellent new magic trick," I said as I went over to figure out how they'd done it.

It was actually a simple mirror trick. The rectangular mirror was under the table, facing the intended audience at a diagonal running from a back leg on one side to a front leg on the other, and Stepan's body was hidden behind it. The mirror reflected the table's front legs, giving the audience the illusion that they were seeing all four legs, through to the back.

Stepan ducked out of his spot, revealing the hole that had been cut in the center of the table. "How did you manage the hole?" I asked. Most of the tools the boys used to build their magic-trick contraptions were in the country.

"Yermak did it for us," Hap said. "We thought Archer was going to catch us, but Stepan provided a distraction." He punched at Stepan, who ducked and grinned. Stepan loved it when the older boys let him be part of their plans.

I heard Dmitri clearing his throat. When I glanced back at him, I thought his eyes were showing a bit more white than they had before, and he was a little paler.

"This is Dmitri Antonovich Sokolov, your new tutor," I said.

I turned to Dmitri. "I forgot to mention that my brothers like magic tricks."

Looks of suppressed glee passed among the three boys. I knew exactly what they were thinking. A new victim.

I introduced them one by one. "This is Miles," I said. I didn't want to point out that it was easy to tell Miles and Hap apart because Miles was so much smaller, even though he was older. I think his illnesses over the years had affected his appetite even before he'd been diagnosed with tuberculosis, and so he'd never grown very tall. "Miles is a wielder of a vicious pen if he doesn't like you. His limericks can be quite rude, and he's always running his hands through his hair, which is why it's a mess all the time."

"Very eloquent description," Miles said, messing up his hair even more. "Do I get to describe you, too? No, never mind. I have a good limerick in mind." He grinned, and I realized I shouldn't have added in the bit about the limericks. I held up my hand to stop him. It didn't work.

"I don't have the rhythm of the last line right, but I'm working on it," he said. He cleared his throat like he was about to give a speech.

> Our Charlotte is prone to shriek and to yell
> We're surprised the house hasn't yet fell
> Every day is a new rant
> It's always, "You can't, can't, can't."
> We hope one day her voice will say farewell.

If Dmitri hadn't been there, I would have thrown something at Miles. Of course I shrieked and yelled when I had a good reason to, and with the boys I had a good reason nearly every day.

I forced myself to smile. I'd pay Miles back later. "You're right. The last line needs work. Let's move on to Hap." At least Hap wouldn't have a limerick on hand to torment me. "Hap was really a happy little baby, hence the nickname. And still mostly happy as long as he has something to draw with and on."

The nickname fit his face, too. Even when he wasn't smiling, he looked content. The corners of his mouth turned up ever so slightly, and that, combined with the broadness of his face, made his looks a sharp contrast to Miles, whose features had sharpened and become more drawn with each bout of illness.

"Last but not least is Stepan, the serious one who knows many, many facts about animals. He'd be glad to answer any questions about them."

Stepan moved forward and held out his hand, standing very straight. "How do you do? I am Stepan Feodorovich Cherkassky."

Dmitri shook his hand. "How do you do," he said, matching Stepan's serious tone. He glanced between me and Miles and Hap. "I didn't know Americans had such red hair. I thought it was more a Scottish trait. Interesting."

"Our father had red hair because my grandmother is Scottish, though our grandfather was American," I explained. "She had the same red hair when she was young."

"It's very distinctive," Dmitri said. "I like it." He sounded as if he meant it, which surprised me. Some people acted as if our hair color were a burden we had to bear, or worse, that redheads were so out of control with their fiery tempers, they'd bring disaster to any family. My red hair had been an additional mark against me with Pavel's mother.

I watched Dmitri examine the room, which I realized was in quite a state. At least the rabbit cage was clean and didn't smell; the rabbits dozed in one corner next to each other. The rest of the room looked like no one had straightened it up in weeks. Miles's manuscripts were piled everywhere, some of the stacks of paper topped with Stepan's tin soldiers. Stepan claimed he couldn't remember history unless he could use his soldiers to set up the battles, though for some reason the soldiers were always accompanied by his collection of Dymkovo toys, the colorful little clay ducks he loved. Sometimes both sides would be made up of ducks, and they'd end up intermingling, grouped in little circles, a nicer thought than actual men throwing themselves into hell.

"I hear your former tutor left quite suddenly," Dmitri said as he hobbled all around, examining some of the books on the shelves and Hap's drawings stuck on the walls. The latest ones were mostly of kikimoras, the strange spirits from Russian folktales that some described as little old women with large chicken feet. Hap's versions of them were rather scary.

"And I heard the reason the poor fellow left was because he thought the house was cursed." Dmitri moved over to the globe and put his fingers on it to make it spin. I noticed again how long his fingers were. His hands were those of a pianist. An image flashed into my head of him sitting next to me on a piano bench, leaning in to turn the pages, his eyes fixed on me. The image was so clear, it was like a memory, though of course it had never happened.

My face felt hot and I put my hands on my cheeks to cool it down. What was wrong with me?

"Yes, he thought he saw a kikimora and found her wet footprints in his room," Miles said. He walked over to a pile of manuscripts on a table by the window, acting as if he had just noticed them. Very casually, he took one off the top and moved it to the bottom of the stack. That meant it was something he didn't want either me or the tutor to read. It was probably some lurid, gothic-type horror story. He and Hap delighted in coming up with outrageous scenarios Miles could write.

Miles turned back to face us. "Monsieur Girard even saw her moving down the hall late one night. A small, dark shape scurrying away from his door." I noticed that Stepan had his eyes fixed on the floor.

"Interesting." Dmitri studied the room like he was trying to memorize it. He went over to a cupboard and opened it. I almost expected a deluge to fall from it, because as usual it was crammed full of a jumble of old games and books and art supplies.

"Stories about kikimoras can be quite frightening to the gullible," Dmitri said as he reached in and pulled out a robe of blue silk with stars embroidered on it. The robe was one Miles used when he told fortunes. Dmitri laid it over a chair, then reached in the cabinet again and pulled a piece of black fabric from under a broken microscope. He held it up and examined it as if he'd never seen fabric before, and then put it over his shoulders like a cape.

"A little short for me," he said. "My older sister was one of the gullible ones. My younger brother and I convinced her our house was haunted. It was too easy to do: strange noises in the night, wrapping ourselves in gray cloth and walking about, that sort of thing. Very childish of us, I know, and we later confessed when we saw how upset she was." He pulled the fabric off and tossed it back inside along with the robe, shutting the door.

I'd never seen all three brothers rendered speechless at the same time. I was impressed despite myself. Maybe Dmitri Antonovich wasn't just full of book knowledge. Though, looking at him, I found it hard to imagine him as a boy playing pranks.

"Why don't we talk for a bit about where you are in your studies?" Dmitri asked, as if he hadn't noticed the boys' reaction.

"Where you *actually* are," I said to them. "Not claiming you haven't learned something you've covered so it will be easy for you the second time around."

"We only did that once," Hap said, sounding indignant. "And that was three or four tutors ago."

Miles picked up another piece of paper, crumpled it up, and threw it in the direction of the fire. It didn't make it that far, but Hap scooped it up and tossed it the rest of the way.

"Yes, don't believe everything my sister says," Miles added. "She's actually the real troublemaker of the family. Would you believe she once ran away, intending to join the circus?"

I put up my hands. "Miles! Stop. I'm sure Dmitri Antonovich doesn't want to hear our family stories. That was years ago."

Stepan piped up. "Maybe the tutor wouldn't want to hear, but he might like to see you juggle on horseback and on a unicycle. That's her talent. She was sure the circus would give her a job. Show him how you can juggle, Lottie."

I closed my eyes for a moment and forced myself to take a couple of deep breaths. When I opened them, I saw Dmitri looking at me.

His mouth twitched like he was trying not to smile. "That is quite a talent," he said. "I'd like to see that sometime."

I absolutely could not picture myself juggling in front of him. I'd drop everything.

Miles's attention was caught by something out the window. "Charlotte, your friend is in the courtyard." He turned around and smiled at me. "When are you going to tell us about your mysterious peasant?"

"Don't be such a snob." I needed to get downstairs and see if the man I'd seen earlier was still watching the house. Ivan would have to be careful when he left if the man was still there. "He's not my mysterious peasant. Mr. Sokolov, my brother is just trying to stir up trouble. Miles, you know very well it's Ivan."

"It's mysterious that Ivan comes all the way to Petrograd to visit you."

I didn't like the sly tone in Miles's voice. I hadn't realized he'd been paying attention to Ivan's visits. "Stop acting like you don't know he delivers the wood." Miles could be so infuriating at times. I knew I shouldn't let him bait me. It was always better to ignore him. "I have to go to the hospital, so I won't be back until after dinner," I said. "Hap, I'm counting on you to let Dmitri Antonovich know the schedule."

When I opened the door to leave, Nika tumbled inside. I knew what she'd been doing.

"Nika, you shouldn't eavesdrop!" I scolded.

She got up and smiled. "I'm not Nika. I'm Sophie."

The twins never gave up trying to fool us. "You are definitely Nika. Where is Sophie?" I asked.

Sophie poked her head around the door. "I'm here, but I'm Nika. We wanted to meet the new tutor."

I noticed that Polina had succeeded in getting them dressed, but they still had orange hands and hair. "Where's Polina?" I asked, wondering how they'd managed to escape from her again.

"Nika, I mean Sophie, spilled milk on her," Sophie said. "She had to go change."

The best way to get them back to Polina without an argument would be to give them a look at the tutor. "Dmitri Antonovich, may I present my sisters, Sofiya Feodorovna Cherkasskaya and Veronika Feodorovna Cherkasskaya," I said. "They're a little hard to tell apart if you don't know them, but Nika has a scar on her cheek from falling out of a tree she wasn't supposed to climb."

The two giggled. Dmitri bowed. "I am delighted to make your acquaintance, ladies."

The twins' eyes widened. Nika grabbed Sophie's hand. "You have a nice nose," Nika blurted out, and then she dragged Sophie out of the room.

Dmitri looked totally bemused. "I've never been complimented on my nose before," he said.

He actually did have a rather nice nose. "Nika has an odd fixation on noses," I told him. "Don't mind them. *I'm* sorry they seem to have lost their manners. I'm sure they'll be back, but just send them away if they are nuisances. Now I really do have to go."

"Charlotte, wait," Miles said. "Have you seen Raisa lately?"

Something was definitely odd. No one knew I had planned to

see Raisa the night before except Raisa. It was too much of a coincidence for Miles to bring up her name when he hadn't spoken of her for months. She said she'd seen him, but I couldn't believe she'd have mentioned we were going to meet. It would put Miles in danger to know about any of our black-market arrangements. I couldn't ask him about it in front of Dmitri, though. I'd have to get to the bottom of it later when I could talk to Miles alone.

"I did, as a matter of fact," I told him. "We met for tea and she gave me a book of poems she thought you'd like. It's in my room if you want it."

He looked away. "I was just curious. When we were working on the magic trick, I remembered how much she liked helping us. I'm not much interested in poetry these days, but maybe I'll take a look at the book later."

Miles never explained any of his thoughts to that extent. It was as if he was making excuses. He never made excuses. This wasn't the brother I knew. "Go," he said. "Sorry, I didn't mean to keep you."

As I went out in the hall and closed the door behind me, I heard Stepan. "Dmitri Antonovich, tell us the truth. How close are the German troops to Petrograd?"

I almost went back in to hear Dmitri's answer, though I didn't know if he'd actually tell the truth. In a way I hoped that if the news was bad, he would lie. I didn't know how Stepan had gotten it in his head that we could be overrun by the German army at any moment. No matter how often Miles went over the map with him to show him that the front line was hundreds of miles away, Stepan couldn't be convinced. He'd been a worried child even before the war, prone to nightmares, which had gotten more frequent the longer the fighting dragged on.

I hated that he had to grow up worrying about war. He'd never forget it. None of us would, of course, except maybe the twins if the war ended soon. My stomach clenched as the anger rose in me, the anger I felt each time I thought of the war. It wasn't fair, any of it, and it was all caused because some powerful men couldn't be satisfied with what they had. They always had to grab more. The worst of it was that we were powerless to do anything but try to keep going until the war ended.

I hurried to my room, shut the door, and then went to the window. The man was still there, though he was stomping his feet and moving around like he was cold and wanted to leave. Ivan would have to be careful, but I knew he'd agree with me—we weren't going to let an Okhrana spy get the better of us. The hospital would keep going, at least. I would make sure of that.

I got the rubles to pay Ivan and put them in a small envelope. I knew the butler thought Ivan and I had some sort of scandalous flirtation going on, and I wanted to encourage that presumption, so I put some of my mother's perfume on the envelope to make it seem like a love note. Since it bulged with the rubles, I'd have to hold it so Archer wouldn't get a look at how thick it was. Even the totally infatuated wouldn't write that many pages.

Before I left the room, I picked up the book of poetry. It was a volume by Pushkin. I didn't remember Raisa ever being particularly interested in poetry, but I supposed she could have turned to it as a distraction from not being allowed her music. I set it back down and headed to the kitchen, wondering if I'd completely misread Miles's lack of interest in Raisa.

I heard Archer complaining as I came down the stairs to the lower level.

"Those hooligans will bring down more and more bad luck on us! Three of the red-haired troublemakers! One would be bad enough.

And not even the general's own children! He should have sent them back to America after that woman died." Archer never referred to my mother except as *that woman*.

I'd heard all of it before. Many times Archer said such things right in front of us, muttering loudly enough to himself that we could hear it. There was no way to stop it. Miles, Hap, and I talked about telling our stepfather, but we knew Papa depended on Archer, so we'd decided just to put up with it. Archer had come to Russia years ago with Papa's first wife, who was also English, and he'd stayed after she died, becoming a fixture in the house.

The housekeeper, as always, tried to defend us. "Mr. Archer! You stop right now! They are good children, just high-spirited, and the general would be lost without them."

"It's all right, Zarja," I said as I came around the corner. "You don't need to stand up for us. I know my brothers are a bit trying."

Archer sniffed. "More than a bit trying. They are a bad influence on Stepan. They're sure to end up in jail someday. Did you know they have been collecting materials to make fireworks? Monsieur Girard informed me, and I took the liberty of confiscating their supplies. Mr. Miles had the audacity to claim it was for a science experiment. They could have burned down the entire house!"

"If it's too much for you, you can always retire, Mr. Archer," Zarja said. "I'm sure the general would give you a generous pension, and then you can go back to England."

He sniffed again. "Someone has to stay and protect this house."

I didn't want to be drawn in to their ongoing bickering. I headed to the back door, waving the envelope so that the scent of it filled the air around me. As I opened the door, I heard Archer mutter, "Just like her mother. Always running after men, even peasants!"

He's just a sad old man, he's just a sad old man, I chanted to myself, determined not to snap at him. It wouldn't do any good, and if he saw me get angry, it would give him a reason to feel superior. I did allow myself to slam the door behind me, but it didn't make me feel much better.

The snow had stopped, but it was still very cold. Ivan was waiting in his sleigh. "Little sister, you should have on a hat," he called as I walked across the courtyard.

"I know," I said, already feeling the chill on the top of my head. Ivan was bundled up in a long sheepskin coat and a fur hat, bits of ice in his beard. He was Yermak's younger cousin, though they looked enough alike that Ivan could be mistaken for Yermak's son. Before the war, Ivan had had the reputation of being the fastest woodcutter in the neighborhood around the dacha, but after he was conscripted and sent to the front, he lost an arm and was sent home. He could still cut an amazing amount of wood, though no one bothered to have competitions any longer. There weren't enough men left, and the women cut the wood they needed, not caring about proving who was the best.

His sleigh appeared to be piled full of wood. I knew that only half of it was wood, stacked onto crates full of food.

"Any problems this trip?" I asked as I handed him the envelope.

"Not for me, though others have run into trouble. Things are getting worse. Too many soldiers have deserted and they are hungry. They'll stop a sleigh full of food and take what they want."

"Don't come if it's too dangerous. Olga and the little ones need you." I felt I had to say it, but once the words were out of my mouth, I tried to keep a flutter of panic down. I didn't know what we'd do without the food. There were such long lines at the shops, and we couldn't buy enough in any one place for all the patients.

He grinned and pounded his fist on his chest. "I'd like to see them try to stop *me*."

"Be careful when you leave," I said. "There is someone in front of the house who may be watching us, but I don't think he saw you since you came through the back. When you come next time, keep an eye out."

"A dirty spy watching the general's house! I'd like to get a hold of that swine and teach him some respect!" Ivan squeezed his fist together like he was crushing something in his hand.

"I've heard things may be back to normal before long," I said, repeating what I heard from Papa almost every day.

"Ah, if only it were so. I hear that too, but I also hear some people claim they can get milk from chickens," Ivan said. "We shall see. The land captains are getting more and more demanding that we prove we don't have any food to turn over to them. No one is happy with that." His face turned serious. "I hope I can keep coming to town, but you should make other plans in case I can't." He slapped his leg. "Enough serious talk. We'll have faith things will improve. And how are the little girls?" he asked. "Olga says she is counting the days until you come in the summer. She can't wait to see them."

"They are fine and healthy," I said, though the panic was increasing. I didn't know how to make any other plans to get supplies.

"Good, good. Where is Yermak? I thought he'd be here to help unload."

"He took my stepfather somewhere. I'll help."

We had a whole system worked out where Ivan would place the wagon so that he could unload the wood he'd brought for the house, and then slide out the crates of food to be carried into the carriage house without any neighbors seeing what we were doing. I didn't trust some of those people. I wasn't even sure I trusted Archer not to report us if he saw.

Yermak had made a special cupboard for the food inside the carriage house so I could take it into the hospital bit by bit as if I'd bought it at a shop along my way. The cook at the hospital knew where the food came from and wouldn't report us, but since there were others in and out of the building all day, it was better to be cautious.

When we had finished, Ivan climbed back up in the sleigh and jerked his head toward the house. "Old Archer is watching us out the window. I see his face is still as sour as vinegar."

"Yes, he doesn't change." I reached up and put my hand on Ivan's sleeve. It would give Archer even more to grumble about. "Thank you," I said. "Stay safe."

"I will. God watches over those who are careful." He flicked the reins. "Wake up, old boy."

As I walked back to the house, I glanced up at the schoolroom windows, wondering how everyone was doing. Dmitri stood at one, looking down at me.

I forced myself to smile and give a quick wave. Even as I scolded myself for being so paranoid about the informants for the Okhrana, a shiver still ran through me. Just exactly who was Dmitri Antonovich, and why was he in our house?

Chapter Six

ARCHER WAS GONE by the time I went back inside, and Zarja jumped at the chance to talk about Dmitri.

"I only caught a glimpse of him, but he's a fine-looking young man," Zarja said. "Those eyes! I'm sure many young girls have gotten lost in them."

She was right—that is, if a girl wanted to let herself get lost in them and had time to think about that sort of thing.

"Lottie, did you hear me? You don't look like you are listening."

"What?" I asked.

"I said he doesn't look much like a tutor. The ones who have been here before couldn't withstand a strong gust of wind, much less your brothers' antics. Maybe this one will stay."

"I love your optimism," I said. "But I don't share it." I wanted to chat, but I was already late. "I'm sorry; I have to go. I have to pick up a few things at some shops, and then they are expecting me at the hospital." I got a basket and then went back outside to load it up with some food from Ivan's delivery.

I decided I wouldn't go the back way. I'd let the man in front of the house see me. Better to act as if everything were normal.

When I went out the front door, I pretended to ignore him as

I walked away, though I did look back when I turned a corner. I breathed a little easier to see he hadn't followed me.

My errands and the walk to the hospital took longer than I had planned. The basket was filled with a cabbage, some flour, and some eggs, so it was heavy, and I had to avoid some streets I normally took because so many troops were out practicing.

I stopped into the pharmacy that supplied us with some of our medicines. I'd made an arrangement with the pharmacist to give him English lessons in exchange for putting us at the top of the list for new deliveries. He wasn't in, so I left a message with a young man stocking the shelves.

"Could you tell him Charlotte from the hospital stopped in? We're running short on hydrogen peroxide." We were about to run out, and I'd hoped to hear that a new supply would be arriving shortly.

"I'll tell him," the man said.

I continued on, trying to walk faster, thinking I was going to be late. I passed one bakery with a huge line of women standing patiently out in front. It seemed that every day the lines for bread grew longer, and our ration cards only allowed a small amount at a time. We were lucky Ivan brought us enough flour that the cook at the hospital could make bread for the patients. We couldn't ask to use the patients' own ration cards. They wanted their families to have them.

When I was almost at the hospital, I heard shouts and saw a crowd gathered in front of a bookstore, one I'd been at before. Rivkin's was owned by the parents of one of Raisa's friends. It was full of books in several different languages and very popular with university students. I pushed my way forward to get a better view. A policeman was trying to keep people back from the entrance. I held the basket to my chest, dreading to find out what was happening.

Two other policemen dragged a boy out the door while a woman followed after them, begging for them to let him go. The boy was struggling, though he was so slender they had no trouble holding on to him. He had blood running out of his nose and his face was all swollen. I couldn't see his features very well, but I thought I knew him. My legs began to tremble.

"I told his mother last week they'd come for him eventually," I heard a woman say.

"What did he do?" a boy asked.

"He spoke out against the czar, and I'm sure he's been associating with radicals. He comes and goes at all hours of the day and night. He should have just stayed with his studies. Now his mother may never see him again."

A third policeman raised his truncheon and hit the young man. The prisoner screamed out in pain and raised his head. I did know him, Samuel Rivkin. He'd been part of our group that had met to go on picnics on the Summer Islands in the Neva. I hadn't seen him since I'd stopped going to school.

"Samuel!" I yelled, trying to get through the crowd. They couldn't be taking Samuel away. He wouldn't harm anyone, and he was younger than me. He was Miles's age.

"Be quiet! Don't draw attention to yourself!" a man near me said. He and the other people close by drew away from me as if I had suddenly developed a contagious disease.

Samuel turned his head in my direction, his eyes searching the crowd. When he saw me, he called out, "Charlotte! Charlotte! Help!" The policeman clubbed him again, and he sagged down between the two holding him up.

I took another step forward without thinking. An old woman grabbed my arm and held on to it with a tight grip. "You can't help. Stay here or they will arrest you, too."

Before I could decide what to do, the two policemen shoved him in an automobile, then got in after him and drove away. The third policeman said something to the woman who had come out of the store. It had to be Samuel's mother. She stuck out her chin and replied to him, but I couldn't make out the words. He hit her then, so hard she fell down against the side of the door frame. It all happened so fast. I hadn't thought he would hit her.

The crowd surged forward, shouting angry words, no longer so afraid. I found myself moving with them, shouting too. The policeman turned to face us, raising his truncheon and yelling for us to move aside. He pushed through the crowd and then hurried down the street, looking back over his shoulder.

I ran to the woman, who was still on the ground. A man reached her before me and helped her up. Her hand was bleeding, so the man pulled out a handkerchief and gave it to her. There was far too much blood for it to be a mere scrape.

"May I look?" I asked her. "I'm a nurse, and I think you might need stitches." She shrank away from me, and I thought she was going to refuse, so I introduced myself. "My name is Charlotte Mason. I've met Samuel and I've been to your bookstore. I really would like to help."

Her skin color had a grayish cast to it, and I was afraid she was going into shock. "Can we go inside the bookstore? You're getting too cold out here."

She let the man help her inside, and from the way he spoke to her, it was clear they knew each other. I saw a shawl draped over the chair behind the counter, so I grabbed it and wrapped it around her.

Once I got the cut cleaned up, I saw it wasn't as bad as I'd feared. While I bandaged it, she sat quietly, but when I finished, she finally spoke.

"You know Samuel?" Tears ran down her face, though she acted as if she didn't notice them.

"Yes. I met him through a school friend. We used to go to picnics together." I don't know why I told her that, but I couldn't think of anything else to say.

"He's a good boy," she said. "He's done nothing wrong." She didn't speak again, just nodded her head when I explained how to take care of the cut.

"Can I do anything else for you?" I asked.

She shook her head, still crying.

The man nodded at me. "She'll be all right. You should go now."

I went outside and stood looking up and down the street. Everything had gone back to normal. The crowd was gone, and the falling snow had covered up any sign of blood. It was as if Samuel hadn't even been there.

The thought of Samuel in prison made my stomach twist. They'd beat him to find out what he'd been doing and who he had been seeing. Had a watcher been monitoring the bookstore? Who had turned Samuel in? I had to tell Raisa what had happened. I didn't know how to help him, and I doubted if she did either, but I needed to see her.

I managed to get a droshky to take me to her uncle's house, but when I arrived, the housekeeper said she'd gone out. She wouldn't tell me where.

"Who are you again?" the woman asked, her eyes narrowing.

"A friend from school. I'll come back later."

"I don't know when she'll be back. It will probably be a waste of your time, and she has a lot of work to do."

"I don't mind," I said, putting on a smile. *Old witch.*

When I finally made it to the hospital, I walked inside and my legs immediately began to shake. The fear I'd held in check rose up, making my breath come in gasps. I tried to set the basket down, but it tipped over and the cabbage rolled out. I picked it back up, willing myself to calm down.

Galina Petrenko, the head nurse, walked in as I was trying to take off my coat. My arms were so shaky they weren't working quite right.

"You're very pale," she said. "Are you feeling ill?"

I managed to get the coat off, but instead of putting it in the armoire, I hugged it to me. "I saw the police arrest someone I know. It was terrible."

"Oh, dear. I'm sorry. Who was it?" Galina had the most soothing voice. I'd seen it work on patients, and it was already working on me. I felt less shaky.

"An acquaintance I met through a school friend. I don't know him very well, but he's younger than me, and they dragged him off and hit him like he was some terrible criminal."

Her eyes widened. "It's getting worse and worse. They can't go on terrorizing us. There is only so much people can take." She sighed and shook her head. "You should sit for a while and have some tea until you feel steadier. You don't want the patients to see you like this."

"Is the doctor here?" I asked.

"Yes, she's just washing up."

I heard Dr. Rushailo's voice. It sounded like she was talking to another nurse.

"I'm all right now," I said. I hung up my coat and smoothed my hair. I didn't want the doctor to see me upset. She was always so calm no matter what went wrong, the way a doctor should be.

Dr. Rushailo walked in, writing on a clipboard. "A girl. Six pounds, four ounces," she said to Galina and me, "and healthy, though it's clear the mother has not had enough to eat for a long time. If the food situation gets much worse, we're going to see smaller babies who will struggle more."

I didn't know how many babies Dr. Rushailo had delivered in all the many years she'd been in practice. It had to have been hundreds, and there were dozens of girls in Petrograd with the first name of Serafima because of her. She delivered most of the babies in the patients' homes except when she referred women to the hospital who had complications. She and my mother had worked hand in hand to get the hospital started.

"Oh, I nearly forgot," the doctor said. "Lottie, I've told the other nurses, but you need to know too. I'm beginning to see some measles cases in the city. We're going to have to limit visitors to just husbands or grandparents. No older children visiting for at least the next month."

I nodded. I knew it would be bad if any of the newborns came down with measles.

"I should go," the doctor said. "Anything I need to know about?"

"No." I never mentioned the food and medicine shortages to her. The doctor had enough to deal with. "But can I talk to you for a moment about my stepfather?" I asked. "I need your opinion." When she nodded, I explained about Papa. "Since I can't convince him to see you, should I try to get him to see another doctor?"

"If he has another episode, definitely. The slurring of the speech and the difficulty walking concern me. I'll give you the name of a good doctor."

She flipped a page on the clipboard, wrote a name on a blank sheet, and gave it to me. "How is the studying going?"

"Fine," I said. I wasn't going to tell her the truth. She'd been so encouraging about my plans and said she'd put in a good word for me with the admissions committee once I passed the entrance test for medical school. The Women's Medical Institute was one of the best medical schools for women in the world, and they didn't often take foreigners, so I needed all the help I could get.

"Good. I know you can do it." She got her coat and put it on.

The rest of the day flew by. I cleaned instruments, boiled the silk thread for stitching up incisions, and gave bottles to some of the babies. By the time I left, it had been dark for hours.

I didn't want to go by the bookstore again, so I took a different route to see Raisa, one that took me past our old school. Everyone had gone home for the day, and the building was dark. I tried to remember sitting inside, practicing our Italian conversation or working out our algebra problems. It all seemed like it had happened in another life.

I walked faster. I needed to see Raisa.

I knocked on the door of her uncle's house, holding my breath to see who would answer. When Raisa opened the door, I had to keep from flinging myself at her.

"Charlotte! I didn't expect it to be you. Is anything wrong? Is it Miles?" Her hand went to her throat.

"It's not Miles. I wanted to talk to you for a minute. Can you come out?"

She got her coat, and we walked to a little park down the block. I waited until there was no one near us and then told her what I'd seen. Her eyes closed and her head tipped back. I knew she was going to faint, so I grabbed her right as her knees buckled. A man on the other side of the park saw us and ran to help. We managed to get her over to a park bench and sit her down.

I put my hand on the back of her head and moved her so that her head was in her lap as the man hovered around.

"It's all right. I'm a nurse," I said to him. "She'll be better in a moment. She heard some bad news." I wanted him to go away before Raisa came to in case she said something he shouldn't hear. I'd never expected her to faint.

He nodded, an understanding look on his face. Three years into the war, bad news had become commonplace.

She came to quickly, and when she looked at me, she put her hand to her throat again. "I feel like I might throw up," she said.

"It will pass soon. Just sit quietly for a minute."

I waited a few minutes before I asked her a question that had been worrying me all day. "Did you know Samuel was associating with some radical group?"

"No," she said. "But I'm not surprised. There are groups everywhere working for change. People have realized we can't wait any longer."

She'd said "we can't wait." It would be just like Raisa to throw herself into one of the groups trying to bring down the czar. She was desperate to do something that might get her father out of prison.

My stomach turned at the thought of what could happen to her. I didn't want her putting herself in so much danger.

I started to ask another question, but Raisa held up her hand. "Don't," she said. "Sometimes it's better not to ask questions."

I grabbed her hand. "Be careful," I said, hearing how ridiculous my words sounded, as if they would make any difference.

"I am." She stood up. "I have to get back."

"Is there something we can do for Samuel?" I asked.

"I'll go see his mother tomorrow and find out if she's heard anything. I can tell her who to go see."

"What should I do?" I felt completely helpless.

"Nothing. Please, Charlotte, don't get involved." She darted away so fast I didn't have time to say anything else.

I headed for home as tiredness washed over me. The weight of the day pressed down on me so much each step was an effort.

When I finally reached our block, I saw the glow of a cigarette a few feet from our front door and a couple of dark shapes. My steps faltered. Another watcher? I didn't know who else would be standing outside in the cold so late.

As I turned around to go a different way so I could reach the house from the back, I heard a burst of laughter and a voice I recognized. It was Osip, our footman, and I knew he was talking to Vladislav, the footman next door. Vladislav worked for another retired general, General Stackleberg, who was a little older than Papa. The general and Papa weren't close friends, though they were cordial. I think the general's wife hadn't liked my mother, so she kept her distance from us, and after the woman died, the man rarely left the house.

"Hello," I called out. Osip replied but Vladislav did not. The man threw his cigarette down and went back into the Stacklebergs' house. He never responded to anything I said for some reason. I knew from Osip that he had worked on one of the Stackleberg estates until all the regular footmen had been called up. He, like Osip, wasn't considered fit enough to be in the army. Osip's eyesight was too poor, and Vladislav had a problem with one of his feet. Osip had said that Vladislav hadn't wanted to come to the city, but the general had insisted, threatening to make Vladislav's family move out of their house on the general's estate.

"Everything all right?" I asked Osip as we went inside. Unlike Archer, Osip actually liked us, and I relied on him for updates on how the household had managed on any particular day. My brothers were good at not mentioning disasters.

"Everything is fine. A quiet day," he said.

"Is . . . is the tutor in?" I didn't know how to ask if Dmitri had quit or not.

"Yes," Osip said. "I hope he doesn't leave until the end of the week. I've made a bet with Vladislav and I've got him lasting five days. Vladislav has him only lasting for three."

After the day I'd had, I didn't think I'd find anything funny, but Osip's words made me smile. Even with everything happening in the city, some things never changed. Osip and Vladislav always bet on each tutor.

"I hope you win," I said as I went upstairs. I tried to be quiet so my brothers wouldn't hear me. If they did, I wouldn't be able to leave the house again without them knowing. They'd want me to play music with them or work on some magic trick.

Once I had changed, I took the baron's piece of paper from its hiding place in my Greek book and put it in a small bag. I'd managed not to think about it during the day while I was at the hospital, but once I'd gotten home, I couldn't wait to get rid of it. I didn't know if I'd be able to burn it at the Tamms' after I showed it to them because there would probably be too many people around, but I'd find a way to make sure it didn't come back into the house.

I also collected some packages I was taking to the Tamms and then went back outside. As I started down the street, two figures burst out of the narrow passageway that ran along the side of the house, nearly knocking me down. One of them dropped a package.

I scrambled away from them, my heart pounding, ready to yell for help, afraid they were men intending to rob me.

"Lottie, what are you doing out here?" a voice said. It was Hap.

"What are *you* doing out here?" I asked, trying to calm down. "It's very late."

Miles picked up the package he had dropped and put it inside his coat. "It's not *that* late. We're going to the Tamms' party, but we had to wait until Stepan was asleep because he'd want to go with us."

"They have what is basically a party every night," I said.

"It's Peet's birthday tonight," Miles said. "It's a *real* party. We have to go."

Hap waved a small bundle at me and then pointed at the package I was holding. "We have a present for him. Did you get him one too?"

"It's a bag of sugar for Celeste. And no, I didn't know it was Peet's birthday."

"Now you know. So let's go." Hap took a few steps down the street.

I knew there was no way I could convince them to go back inside. As I was about to follow, Dmitri came out the front door wearing a coat and hat. He paused on the step, looking shocked to see us.

"Dmitri Antonovich!" Hap called. "We're going to a party. Do you want to come along? You should meet our friends the Tamms. You'd like them."

I wanted to shake Hap. We couldn't take a stranger to their apartment. Even though I knew the Tamms were not radicals, I didn't know about the people who came and went to all their parties. Dmitri might misunderstand a stray remark.

It was obvious Dmitri was planning on going somewhere. With his leg injured, it wasn't likely he'd just decided to take a stroll in the cold and the dark.

"I was just about to . . ." Dmitri paused and then said, "Yes, I would like to go, but I don't have an invitation."

"The Tamms won't mind. Half the people at the party won't have an invitation either," Miles said.

"If you are sure." Dmitri looked at me.

I had to try something to get him not to go. "It's not going to be much of a party. Just ordinary people gathered together in a small apartment."

"What are you saying, Lottie? They are terrific people!" Hap exclaimed. "You have to come with us. We were going to walk"—his gaze turned to Dmitri's cane—"but since we've run into Lottie, she'll have money to hire droshkies."

It appeared Dmitri was coming to the party. I prayed it would be the one night that no one but us showed up.

Chapter Seven

I TOOK SOME money out of my bag and handed it to Hap. "Go down to the end of the block and hire some sleighs to come pick us up. See if you can find one big enough for all of us." There was no sense in making Dmitri walk even that far, since the izvoschiks would be eager for a fare.

When two small droshkies pulled up in front of the house, Hap leaped into the front one. "I couldn't find a bigger one. Come on, Miles. Lottie can ride with Dmitri Antonovich."

Each droshky for hire had room for two passengers, but it was always a tight fit. I got in first and then Dmitri struggled in, apologizing for bumping me with his cane. Our izvoschik urged his horse forward as if we needed to catch up with Miles and Hap's sleigh, which was already halfway down the block. Both Dmitri and I were nearly thrown out.

When we got our balance back, Dmitri put his arm around me. It was considered polite in Petrograd for a man to make sure a woman passenger didn't fall out of the poorly designed sleighs, no matter how slightly acquainted they were. I pretended I didn't even notice. You weren't supposed to react. Usually I didn't notice, but I was intensely aware of Dmitri next to me. I held myself very still, remembering other rides where I'd wanted Pavel's arm around me. I pushed that thought away as quickly as it had come. It wasn't as if Pavel and I had even had time to become that close, just a few dances and walks before he'd gone to the front. I needed to stop dwelling on those memories.

The two drivers kept shouting for people and automobiles to get out of the way, as drivers always did, though it was late enough that there were not many people on the streets. The shouting kept me from feeling like I had to make conversation with Dmitri. I wished I could ask him where he'd been planning to go. If we hadn't run into him, we'd probably never have known he'd left the house. There was no reason he'd have had to tell anyone. Even when tutors lived in, it wasn't as if they had to account for every moment of the day. It was the perfect setup for Dmitri to go out at night and report our doings to someone. I spent the rest of the ride scheming ways to find out more. I wasn't going to rest easy until I knew more about him.

The Tamms and their extended family had an apartment in the building next door to the theater. We got out of the droshkies and heard shouts from inside the theater. The performance should have ended some time before.

"Sounds like something is wrong," Miles said. He pulled open the door.

"I smell smoke," Hap said as he dashed inside.

Miles tried to follow but I grabbed his arm. "Don't go any farther," I ordered him. "You don't want to breathe in smoke." He didn't listen, pulling away from me. I hurried after him into the tiny lobby and then into the theater itself, leaving Dmitri to follow us.

Smoke billowed from something on one corner of the stage. Two stagehands tossed buckets of water on the source of the flames. I couldn't tell what it was.

Kalev Tamm stood next to them, trying to wave some of the

smoke away. "That should do it. No major damage." He sounded calm, but then, he always did—a good trait for a theater manager, according to my mother.

One of the actors began to shout at another stagehand, who cowered in front of him. "My cape could have caught on fire!" the actor thundered. "How was I to know you'd spilled the lightning powder before I threw down my cigarette?"

"I'm sorry," the boy said, wringing his cap between his hands.

"It's all right," Kalev said. "You can get back to cleaning up. These things happen." The stagehand ran offstage like he wanted to be gone as quickly as possible. Kalev's calming voice didn't have as much of an effect on the actor. The man stomped away

"Kalev, what happened?" I called out.

"Lottie! I thought I'd see you at the party, not here."

"We heard shouting and smelled smoke," Hap said.

"The stagehand spilled some of the powder for the new lightning machine. He didn't know it was so flammable. One tiny burning ash and poof!" Kalev threw his hands up. "Unfortunately, he spilled it right by the broom, and the broom caught fire rather fast."

"Lightning machine?" Hap said as he went up onstage. I could imagine the gleam in his eyes. He loved all the special-effects machines in the theater. He would quit his studies in an instant to be a stagehand if Papa would allow it, which of course he never would.

Dmitri followed him onstage, though it took him some effort to get up there. I made the introductions.

"Any friend of the Masons is welcome here!" Kalev said to him. His eyes flicked between me and Dmitri. I realized I'd forgotten to add that Dmitri was a tutor. I could tell that Kalev was wondering if Dmitri was someone important to me. He'd known about Pavel, and I was sure he'd heard from Celeste how I'd cried when I learned of Pavel's death.

Before I could explain about Dmitri, Hap took over the conversation. "Now that you've said hello, where is the lightning machine?" he asked.

"It's over here, but it's not working right." Kalev gestured to a tall metal box, open on one side, that had some screen contraption inside it with a spirit lamp at the base. He began explaining in great detail how it was supposed to work. Kalev loved special-effects machines as much as Hap.

I was surprised when Dmitri spoke up. "The spirit lamp is probably too far away from the screen. The powder needs more heat to ignite. It can be fixed if you raise the lamp up on some bricks or something. Or possibly the box is too deep and is muffling the effect. There are several things you can try."

"You sound like you know what you are talking about," Kalev said. I could hear the surprise in his voice. I knew he didn't think much of the elite regiments, because he'd said their whole purpose before the war had been to parade around during ceremonies in fancy uniforms.

"I planned to study engineering and architecture before the war," Dmitri said. "I don't know that much, but I've always liked this sort of problem. It keeps me thinking, so when I go back to school I won't be stale."

I didn't understand. Dmitri would never be able to study those subjects as long as he was in the Horse Guard, even once the war ended. Men didn't just quit. It was a lifetime job. He had to know that. As I was trying to work out why he'd said that, I caught myself. It wasn't my problem what he did with his life. As Miles too often reminded me, I should stick to my own problems instead of trying to take charge of other people's.

"I want to see how it works," Hap said.

"You've given me some ideas," Kalev said to Dmitri. "Since Hap wants a demonstration, let's try a few things. Lottie, Miles, tell Celeste we'll be along shortly."

I knew that "shortly" could mean an hour or more. At least it would give me time to talk to Celeste. I had to get rid of that piece of paper, and once I'd heard from Celeste that the baron's accusations against them were all nonsense, we could figure out how to keep interest away from them, and from me.

The dvornik, Hugo, let us into the apartment building, greeting us like we were long-lost relatives. He was an elderly man who looked so much like Papa they could have been brothers, though their lives hadn't been anything alike. Hugo had been an actor until the infirmities of old age caught up with him and Kalev got him the job. Since dvorniks oversaw who came and went in the apartment building, Hugo got to live in a small room of his own right off the front door.

I pulled out the bag of tobacco I'd purchased earlier in the day and handed it to him. "They only had Mahorka left. I'm sorry. I know it's not the best brand."

He took it and held it up to his nose. "Ah . . . any tobacco is greatly appreciated. You are a good child, Charlotte Danielovna," he said.

"It's nothing," I said. "I hope you enjoy it."

The voices and music from the apartment above were so loud, they spilled down the stairs. My spirits lifted a little, even with the knowledge that I had the paper in my bag. I loved visiting the Tamms. They made their home feel like it was ours, too. We went up and Miles opened the door, not bothering to knock. The Tamms' parties were too loud for anyone to hear the knocking. A wave of noise and smoke and heat hit us along with the smell of sausages grilling on the stove.

The room was lit with only one electric bulb dangling from the ceiling, encased in a painted glass shade. It was so crowded people could barely move. We edged our way through. Miles found Peet, who was playing the piano, surrounded by a group of friends. I made my excuses to people as I passed them to get to the kitchen, which was almost as crowded. Celeste stood at the stove, turning the sausages, but when she saw me, she put down the tongs she held and took my hands, kissing me on both cheeks. I immediately felt warm inside and out.

"I'm so glad you came!" she cried. "We haven't seen enough of you."

"I've been so busy at the hospital." I told her about the problem at the theater and then handed her the bag of sugar.

"Sugar! A whole bag! It's a treasure. But you don't have to bring something every time you come to see us. We wouldn't even have a theater without your mother's help."

"I know my brothers eat everything in sight wherever they go. This is just to help feed them." The price of sugar had gone way up over the last few months, and I knew Celeste never turned anyone away who needed a meal.

"Are Hap and Miles here? Peet was afraid they wouldn't be able to come. He saved them some of his birthday pie."

"They're here, though Hap is still over at the theater with Kalev. They didn't tell me they were planning on coming. I caught them sneaking out of the house."

She laughed. "But at least they were sneaking here! Much better than many places they could go. How is Miles?"

"The same. Dr. Rushailo is trying some new treatment she's read that has helped other tuberculosis patients, so we just have to hope he won't catch a bad cold this winter." Since my stepfather never asked the name of Miles's doctor, I never mentioned I'd arranged for Miles to see a woman.

"I say a prayer for him every day." I felt a little pang at how worn down Celeste looked. Her graying hair was coming loose, frizzing from the heat of the kitchen. The years of hard work had taken a toll on her. Even though she looked happy, I found it hard to believe she and my mother would have been the same age had my mother lived. My mother had told me Celeste had been considered the most beautiful young actress in Paris the year they met. Wealthy men pursued her, promising jewels and apartments. She turned them all down, walking away without a look back to marry Kalev, a young Estonian who was just a stagehand determined to have his own theater one day.

The sausages on the stove began to smoke. Celeste pulled them off the burner.

"I need to talk to you," I said.

"Can it wait a few minutes? So many people here tonight!"

I didn't want to wait, but I couldn't just drag her out in the hall to talk. "What can I do to help?"

She put the sausages on a platter. "You can carry these out. I need to bring some more water for the samovar."

I edged my way back through the crowd, hoping I wouldn't spill the sausages. They made it safely to the zakuski table that held the rest of the food, though they were gone almost immediately as the people who had followed my progress snagged them.

"Who is that?" I heard Celeste's voice behind me.

I looked over to see Kalev, Hap, and Dmitri at the door. Kalev was introducing Dmitri to two young actresses from the theater troupe. Even at a distance I could tell that one of the women was practically cooing over him. She touched the epaulet on his tunic like she'd never seen one before.

I explained to Celeste about the tutoring.

"Very interesting and very handsome! Horse Guard? We don't usually have one of those at our parties. They are a little too high and mighty for us. He looks like an intriguing young man. Rather brooding and mysterious."

I didn't have time to think about Dmitri. "I really need to talk to you," I said. "Can we go out into the hall where it's quiet?"

"Charlotte, over here!" Peet called.

A man took hold of Celeste's waist. "You should stop cooking," he said. "Dance with me."

Celeste laughed and removed the man's hands. "Where? On the ceiling? There's no room anywhere else."

"Charlotte!" Peet called again. I saw that Hap had taken his harmonica out and Miles was tightening a string on a borrowed balalaika.

"Let me cook the rest of the sausages," Celeste said to me. "You might as well humor Peet while I'm busy. He won't stop badgering you until you do. Then we can talk." She smiled and then twisted around so she could move between two different groups of people.

I went over to the piano. "Happy birthday, Peet," I said when I got close enough that I didn't have to shout.

Peet got up from the bench. "Thank you! You can take over at the piano. Hap says the three of you have some new songs he arranged. I'd like to hear the Mason family serenade me for my birthday. Don't say no." He smiled, looking so much like a miniature Kalev I could understand how his father had charmed his mother so many years ago.

"I'll play, but I don't think anyone will hear us over the noise!" I sat down. "What are we starting with?" I asked Hap.

"'Kalinka,' then 'As My Mother Wanted Me to Marry,' and then 'Oh, Dear Snow.'" Hap loved Russian folk songs and was determined to transcribe as many as he could.

We launched into the first song, and several partygoers began to sing. I sang too. I couldn't often push away the worries and the to-do lists that always filled my head, but when we played, they took up less space.

I don't know what made me glance up in the middle of the second song, but I did, and I saw Dmitri staring at us with an intensity that made me miss a couple of notes. He wasn't singing with the others.

Miles kicked me. "Concentrate," he muttered.

I glared at him but went back to paying attention to the music, or at least trying to. I didn't dare look in Dmitri's direction. When we finished the third song, I saw that Celeste had come back into the room, so I pushed the bench back.

"We've got some other songs," Miles said.

"I need to talk to Celeste. Go ahead and play them without me."

I ignored Miles's protests. Celeste saw me and waved toward the hall. It was a relief to leave the apartment and breathe in some fresh air. Too many people were smoking inside the apartment and I didn't like the smell.

"What do you want to talk about? You sounded so serious earlier." Celeste asked.

I took the paper out of my bag and handed it to her. As she was reading it, I plunged right into an explanation. "Someone gave me this and warned me to be careful associating with you because I'd draw the attention of the Okhrana. That sounds like you've come to their notice." My voice faltered. I saw Samuel's bloody face in my mind. "I'm scared for you. I couldn't bear it if anything happened. Do you know who wrote this?"

Her eyes shifted away from mine just for an instant. The corners of her mouth turned up, but it wasn't a real smile. She hugged me and then took a step back, crumpling up the paper. "I'll get rid of this. Lottie, you don't sound like yourself at all. I've never known you to jump at shadows. Theater people talk and talk and talk. You know we like the sounds of our own voices. It means nothing. The Okhrana are suspicious of everyone. I don't want you to worry about us. You have enough of your own worries."

She sounded so reasonable. It was true that artists and writers were always viewed with suspicion. Neither Celeste nor Kalev would do anything to jeopardize the theater. They'd worked too hard. The baron was trying to unsettle me by making insinuations. I couldn't let him do that.

More voices came from below as a group of people clattered up the steps. A man's voice rose over the noise, someone speaking English with an American accent.

"Him again!" Celeste pushed her hair off her face. "If you want to help, you can talk to the American." She nodded in the direction of the stairs. "He's just arrived in the country. I don't even know who brought him here last week, but he's been here almost every night since then because he says he's 'mad about theater.' He doesn't speak Russian and his French is atrocious, so he can't talk to that many people."

The group reached the top of the stairs and Celeste introduced everyone, but I didn't quite catch the man's name. He certainly looked like an American: extremely tall with a lanky build, fair-haired and already balding, though he appeared to be only a few years older than me. I don't know why the young Americans I met would never be mistaken for Russians. I suppose it was because they smiled too much. This one was grinning away as if he'd never been happier.

We were swept back into the apartment by more new arrivals coming in behind us. I saw a few people leaving, otherwise we literally would not have found space for any more.

The American and I ended up back near the zakuski table, which at this point was nearly empty. I noticed Dmitri across the room. He was leaning down, listening to one of the actresses. She was very pretty, and whatever she was saying made Dmitri smile.

"I'm so glad I've met another American!" the American yelled in my ear, making me jump.

I struggled to find a way to respond to that. "How long have you been in Russia?" I asked.

"A week. It's sure something! The people are so friendly. A fellow brought me here last week and I felt so welcome, I just had to come back. I'm mad about the theater. Did a bit of acting in college."

"What kind of work do you do?" I thought perhaps he worked in a bank. There were scores of young men sent to work in the foreign banks in Petrograd.

"I'm a newspaperman. The *St. Louis Chronicle Dispatch*'s first-ever foreign correspondent." He pointed at himself. "That's me. Had a tricky time getting into Russia, and once I got here, I had an even worse time finding somewhere to stay, even with a cousin working at the embassy! All the foreigners who want to go home are too scared the Germans will torpedo their ships, so the hotels are jam-packed. Guess where I'm sleeping?" He grinned.

The conversation was taking a bit of an odd turn, but I decided I'd play along. "I can't guess. Where?"

"The billiard table at the Hotel de France!" He seemed so pleased with this bit of hardship that I had to smile.

His next words were drowned out when a man across the room began to speak in a loud, deep voice. The speaker was a big, burly man a head taller than the rest of the crowd. He shook his finger at a man next to him. "You can't stick your head in the sand!" the man bellowed in Russian.

"Not that fellow again!" The American threw up his hands. "He'll shut down the party if he carries on. I met him here a few days ago and he wouldn't stop yelling. He's some sort of playwright who writes political plays."

Political plays. That didn't sound good. The Tamms didn't put on political plays. I'd heard that the only theater people who did so staged them in random spots without any advertising. It was too dangerous to do it any other way.

The playwright's voice grew louder. "We can't wait much longer! We need peace before the country is destroyed. We must have a new government!"

"What in the devil is he saying?" the American asked.

The man continued, practically roaring, and I translated. "'The traitoress empress should be locked up in a convent or sent away. Who knows what all she's done to help the Germans? She's going to let them have our country if she's not stopped.'"

Even though I was just translating, I felt like I should not be saying the words. I couldn't believe the man was talking in front of so many people, most of whom he probably didn't know. Such words could get him arrested.

I looked around to find Dmitri. I didn't see him anywhere. I didn't see the actress, either. It was so hot, I couldn't get enough air, and the scent of the greasy sausage plate mixed with the cigarette smoke made me queasy.

"I have to go," I said to the man. Without waiting to see if he replied, I pushed my way through the crowd, trying to spot Hap and Miles.

I got to Hap first. "Have you seen Dmitri?"

Hap shrugged. "Not for a while. I suppose he left."

"We need to go too. It's getting late." If Dmitri was still around somewhere, he could find his own way home.

Both Hap and Miles protested, but when I said they'd have to walk home in the cold if they wouldn't go with me, they gave in. I noticed that the package Miles had been carrying was still sitting on the floor next to the piano.

"We can wait long enough for you to give Peet his present," I said, pointing at it.

Miles mumbled something.

"What?"

"He can open it later. Let's go."

Downstairs, Hugo dozed in his chair, not stirring at all as we slipped through the front door, trying not to let in any more of the frigid air than necessary.

When we got outside, I noticed a man across the street standing in a doorway. I couldn't make out his features but I could see the glowing tip of his cigarette. I wanted to bolt back inside. I turned away, not wanting the man to see my face, and then I noticed that, as usual, Hap didn't have on a hat. Standing under the streetlamp in front of the theater, his red hair was practically a beacon, and when he and Miles began talking about the party in English, their voices carried in the quiet night air.

"Find us a ride," I said to Hap in Russian so he'd stop talking, even though I was sure that if the man was there to watch us, he would have already noticed everything about us that stood out.

I pretended to listen to Miles while we waited, and nearly pushed them both in the sleigh when it drew up, glad Hap had managed to find something big enough for all three of us.

We pulled away and I resisted the urge to turn around, though my shoulders tightened as if I could feel the man still watching us.

"Lottie, you aren't listening," Miles said.

"What?"

"I said, how are you going to answer Elder Red?" Miles's voice was raspy. It always was after he spent any length of time in a smoky room.

"What?" I asked again. Elder Red was what the boys called our grandmother, our father's mother. I didn't understand why Miles was asking about her at that particular moment. When we received our infrequent letters, I responded, though her letters were a litany of complaints. She'd hated my mother, and I was never sure she even wanted us as grandchildren.

Miles coughed, but got it under control fairly easily. "Didn't you get a letter too? Elder Red said she was writing to you in the one she sent to us. Ours was full of fire and brimstone, even more than usual."

Hap threw his fur onto Miles. "Here, I don't need this. It's not that cold. Charlotte, we decided you're going to have to be the one to write her back and tell her we aren't coming."

"Wait. She wants us to come visit her?" The few times we had seen her, she could barely contain her irritation at our existence. She never came to accept that her son had married a young actress he'd met on a business trip to France instead of marrying someone from an approved "good" family, and had then had the audacity to produce three grandchildren without impeccable pedigrees.

"No, she wants us to come live in America," Miles said. "Our letter was full of dire predictions about our futures if we stayed here.

You'll tell her no, of course, but find a way where she won't cut us out of the will."

"Start over," I said. "You must be leaving out some parts."

"We're not," Hap said, repeating Miles's version of the letter.

The sleigh pulled up in front of the house and Hap jumped out. "Don't just sit there," he said. "Pay the man."

I followed them inside and they threw off their coats and their felt boots and were racing upstairs in the time it took me to unbutton my own coat.

"Has the tutor come home yet?" I asked Osip, trying to keep my voice casual. I had more than my grandmother's letter to worry about.

"No, he's not back. You have a letter. I'm sorry I forgot to give it to you earlier." Osip went over to a hall table and brought me an envelope that had been lying on a tray.

"Thank you. Good night, Osip," I said as I went upstairs. The letter felt heavy in my hand. A familiar pang of pain hit my right temple, one that happened every time I faced a letter of hers. Once in my room I decided just to get it over with, so I ripped the envelope open.

My grandmother's handwriting was tiny and precise.

Dear Charlotte,

I don't wish to be so blunt, but I see no other choice. Your desire to be present as your half sisters grow up is admirable, but there are others who can oversee their upbringing. You only have a few years as an eligible young woman, and you shouldn't waste them in such a foreign place.

I was shocked to hear of your plans to go to medical school. What kind of influences are you under to come up with such a scheme? You will doom yourself to a life of toil, and no man will want to marry a doctor. It is beyond absurd.

Nursing is fine for young women in time of war, and again, admirable, but it is not meant as a career for the women of this family. If your father were alive, I'm sure he would not approve.

I must insist you make plans for your immediate removal from Russia. I allowed you to stay in the aftermath of your mother's death because I thought you needed time in a familiar place to deal with your grief. But it's been over a year now, and it's time for you three to move on with the rest of your lives.

I fear you will resist this, so I am going to have to make this an ultimatum in the hopes you will come to realize that what I am doing is for your own good. Come back to the United States or I will remove you and your brothers from my will. I'm sure your mother wasted the rather substantial fortune that your father left her, but I don't want to see my grandchildren suffer from her poor decisions. Come back to the United States and we will make suitable arrangements for your and your brothers' education. If you want to go to an appropriate women's college, that can be arranged.

Think over this letter carefully before you respond. I know you have inherited your mother's stubbornness. You must work to overcome that.

Your affectionate grandmother,
Elizabeth Mason

I threw the letter down, my head throbbing so much I could barely see. I didn't care about her money. I could support myself as a doctor. I certainly wasn't going to go back to the United States so that a grandmother I didn't know could control my life.

I would tell her I wasn't coming but I would not speak for my brothers. They were going to have to do that themselves.

I went to the window and looked out. No sign of Dmitri. I stayed there for a long time until the cold drove me to my bed.

Chapter Eight

WHEN I WOKE, I jumped up and went back to the window. There was no one standing outside. I didn't know if that was a good sign or a bad sign. It could have meant the secret police had already decided that since we'd been at the Tamms', we were definitely on the list as agitators.

I needed to know when Dmitri had gotten home. Had he left the party with the actress? Where had they gone? I ran through some possibilities in my head until I realized how ridiculous those thoughts were. I should have been far more worried that Dmitri had gone somewhere to report the presence of potential anti-czarists at the party. The Horse Guard, after all, was one of the most loyal of the czar's regiments. It was time to get more information about Dmitri Antonovich.

When I went downstairs, I heard Osip and Archer arguing in the dining room.

"You are a lazy good-for-nothing!" Archer said in a loud voice. "You should have been done polishing the silver yesterday. You're ruining the whole schedule."

"I was busy polishing the brass," Osip said in an equally loud voice. "There are not enough people to do all the work here anymore.

I don't want to do a maid's job. Vladislav says we should only have to work eight hours a day and be paid enough so we can drink champagne just like the rich."

Archer's voice grew louder. "Vladislav doesn't know how to do a decent day's work. He's lucky he has a job. *You're* lucky you have a job." Osip began to protest, but Archer cut him off and kept talking. "You'd be out on the streets without this. You may still be out on the streets if I decide you're more trouble than you are worth."

"Just you wait!" Osip shouted. "Revolution is coming—then we'll all have apartments of our own and all the food we want to eat."

Archer laughed. "You fool! No one is going to just give you an apartment."

"You wait." I heard Osip stomping away.

I didn't think Archer would actually fire Osip. He'd have to hire someone else, and he was very particular about who worked in the house. Although there were certainly plenty of men needing work, Archer wouldn't hire anyone who didn't fit his idea of the perfect servant. He did give too many tasks to Osip, but since my stepfather left Archer in complete control of running the house, it was one area neither my mother nor I had ever tried to intervene in.

I knocked on the door to the library and then went in. It smelled so strongly of cigars I wanted to open all the windows and let the room air out. Without my mother around to protest, Papa smoked far too many cigars. He sat at his desk, writing in his usual slow and careful way, a cigar sitting in an ashtray next to him.

"Good morning. How is the writing going?" I asked, praying he would not confuse me with my mother again.

He looked up. "Lottie! I suppose you are off to the hospital? I'm happy to report that the writing is going very, very well. I've finished the war with Turkey." He didn't slur any of his words and he seemed like his old self.

"Wonderful!" I said as I pulled up a chair.

For a moment he seemed a bit taken aback by my enthusiasm, and then he smiled. "It's a most interesting time period. It seems like it all happened just yesterday, though most people would consider 1878 a long time ago."

1878. That meant Papa had almost forty more years to cover in the memoir. At least he'd have something to occupy him for a long time.

"1878, you say? You would have been about Dmitri Antonovich's age then, wouldn't you?" I asked. "Is Dmitri related to Prince Shulga?" Not the smoothest transition, but my stepfather loved talking about family connections almost as much as he loved talking about battles.

My ploy worked. "A cousin by marriage," Papa said. "Dmitri Antonovich is the great-nephew of the prince's brother-in-law, Count Lieven."

I tried to untangle the meaning of that while Papa continued to talk.

"The boy has a sad history. His parents and siblings died of cholera in the 1910 epidemic."

My throat tightened. Dmitri had lost his entire family. I'd heard about the cholera epidemic. That was a year before we'd come to Russia, but people still talked about it because so many had died. I'd never heard of anyone who'd lost their whole family. That would be like being plunged into a bottomless pit. I didn't even want to think of the horror of it. How had he survived?

I realized my stepfather was still speaking. "And then, after the count's own grandson died, Dmitri Antonovich became his heir, so the count arranged for the boy to take his grandson's place in the

Horse Guard. The family has always had someone serving in that regiment."

I forced myself to focus on what my stepfather was saying. It explained why Dmitri's university career had been cut short, but it didn't explain everything. "Why does he want to tutor? I'd think he'd recover much faster at home. Or he could be working in a staff position for his regiment. Don't they find desk jobs for injured soldiers?"

"I don't know. Something about a problem with the officer in charge of the regimental office who has a grudge against the count."

Archer's voice from the doorway startled me. "Baron Eristov is here to see you, General."

My heart skipped a beat. The baron had never come to the house before, as far as I knew.

Before my stepfather could respond, loud voices came from upstairs. "I want to go first!" Hap shouted.

"I'm already here!" Stepan shouted back. I hurried out the door to tell them not to yell, but as I came into the hall I heard glass breaking. I saw the baron by the door, and then a motion made me glance up. Hap dropped something made of rope over the railing on the upper landing. It hit the floor along with the sound of more glass breaking. He swore. Stepan leaned so far over the railing I thought he might fall.

"What are you doing?" I tried not to shriek. I don't know when I'd taken up shrieking as a means of communication, but I found myself resorting to it all too often.

The boys came pounding down the stairs.

"A physics experiment," Stepan said. "We're supposed to figure out a way to cushion the fall enough so the glasses won't break." He picked up a small contraption made of sticks and string that vaguely resembled a misshapen birdcage. "Mine worked better than Hap's. My glass only broke into four pieces."

"Where is Dmitri Antonovich?" I asked.

"He had to go out," Stepan replied. "I already know how I can modify mine."

Archer gave the loudest sigh I'd ever heard. "I'll get Zarja to clean up," he said.

"Don't put on that face, Lottie," Hap said. "We're doing something very educational. You should be pleased."

Osip burst out laughing and then covered his mouth, still shaking with mirth.

"Hello, Baron. That's true, Lottie," Papa said as he walked over and picked up Hap's contraption. "It is educational, though rather an unconventional way to learn. Very clever. A little adaptation will make it better. More rope wrapped around, perhaps."

Before he could add anything to his evaluation, screams erupted from the upper floor. The twins. Their screams were unmistakable.

"Is something wrong?" the baron asked.

"Just our little sisters," Hap said. "They scream a lot." This was true. He pointed at one part of his rope bundle. "I guess I didn't add enough here."

I realized something odd. Someone was missing.

"Where's Miles?" I asked.

"He wrote a new story he's reading to the twins," Stepan said.

I went toward the stairs, my irritation rising. "He's not supposed to read them his stories. They get frightened." They actually became so terrified they'd have trouble sleeping and then they'd end up in my bed. The way they flopped around would keep me awake all night.

"Don't act like an old lady, Lottie. They like his stories," Hap said. "You're turning into Elder Red." He laughed. "Dmitri was surprised to find out you were a few months younger than him. He thought you were old, like twenty-five. We told him you used to be fun, but I'm not sure he believed that."

"Yes, old," Stepan echoed. "People like to be scared," he added, "and Miles is really good at scaring."

The screaming grew louder, and then I heard a door open upstairs. The twins came into view, running along the landing and then dashing down the stairs, looking behind them as they ran. It was a miracle they didn't take a misstep and fall. I yelled, trying to get them to slow down. They didn't, and when they reached me, they grabbed my skirts, trying to hide behind them.

A figure dressed in rags with long, straggly gray hair came flying down the stairs after them, someone who appeared to be an old hag but who ran exactly like Miles. I recognized the wig. It was the one Miles wore when he was doing his fortune-telling routine, but he'd made the hair all wild in its current appearance.

"I shall get you, my little ones!" the creature shouted in a high-pitched voice. "You can't escape from me!"

Both twins continued to scream, but it turned into that sort of happy screaming they did when they were excited.

"Miles! Stop!" I yelled.

He came toward us, his arms outstretched and his fingers curled like claws.

"Miles! We have a guest!"

Miles slid to a stop and looked around. When he spotted the baron, he pulled off the wig.

"Oh, I didn't know," he said in his regular voice. "How do you do?"

The baron seemed to have lost the power of speech. Miles gave the tiniest of shrugs and grinned.

Osip broke out into laughter again, laughing so hard a few tears ran down his face. He tried to speak but ended up gasping until he finally managed to choke out a few words. "He looks just like my old grandmother."

I heard a strange hissing noise coming from the baron. When I glanced back at him, I saw him glaring at Osip, his face an alarming shade of red. A vein throbbed in his forehead. Osip was too busy laughing to notice.

"Don't mind the children." Papa said to the baron as he waved in Miles's direction. "We can talk in the library." He chuckled. "We have quite a lively household."

It always struck me as odd that my stepfather still considered Miles and Hap to be children, though he'd certainly commanded young men Miles's age when he'd been in the army. I'm sure he hadn't been lenient with those boys, but he never rebuked Miles or Hap. It was as if he still saw the two of them at the ages they had been when he'd married my mother, forever young boys running about the house whooping with excitement.

The baron looked as if he was going to say something, but the bell rang before he could speak. Osip, still chuckling, opened the door and Dmitri came in, limping much more noticeably than he had been the day before. I hoped the wound hadn't become infected. He really needed to stop going out for at least a few days.

"Dmitri!" Stepan shouted. "We need help with our experiments."

I didn't think Dmitri heard him. He was looking back and forth between the baron and me.

"Good morning, Dmitri Antonovich," the baron said. "I'm glad to hear you accepted the tutoring position. I also heard your great uncle is very ill in Paris. Have you any news?"

"Nothing recent," Dmitri said. His tone was sharp, and he didn't add anything to those two words.

The baron obviously knew Dmitri. I remembered what Papa had said at the party about telling the baron to send the young man over to our house. I hadn't thought about which baron he was referring to, but it must have been this one. I looked over at Dmitri. His face was grim.

"Dmitri, come see what we made!" Stepan shouted again.

Dmitri's gaze turned to the broken glass on the floor. "I thought you were going to wait to try this until we could discuss some of the factors you needed to consider," he said.

Stepan nudged around the pieces of glass with his foot until they were in somewhat of a pile. "We didn't want to wait. Let's get some more glasses. I have another idea."

"No," Dmitri said. "That is not how an actual engineer would proceed. You need to analyze your mistakes first."

"Listen to your tutor," Papa ordered. "This way, Baron."

"I'd like Miss Mason to join us," the baron said. I saw Dmitri's head jerk around toward us.

I felt a pain in one of my eyes, a sign the headache from the night before was trying to creep back in. Whatever the baron wanted with me, it wouldn't be pleasant. I took a deep breath and put on a smile as if I were delighted with his presence.

Papa twisted one end of his mustache, something he did when he was thinking or confused, though I knew he'd be too polite to ask the baron why he wanted me included in their talk. He motioned again toward the door of the library and then led the way inside. I came last, glancing back before I went in. Dmitri was still watching us. I couldn't read the expression on his face.

The baron asked me to shut the door. I came in and sat in one of the chairs in front of Papa's desk. The baron refused a chair, standing next to me with his hands clasped behind his back.

"How are you?" Papa asked.

"I'm sorry I don't have time for pleasantries," the baron replied. "I'll get right to the point. The political situation is deteriorating, and that means there will have to be a severe crackdown on dissent or the czar will fall."

"How could the crackdown get more severe?" I asked, not believing what I'd just heard. "I saw a boy who had been beaten yesterday. The police dragged him away for voicing his opinion."

The baron ignored me. "The army's losses are staggering, though we don't want the people to know. If the czar is forced to give up the throne, there is no one to take his place who will be any better. Even if the czar's son were not still a child, the boy is sickly and would never make a strong ruler."

Hearing those words from a man in the baron's position was shocking. Even with all the gossip, the official word was always that the situation was under control, and that Russia was strong and would triumph in the end. I'd thought that a revolution would mean the czar would give some power to the people, to hold elections and have representatives, not that he'd be gone altogether.

I looked over at my stepfather. Papa frowned, his face creasing so much he suddenly appeared ten years older. When he spoke, his tone was different. It was sharp, and I could see him as the military commander he had been.

"I didn't know the situation was that bad, and of course steps must be taken. What can I do? I'm ready to step back into a post at anytime." He put his hand on his heart. "I will always serve the czar."

I wanted to protest. There was no way he could go back to the army.

The baron held up his hand. "That won't be necessary, though we may call on you for advice."

Papa slumped a little, as if he were a scarecrow with his stuffing removed. "Then I'm confused. What can I do for you?"

The baron turned his attention to me. I squeezed my hands together.

"I thought you should be made aware of what is happening in your own household. Last night, your stepchildren were seen leaving a place that known agitators frequent."

I tried to keep a calm expression on my face. Why had the baron bothered to come to the house to tell Papa that? If the government was practically falling apart, we could hardly be considered all that important.

Papa turned to me. "What is he talking about?"

"We went to a birthday party at the Tamms'," I said. "There were no agitators there, just theater people." I forced myself to laugh, as if the thought that there was anything else happening at the party was a ridiculous idea.

Papa nodded. "Ah, of course, the Tamms. Yes, as Lottie says, the Tamms are just theater people. My wife was very fond of that family. If an agitator goes there, it has nothing to do with the Tamms. I know they are a little too free in welcoming people to their home, but that is only because of their generous hearts. Believe it or not, I went there myself once. Very jolly time."

The baron spoke through clenched teeth. "Anyone can be an agitator. They don't advertise the fact. Miss Mason, can you say you've never met a traitor at the Tamms' house? If you have, now would be a good time to say so."

I hadn't actually met the playwright. "I've never met anyone at the Tamms who spoke against the czar."

The baron raised an eyebrow and then gave a smile that was more of a sneer. "That's surprising. A man was arrested just a few hours ago, a playwright. He was at the Tamms' last night, and there is a report he was definitely making his views known. Somehow you didn't hear him?"

I couldn't believe I'd fallen right into the baron's trap.

I squeezed my fists so hard my nails bit into my hand. "I didn't hear every conversation nor meet every guest," I said. "Their parties are very crowded." Who had reported the man, and how had the baron found out so quickly? The baron had to be working closely with the secret police. But if he was, I still didn't understand why he had warned me the other night.

The baron pulled a piece of paper out of his pocket and unfolded it. "The playwright also had in his possession several dozen leaflets that he's admitted he was going to distribute. He hasn't yet said where he got them, but he may soon realize it is better to cooperate. This is a bit different from ones we've seen before. However, there are some interesting features that are similar to other ones passed around last week."

He handed the paper to me instead of Papa. "As I told Miss Mason the other night, most of our revolutionaries quote the French, not the Americans."

I took the paper, trying to keep my hand steady as I held it up to read. There were the usual claims that the czar and czarina were leading the country into ruin. Down near the bottom I saw why the baron had mentioned Americans. The very last statement read *We have it in our power to begin the world over again. —Thomas Paine, American revolutionary.*

This time my laugh was real. "Surely you don't think I'm behind these?" I handed the paper to my stepfather. "That's absurd."

I saw the vein throbbing on the baron's forehead again. "It is no laughing matter. For the well-being of your family, I would suggest that none of you visit these theater people until the situation is brought under control. Or, even better, send your stepchildren back to America, at least for the time being."

"No!" I burst out. "Papa, we don't want to leave." I felt hot, like the anger inside me was going to catch fire. The baron was a vile man, and I wanted him out of our house.

Papa tossed the paper down on his desk. "They're not going anywhere. What nonsense!" His voice was shaking. I examined his face, trying to determine if he was feeling ill again. "I'm sure the baron didn't mean to imply you'd written it, Lottie," Papa said. "But he is right. Best to avoid the Tamms for a few weeks. It won't take long to get the country back on the right track. Then you'll be able to see your friends as much as you want."

The baron cleared his throat. "There is one more issue."

I tensed, waiting to hear him accuse me of black-market activities.

"People are talking about the hospital your wife founded," he said.

"Yes, they do fine work," Papa said. He sounded impatient, like he wanted the baron to leave.

"No, you don't understand. The facility could be put to better use. You should consider turning it into a real hospital for patients who actually need the care. Hospitals for our soldiers are overwhelmed with patients. I'm sure a doctor could be found who would be happy to run the facility. It could only enhance your reputation."

"We're not closing the hospital!" I shouted. I didn't know how much longer I could sit in the room and listen to the man.

Papa got to his feet. He straightened up as if he were standing at attention.

"I think you overstep yourself, Baron." There was a coldness in my stepfather's voice that I'd never heard before. "My reputation needs no 'enhancement,' as you call it. I have spent my life in service to the empire. No one would question that. And as for the hospital, my wife dedicated many hours and much work to it. It will remain as a tribute to her. She was a wonderful woman. Pity you never married, Baron. Perhaps then you would understand. Now, if you don't mind, I must get back to work."

The baron stared at Papa, disbelief written on his face.

I wanted to clap. I'd never felt more proud of my stepfather.

The baron picked up the leaflet, folded it, and put it back into his pocket. "I'll see myself out." His face had turned so red I feared he was going to have an attack of apoplexy.

"It would be rude of us to let you do that. Lottie will show you out," Papa said. "My children know their responsibilities even down to the smallest of duties. Lottie, please come back once the baron is gone. I may need your help."

I saw him take hold of the edge of the desk with one hand. I stood up and nodded my head, then walked out the door of the library as fast as I could, wanting to get the baron out of the house so I could see if Papa was actually feeling ill.

The baron followed me, though he didn't speak.

Osip stood by the door, the baron's cloak in hand, as if he had known the man wouldn't stay long.

The baron snapped at him. "If you were my servant, you'd be out on the street after the sort of behavior I witnessed here today." He spun on his heels and stalked out the door.

As soon as the door was shut, Osip made a rude gesture at it, or rather at the baron on the other side of it.

At another time I would have laughed, but I was too worried about Papa. I hurried back into the library to see him sitting there gazing down at an empty spot on his desk.

"Papa, are you ill?"

He looked up at me. "Lottie, please be careful." His voice was so low I had trouble making out the words. "I can put on a good show, but I don't know if I can really protect you. I'm just an old forgotten man now, and the Okhrana are ruthless."

I sank down in the chair. "I didn't have anything to do with that leaflet! Surely you know that."

"I know you didn't, but that doesn't matter. The secret police fabricate evidence if they need to show they are successful. They can try to make an example of you to scare off others. Since you are an American and female, I don't think they'd send you to prison, but even an interrogation would be terrible." His voice trembled. "They wouldn't just question you. They could deport you, and you'd never be allowed to come back."

"But I don't know how to convince the baron he's focused on the wrong person. It's all so ridiculous!"

"If you see him again, just be polite. Perhaps it is better that you laughed. It made you sound innocent."

"I am innocent!"

"I know. I know. But do avoid the Tamms. They will be watched even closer now."

"I'll be careful." I couldn't promise I wouldn't see them.

He nodded and leaned back in his chair, rubbing his face with his hand. "How I wish I could turn back time. I would have been a voice against so much, back when I had a voice that mattered."

"Your voice does still matter." I stood back up. "Thank you for supporting the hospital. It would make Mama happy if she knew."

He gave me a faint smile. "I'm glad you are keeping it going, though I know it is a big responsibility for a girl your age. I hope it's not too much."

"Dr. Rushailo and the more experienced nurses are really the ones who do the most work," I said. "I should go, though. We are short of help."

"Yes, go. Everything is fine here, especially now with the new tutor." He chuckled, and I was happy he didn't seem as upset. "Physics experiments with glasses! What an idea!"

I left him still chuckling. Out in the hall, Osip was cleaning the floor where the wet snow had been tracked in.

"Why was the baron so furious at you?" I asked. "He's never even seen you before, has he?"

Osip shook his head. "I suppose because I made myself noticeable when I laughed at Miles. Servants aren't supposed to do anything that draws attention to them. At least that's what Archer tells me all the time. That won't be true much longer."

"Watch your words." Archer's voice rang through the hall. I hadn't heard him come in. He was wearing a coat and a hat, which struck me as odd. I rarely saw Archer leave the house. "I have never seen the Cherkassky name so disgraced," Archer said. "I will speak to you later. I will be out for about an hour. See to your duties." He walked out the door, not acknowledging my presence.

Osip made the same rude gesture at the door he'd made earlier. "When revolution comes, he will regret all he's said to me."

"Do you really think there will be a revolution?" I asked. I didn't know why I was asking Osip. He wouldn't have a better idea of the situation than anyone else, but I wanted to hear something that would convince me we weren't always going to be stuck waiting and wondering.

"How could there not be? The people are done with being crushed under the czar's rule. Everyone talks of nothing else."

I decided I could trust Osip. I told him about the man watching the house. "Would you let me know if anyone approaches you asking questions about us? The baron has this bizarre idea that I'm one of the dissidents working for revolution."

Osip laughed. "You! Doesn't he know you spend all your time at the hospital?"

"You'd think he could find that out. If he comes back, you should be careful too. I'm afraid he's working with the Okhrana. Don't do anything to draw attention to yourself."

"I'm not afraid of him!"

"I know, but that may not matter." I had a question that needed to be asked no matter how odd Osip thought it sounded. "What time did the tutor return last night?" Someone at the Tamms' had to have reported the playwright almost right after he'd spoken those words. It sounded as if he was arrested right after the party and interrogated so quickly. I really didn't want Dmitri to have been that someone.

Osip didn't act like he thought the question unusual. "He came in around four o'clock and then was back out early this morning. From the pain on his face when he walks, he should stay in one place more."

I thought so too, but I couldn't exactly demand he not go out. Even though Dmitri didn't seem to be friends with the baron, that didn't necessarily mean they weren't both working for the secret police. It was a giant organization, and I'd heard they purposely kept the knowledge of who was working for them secret, even from their own members.

Was Dmitri that good an actor that he would come into our home and pretend to want to tutor my brothers as a means to spy on us? I didn't think he was, but I wished I could be sure. If I was wrong, it could be disastrous for all of us.

Chapter Nine

I FILLED ANOTHER basket with food to take to the hospital and went out. I assumed I could take a tram partway, but none of them were running, and there were no droshkies on the streets. There should have been droshkies everywhere. I stopped a woman passing by a tram stop and asked her if she knew what was happening.

"The drivers for hire are afraid to come out on the streets. They're afraid something is going to happen. And the trams have stopped because they aren't getting paid enough." She noticed my nurse's veil under my hat. "Do you have any news about the war? Do the soldiers tell you how it's going? I haven't heard from my son in months." Her voice broke and she covered her mouth with her hand.

"No, I'm sorry. Our hospital only treats women."

Her shoulders sagged, and she shuffled away from me without another word.

There were so many soldiers around, the city was almost like an army base. One of the squares had been turned into a drilling ground for new recruits. As I walked, I watched them take turns racing at a bizarre stuffed figure that had wooden poles sticking out all over it. Each time a recruit reached it, he would try to stick it with his bayonet without barreling into one of the poles.

I couldn't watch. I knew what damage a bayonet could do to an actual human being. The squares should have been full of vendors out with little carts selling fruit from the south and handmade toys and baskets, and people laughing and talking with their friends. There was no more of that, and the only sounds were the shouting of the officers. Our city had been turned into something so ugly I barely recognized it. I was beginning to fear that Papa was wrong about everything returning to normal soon.

When I got to the hospital, Galina came to find me as I was putting the food away in the pantry. "Charlotte, Irina Igorneeva's husband is here. He's demanding his wife come home. She's crying."

I tried to contain a sigh. We'd had this same sort of situation too many times before, even the very first day the hospital opened. I remembered my mother getting angry at a man for ruining the little celebration we'd had.

As I followed Galina into the ward, I heard the man before I saw him. He was shouting, of course. They always shouted. The other patients were trying not to notice the scene playing out at Irina Igorneeva's bed. Her husband was not a big man, but I stopped when I saw his black uniform. He was a policeman. We'd never had to deal with a policeman husband.

I didn't want to approach him, but I knew the others would be waiting for me to do something. It had always been my mother's job, and they had just expected it to become mine. Because my mother and I were foreigners and patrons of the hospital, the husbands were less likely to try to bully us.

The man turned on me when Galina explained who I was. "She needs to come home now!" he said. "Other women have babies and get right back to work."

I took a deep breath and tried to sound stern. "Not all women can get out of bed right away. It will just be a few more days before she's home."

He made a sound almost like a snarl and motioned to his wife's breakfast tray. "It's her job to stand in line for food and get something on the table for me. She's just lying here being treated to all this food while working men don't have enough." He grabbed a hunk of bread off the tray and stuffed it in his pocket.

I'd learned from watching my mother that harsh words were the best way to stand up to these sorts of men. "If she leaves now, she's likely to collapse at home," I said. "Then what will you do? Now I want you to leave. We have work to do and your wife needs to rest." I moved so that I stood directly between him and the bed and crossed my arms over my chest. I was too close to him, and I could feel sweat forming on my back.

He glared at me, and I forced myself not to shift my eyes away from him. After what seemed a long time, he gave a snort, then mumbled a few derogatory words about women as he spun around and marched out of the room. I waited until I heard the sound of the main door closing to find the nearest chair so I could sit down.

"Now, don't cry," Galina said to Irina Igorneeva as she adjusted the woman's blanket. "I'll bring the baby to you. You don't want to upset the child."

The woman gave a weak smile and wiped her tears. I got back up and hurried out of the ward, wanting to go hide in the office, not trusting my voice to speak to anyone. I could manage to stand up to those men, but once they were gone, I always felt sick to my stomach, the sort of sick I got that threatened a major headache. I didn't want any of the other nurses to know. They expected me to be just like my mother, but I was not nearly as strong as she had been.

I had only been in the office a few minutes when Galina came back. "There's someone to see you." She was smiling. She wouldn't be smiling if it were another problem person.

I had to make sure. I didn't think I could face one more. "Not another husband, I hope."

"No, a young American. I think he said he met you at a party last night but his French is very bad. He's, um, quite an energetic young man. He shook my hand so hard I thought my teeth would come loose."

A young American. The journalist. How had he found me? And why?

"I'll go talk to him," I said as I got up. "Thank you."

When I reached the main hall, the man saw me and broke into a grin. "Hello, Miss Mason! Carter Jenkins. From the Tamms' party?"

"Yes, hello, Mr. Jenkins. I'm . . . I'm surprised to see you here."

His grin grew bigger and he did a little motion with his feet like he was dancing a few steps of a jig. It was a strange action, but he acted like he didn't even realize he was doing it. "I did some investigating," he said. "That's what I do, you know, and I heard all about this little hospital. I thought it would make quite a story for the folks back home, about your mother starting it and all. Since she was an American and here you are an American too, still running it and just a girl. That's sure something!"

The man radiated so much energy it was a bit overwhelming. "I don't know," I said. "I don't think it's all that interesting." I'd have thought he would want to be covering political news.

"Oh, it is interesting. Most Americans have no idea how many of their compatriots are even living here. And with revolution about to break out any day, you just carry on. I like to do special-interest features. My father—he's the editor—says I have a real knack for them. I wouldn't bother any of the patients. When you have time, I could ask you a few questions and maybe look around a little to be able to describe the place?"

"There's not much to see. It's a very small hospital with room for sixteen patients and their babies, and right now we only have a few patients."

"That's still something! And having a hospital in a mansion is something too." He pointed up at the intricately decorated ceiling. "This doesn't look like any hospital I've ever seen!" One of the nurses walked by, and Carter stuck out his hand. "Hi there. I'm Carter Jenkins. Nice to meet you!"

The poor woman gave a start. Americans were so much more effusive than Russians, and I didn't know how many Americans this particular nurse had ever met. She took his hand somewhat gingerly. He got a firm grip on it and pumped her arm up and down. "I hear you are doing good work here."

"She doesn't speak English," I said, and then translated his words to her, adding, "Don't mind him. Think of him as a big American puppy."

"I hear a baby crying," she murmured to me, pulling her hand out of his and hurrying off.

"I need to learn me some Russian," Carter said. "We don't have to make it a formal interview, Miss Mason. What do you like to do for fun? Say, do you like skating? I hear that's very popular here. We can go skating and I can sneak in a few questions along the way."

I loved skating, but I hadn't had time for it in a long time. I was about to say no when Hap's words came back to me. *Dmitri thought you were old. We told him you used to be fun.*

All of a sudden I really wanted to go. "Tomorrow," I blurted out. "Yes, I'll go skating with you. Tomorrow."

"Well, that's wonderful!" Carter said. "I'll come by your house. Just tell me an address."

"We're on the French Embankment, number twenty-four."

He wrote it down in a little notebook. "Now, how about I have a little look around?"

The man was so eager I gave in and showed him around the hospital. Though none of the patients spoke any English, they didn't appear to mind his presence. They actually seemed to enjoy it, because he really was like a large puppy, excited over the smallest of things. He asked so many questions I eventually had to shoo him out the door so we could get some work done.

After he left, I spent the next several hours getting the books in order. When I finally headed home, the streets were still crowded, which was strange because it was so cold. Many people didn't appear to be going anywhere. They were just milling about in small groups. Some had started fires on the sidewalks and were huddled around them. There were no sounds of laughter or even loud voices. I walked faster, wanting to be home in the light and the warmth.

A small group of men from the Horse Guard rode by in perfect formation, not speaking, the only sound the clinking of the bridles and the soft clopping of the horses' hooves muffled by the snow-covered streets, which for some reason no one had attempted to clear.

I had a hard time imagining Dmitri among those men. Did he miss the comradeship? Pavel had spoken of his fellow soldiers all the time. They were closer to him than his own family. Dmitri seemed too aloof for that, but perhaps it was because he'd been at university first.

I was still thinking about Dmitri when I reached home. As I went in, I hoped I would be able to get to my room without anyone needing me, but Hap was waiting for me.

"Finally!" he called as he came out from the sitting room. "Miles and Stepan and I have a new song to practice."

"I'm so tired I don't know if I can learn anything new," I warned.

"Don't be an old lady! You can't be that tired. We want Dmitri to hear the song."

So Dmitri hadn't gone out again. I decided I wasn't that tired, so I followed Hap into the sitting room.

Dmitri sat by the fire with a sketchbook in his hand, his injured leg stretched out in front of him.

When he saw me, he stood up. "No, please, sit back down," I said. "Unless you'd rather not hear us make a racket while we are practicing."

"I like music. I'll stay if you don't mind." He sounded very formal.

"No, I don't mind at all." I felt like I should sound formal too, though it made me feel awkward. "I didn't know you were an artist."

"I'm not," he said. "But I draw plans for buildings I'd like to build some day."

I could see the outline of a building that looked like it was surrounded by huge gardens. "What kind of building is that?" I asked.

"It's a dacha," he said. "Not very interesting, I'm afraid."

I moved closer. "May I see?"

He handed the sketchbook to me, though I could tell he was reluctant. "I love our stepfather's dacha," I said. "It's so wonderful with all the big windows and the open rooms and the breezes blowing through. There are wonderful gardens there too, and a fish pond and . . ." I realized I was talking too much.

Dmitri's face lit up. "That's exactly the kind of place I want to build. These buildings in Petrograd are beautiful, but sometimes it feels like we all live in the past or in a museum."

I'd never seen his face so open and happy, and I was intrigued that architecture was such a passion to him. But once again I was puzzled that Dmitri seemed to be planning to go back to school, as if he could leave the Horse Guard. I wished I knew him well enough to ask him about it.

"Lottie, stop talking and let's play," Hap grumbled.

I handed the sketchbook back to Dmitri. "I'd like to look at more of these sometime, if you don't mind."

"I would be happy to show you, if you're sure it won't be dull." His eyes held mine. I couldn't look away.

"Lottie!" Hap's voice again.

"It won't," I said.

I sat down at the piano, trying to clear my head. I had stopped taking lessons when my mother was sick because I couldn't concentrate on practicing the long classical pieces anymore. Every time I did, thoughts of what I needed to do at the hospital or complaints from Archer about the boys or the twins filled my head until I couldn't hear the music.

At least the pieces Hap liked were short and easy, and I thought I could manage them. But once we started to play, I fumbled far more than usual. Both Hap and Miles grew exasperated with me until I forced myself to shut down all my other thoughts.

When we'd finished playing all the way through without a mistake, I got up. "Enough for tonight."

Dmitri had gone back to sketching, or at least holding the pen, but he didn't seem to be making any marks on the page. I really, really wanted to see what he had drawn. I wasn't paying attention to the boys' talk until I heard Stepan say my name.

"Charlotte, Archer says you all should go back to America now," he said as he moved over to the piano, plinking at one note a few times. "But you won't go without me, will you?" His voice wobbled.

"What?" My heart clenched at the worry in his voice. "Don't listen to Archer," I said, trying not to let my irritation show. "He's always trying to get rid of us, you know that."

"He says you should go because the Germans will be here soon and murder us all in our beds." Stepan didn't look up from the keyboard.

I couldn't believe what I'd just heard. "Archer told you that?" I wanted to go find the man and demand what he thought he was doing scaring a little boy like that.

"Not to me, exactly. I overheard him telling Zarja that." Stepan plinked another key.

"It's not going to happen." Dmitri shut the sketchbook with a loud thump. "We've had some setbacks, but we'll never stop fighting. Archer has no idea what he's talking about."

Stepan looked up at Dmitri. "He says you shouldn't be here either. He says you should be with your regiment at the front even if you can't fight because it would be more useful than wasting your time with Miles and Hap because they aren't worth your time."

Dmitri went rigid. His eyes narrowed, and I could almost see the anger radiating off him.

I struggled to keep my own anger in check. "Stepan, you know how Archer is. He always thinks the worst is going to happen."

"I know he's like that." Stepan's voice trembled. "But maybe sometimes the worst does happen."

I went over to him. "The Germans aren't going to get here. And you don't have to worry about it. That's not your job. Dmitri knows what he's talking about. Archer doesn't. We're all together and we are safe."

I heard giggling from the hall. The twins. They should have been in bed long ago.

"Hello!" Nika called out as they bounded into the room. "We have a surprise!"

Sophie carried a small tray with a single glass on it full of a pink, cloudy liquid. Some of it sloshed out when she set it on the table next to Dmitri. "We brought a special drink for Dmitri Antonovich to make his leg better."

"What's in it?" I asked.

The twins looked at each other. Nika spoke up. "Only milk and jam and a medicine Polina got from her babushka."

While I didn't think any of Polina's medicines were poisonous, I'd be hesitant to consume some of them. Before I could warn him, Dmitri took a sip.

His jaw moved in an odd way and I realize he was trying not to gag.

"It's . . . it's very thoughtful of you," he said after he managed to swallow. "I'll sip it slowly as I draw to make it last."

"Do you feel different?" Nika asked eagerly.

"Um . . . yes, I feel better," Dmitri said.

"Don't you think Lottie is pretty?" Sophie asked.

Miles burst out laughing and Hap made a sputtering sound.

"Sophie!" I was mortified.

"Charlotte Danielovna is very pretty," Dmitri said solemnly.

I didn't know where to look or what to say. Luckily, Papa saved me. He walked in and held his arms out as if he wanted to embrace us all.

"Very cozy," he said. "I like to see all you children together." He of course didn't notice that it was very late for Sophie and Nika. "Dmitri, let's have our talk now. Lottie, why don't you come in with us. Dmitri Antonovich and I are going to talk about the boys' lessons now that he's had a chance to see what they know and what they don't."

The "what they don't know" column was much longer than the "what they know" one. I was curious to hear what Dmitri would say, so I followed them into the library.

Once we were settled, Papa started with Miles. "I know his illness has led to gaps in his knowledge, but if he applies himself, he can catch up, and he'll be well enough to attend university someday."

"It's difficult to convince him to study subjects he's not interested in." Dmitri chose his words carefully. "He's quite occupied with studying American history right now, to the exclusion of everything else. He's writing a comparison of the American government under British rule to the Russian government."

"Oh, he's back to that?" Papa chuckled. "You should have seen him when he was a just a twig of a boy. He'd go around shouting 'Give me liberty or give me death!' Something some radical American was famous for saying."

My breath stopped. It couldn't be. Just because Miles could quote American revolutionaries didn't mean he was writing seditious brochures. My mind went into a whirl as I tried to think of all the reasons it couldn't be him. How could he get them printed? And he couldn't distribute them. I assumed most of the radicals were from the universities, meeting in secret spots around the city. Surely I'd know if he sneaked out at night.

Except I wouldn't have known he was sneaking out to the Tamms' party if I hadn't run into the boys. As much as I didn't want to believe it, there was no escaping the possibility that Miles was the one behind the brochures. My stomach turned over.

"Lottie, you look like you've seen a ghost!" I heard Papa's voice, but it sounded far away. "What's wrong?"

"Nothing, nothing," I choked out. I got up, bumping into the chair in my haste to get out of the room. "I need a drink of water and I want to check on the twins. You don't need me for this."

As soon as I was in the hall, I ran into the sitting room. Only Miles and Hap were still there. "Miles, I have to talk to you!"

He'd moved over to a desk and was writing. "All right. Talk," he said, putting down his pencil.

"No! Not here. Dmitri will be back up soon. Come to my room."

He got up and I grabbed hold of his arm, dragging him up the stairs and ignoring his complaints. When we got to my room, I pulled him in far enough to shut the door.

"What—" he started to say.

"Don't tell me you've been writing flyers calling for the overthrow of the czar!"

He blinked a few times. "I won't tell you if you don't want to know."

"How could you!" I yelled, and then realized how loud I'd been. "You're not a child anymore, even though you act like one."

He clenched his fists together. "How could I? Don't you see? Russia is falling apart! People are starving; soldiers are deserting. If we continue as we are, the Germans will win. We won't have a czar, and we won't have anything else, either."

My head began to pound. "How are flyers going to do any good, besides getting you arrested?"

"What else can I do?" He hit himself on his chest with his fist. "I know what's going to happen to me. I'm not going to spend the time I have left watching everyone else out there actually doing something!"

The headache hit me full on. We never talked about the future. We always pretended there would be a cure. Hearing him say it meant we couldn't pretend. I wrapped my arms around myself, the headache bringing on such nausea I thought I would throw up. I wished I'd never said anything.

"And what about you?" he said. "You don't think of the danger to yourself with your little black-market arrangements!"

I sank down on the bed.

"Oh, you didn't think I knew?" Miles gave a harsh laugh. "I see you out the window. It wasn't that hard to figure out why Ivan would come to the house and park his cart right by the door of the carriage house and then have to carry the wood all the way across the courtyard to stack it. And I've seen you go into the carriage house with an empty basket and come back out with it covered and obviously heavy. You aren't out there just chatting with Yermak. Why do you get to do something important and I don't?"

I didn't have an answer for that.

"I hope you haven't involved Hap in this," I said, trying to shift the subject away from me.

He looked down at the floor. "No, not really."

I had hoped he would say no, but that vague answer told me I needed to know more. "What does that mean?"

"He knows what I'm doing, but I've never let him go with me to any meetings. He cares too, Charlotte, so don't go and yell at him."

"Meetings? You've been going out to meetings?" I was horrified. People could identify him.

"A few. Nobody uses their real names. It's not that dangerous."

Except for someone with bright red hair, who spoke Russian well but would never be mistaken for a Russian.

"How are you even getting the flyers printed? If you are the one who is taking them to someone with a printing press, then someone has seen you and can report you." I paused, suddenly realizing what I'd been missing. "Raisa has been helping you, hasn't she?" I put my hand to my head, though it did nothing to stop the throbbing. "She still has access to her father's printing press." I couldn't believe my best friend had kept such a secret from me and put my brother in danger at the same time. Was she even my friend at all?

"Yes, I asked her to help," Miles said. "She was glad to be able to do something. The sooner revolution comes, the sooner her father will be let out of prison. Don't go yelling at her, too."

I had to think. No matter how much I wanted to yell, I knew it wasn't going to help. And the more I knew, the better I'd be able to find a way out of the mess.

"How did the playwright at the Tamms' get hold of one of your flyers?" I asked. "The baron showed us one today." I told him about the baron's visit, trying to keep my voice steady. Panicking wouldn't do us any good.

"I don't know the playwright and he doesn't know me," Miles said. "It's an arrangement. I leave them at the Tamms' and someone picks them up during one of their parties. I don't know who. Peet has seen the man but doesn't know his name."

I remembered the package I had assumed was a present for Peet. The pain in my head increased. "So Peet is involved too?" I didn't even really need to ask.

"Yes," Miles said before he began to cough—deep, wracking coughs that he couldn't get under control.

I got up and tried to help him to the bed, but he pulled away from me, waving me off. Hap burst into the room and wrapped his arms around Miles, supported him so that he stayed upright. He said something to Miles, but I couldn't hear what it was over the sound of the coughing. I lost track of counting the seconds. I thought he'd never stop.

When the coughing finally eased, Miles sagged a little and closed his eyes. "Come on, Miles," Hap said. "You and Lottie can talk more tomorrow."

Miles nodded, not looking at me.

I sat back down on the bed after they left. If I knew anything about my brother, it was that it wouldn't be easy to convince him to stop with the flyers. But if he was caught, being Papa's stepson wouldn't help him. Just like Papa had tried to warn me that morning, even the children of prominent people could be charged with crimes against the state. The lucky ones managed to bargain or bribe their way to exile, but the rest were imprisoned like ordinary people. I couldn't bear the thought of Miles being dragged out of the house, beaten and bloody like Samuel.

I realized we'd have to take a drastic step to keep him safe. Miles had to leave the country. There was no other good option.

Chapter Ten

I WENT TO bed and slept for small stretches of time, my mind too busy running through different possibilities to stay asleep for long and my head still gripped with pain. If Miles left, Hap would have to go with him, in case Miles got sick along the way. With the war on, it would be a long and difficult trip. And if Miles fell ill, they'd have to stop wherever they were and stay until he was better, and he would need to be under a doctor's care.

I knew he wouldn't want to leave. He and Raisa were so sure revolution was coming—and so sure it would be a good thing— but I feared their hopes weren't based on reality. I'd heard about the attempts at revolution that had happened before we'd come to Russia. They'd all been crushed easily. Even if a new revolution came, there was no guarantee everything would immediately get better.

Could I really let them go without me? I'd never been apart from either brother, and I'd promised my mother I would take care of them. But I had to take care of Nika and Sophie and Stepan, too. They needed me more. Papa was too old to manage them without me.

I felt like I was being torn in two. My head hurt so much I got up and found some aspirin powder, mixed it with some water, and swallowed it down as fast as I could to get rid of the bitter taste.

At some point I fell asleep, and when I woke up hours later than I normally did, the headache was gone and my mind was clear. I realized that even if we had to be split up, it was the best choice. Making the decision made me feel much better. We could do what needed to be done.

The trickiest part would be to figure out the right route. Going west across the Atlantic was dangerous, but going east across Russia and the Pacific was a much longer trip.

I got up and got dressed, telling myself that if I could get everything organized, they could leave within a week. Then they would be safe.

As I was putting up my hair, Sophie and Nika burst in.

"Dmitri likes kittens!" Nika shouted.

Sophie climbed up on the bed and began to jump. "Yes! He says they are his third favorite animal after horses and dogs!"

"Third favorite? That's nice," I said, concentrating on my attempt to get my hair to stay in a bun. I wished there weren't such strict expectations that women had to wear their hair up in public. I wasn't very good at controlling my hair. "You haven't been bothering him, have you?"

Sophie flopped down. "No. We've been keeping him company while the boys are working on their math problems."

"I'm sure Dmitri is overjoyed with your company."

"He is," Nika said. "And Anna's stable cat has kittens. Last time we were there we played with them. They are so cute! I liked the gray one and Sophie liked the black one, but the others were pretty too. Why doesn't Bobik ever have kittens?" Bobik was the fierce old tomcat who lived in our stable. He liked the horses, but he didn't think much of humans.

"Because he's a boy." I jammed another pin in my hair. "You know that boys don't have babies."

They were quiet for a moment, but I could imagine the wheels turning in their heads. I waited to hear what would come next.

Sophie got an idea first. "If Dmitri got a kitten, Papa couldn't argue, because it wouldn't be our kitten—it would be Dmitri's."

That was an easy one to counter. "But Dmitri won't bring a kitten into a house that isn't his. I'm sorry. Papa isn't going to change his mind."

"Does Dmitri like you, Charlotte?" Nika asked as she opened up a perfume bottle.

I took it away from her, set it on the other side of the dressing table, and then twisted around so I could see the back of my hair in the mirror. It would have to do. "Like me? I don't know. I don't think he dislikes me."

"Does he look at you with longing eyes?" Sophie asked.

"Where did you think up such a thing?" I asked. "Has Miles been reading you some of his stories?"

"Polina said that's what boys in love do, they look at you with longing eyes, but she couldn't explain it very well. What are longing eyes, anyway?"

"I'm not sure, but whatever they are, Dmitri does not look at me with longing eyes. Don't be silly."

"He might. Maybe even today." They both giggled.

Before I could ask what about today was special, Hap bounded into the room, nearly knocking over Nika. He grabbed her just in time and set her on her feet. "There's someone here to see you, Lottie. An American. He says you're going skating with him. What's going on?"

I'd completely forgotten about Carter.

"You're going skating with a *boy*? You can't!" Sophie screeched. Nika ran around and grabbed the perfume vial off the dressing table and clutched it in her hand, I suppose to prevent me from putting some on for the boy.

"Why not? I thought you wanted me to get married," I teased.

"No!" they both cried.

"You can't marry just any boy!" Sophie declared.

"Is he handsome like Dmitri?" Nika asked.

"It doesn't matter what he looks like. He seems nice enough." And he was exactly the person I needed to talk to. He'd just made the trip from America, so he could tell me the best way to go about planning the boys' trip.

"Is his nose as nice as Dmitri's?" Nika added. "Dmitri's nose is beautiful."

"I haven't noticed Carter's nose." I didn't want to get into a nose-comparison discussion, and I really couldn't recall the American's nose.

Hap scowled. "Why?"

"Why what?"

"Why are you going skating with him? You don't do that sort of thing."

"That sort of thing? Who told me a couple of days ago I was acting like an old lady? This is what people my age do. They go skating. They see friends."

"I suppose," Hap said. "It's just weird for you."

I was beginning to feel ganged up on. "Aren't you two supposed to go play with Anna Andreevna today?" I asked the twins.

"Yes, but Polina isn't feeling well," Nika said.

"She told us she would walk us there once she feels better," Sophie added. "We told her we'd be quiet until then."

"I'll take you on our way. Come on, let's get your coats and boots." It took so long to find my skates and get the twins ready, I thought Carter might have given up and left, but he was still there when we finally went downstairs, gazing up at the ceiling as he had at the hospital. For some reason, he held a good-sized piece of fur in his hands.

As I was saying hello to Carter and explaining the twins while I was trying to get their coats on, Miles and Dmitri came out of the library, carrying stacks of books.

I didn't want to give Miles a long explanation about where I was going and with whom, so I said, "I can't wait to get on the ice. Let's go."

"Lottie!" Miles called.

"I'll talk to you later," I said as I grabbed hold of Carter's arm and practically dragged him out the door. "Come on, girls."

Once we were outside, I stopped long enough to adjust the shawls around the girls' heads and faces.

Carter shook the piece of fur he held and shaped it, then put it on his head. I stared, and the twins giggled. It was the largest hat I'd ever seen. Fur hats were very common in Russia, but this one was so big, a cat could have curled up on top of it and made a nice bed.

He noticed me staring. "You like my hat? I got a good deal on it. I needed a hat. My ears were getting cold all the time."

The twins giggled again.

"It's very nice," I said as loudly as I could to drown them out. "We have to go this way to drop the twins off."

The twins were a little too quiet for the first part of the walk. They followed behind us, and every time I looked back, two sets of eyes were focused on me.

When we stopped at a street crossing, Nika came around in front of us and stood looking up at Carter. "When are you going back to

America?" she asked. "Most people get tired of visiting here. They like it better in their own countries."

Carter shifted from one foot to the other and then glanced over at me before answering Nika. "I'll be here for a while. There are lots of stories to write."

Nika gave a very loud sigh. "You might find it's too cold here to stay. Sometimes foreigners don't notice that their fingers and noses have frozen until they turn black and fall off. You should go back where you came from."

"Nika! You're being rude! That doesn't happen to people in Petrograd." I turned to Carter. "Though if a Russian approaches you and starts talking and pointing at your nose, that means you are showing the first signs of frostbite. They do look out for foreigners."

I slung my skates over my shoulder and then took hold of Nika with one hand and Sophie with the other. "Let's cross. Do you have any brothers or sisters?" I asked Carter.

He shook his head. "Only child." I had to bite my tongue not to offer him a few of mine.

When we reached the grand duke's house, Anna Andreevna was waiting for us with a girl dressed as a nursemaid who looked very much like Polina, small and fair. "This is Nadia," Anna announced as she danced around. From the looks of Anna's flushed face, she'd been dancing long before we arrived. She ran over and hugged both twins. Somehow they all three managed to get their arms around one another and spin around, singing loudly.

"Hello," I said to the girl over the noise. "My sisters were very excited to come over today." I wondered where Anna's governess was. She was good at making sure the three didn't get up to too much mischief. "I wanted to say hello to Mademoiselle Bessette. Is she here?"

"She is, but she's ill, miss. She said that if it's all right with Polina, I can watch the little girls while they play."

I wasn't sure she could manage all three, but I did want to talk to Carter without extra commentary. "All right. Mind Nadia, girls." They weren't listening.

When we got back outside, Carter said, "I've got directions to a private skating area that the English use on the Neva."

"No, we don't want to go there. It's too small." I found myself actually looking forward to skating. It had been too long. "I've got a card to get into the skating area in front of the Tauride Palace. It's where Russians go and it's much better and bigger. The czar's daughters skate there sometimes." I thought Carter would be intrigued by that bit of information, and he took up the topic of the czar's daughters with great enthusiasm as we walked.

I wanted to start asking him questions right away about traveling, but as we moved out of the residential area into the main part of Petrograd, we heard a big crowd singing in the distance. The streets were so packed with people I couldn't tell where the song was coming from. There were a few more droshkies back on the streets, but they were all occupied. I told Carter I was fine with walking, so we continued on, winding our way through the crowds.

"Look over there," Carter said. "Demonstrators on the bridge." He pointed to a large group of people singing and carrying red banners as they came across the Nikolai Bridge. Some of the czar's Cossack troops had positioned their horses at the end of it to block them from getting all the way across.

"Isn't that the song the French sing? The 'Marseillaise'?" Carter asked.

"The tune is the same but it has different lyrics, ones a Russian wrote." I translated a little of it. "'Stand, rise up, working people! Arise against the enemies, hungry brother!'"

"So is this it?" Carter asked, doing his strange little jig and nearly falling on the packed snow.

"'It'?"

"The revolution! The journalists I know are taking bets on when it will break out. The best guess of the people who have been here for a while is next week, though one fellow told me I shouldn't go skating today in case it started early."

I was shocked to hear they'd been taking bets as if the total upheaval of a country were a sporting event. "I've never been in a revolution, but if it happens, it's not going to be some spectator event where, when it's all over, the participants shake hands and go home." The thought of fighting breaking out in the city terrified me. People would be hurt, and the hospitals were already packed with wounded soldiers.

The Cossack troops were riding back and forth in front of the crowd, which had stopped, and the troops were laughing and joking with them. It almost seemed like a celebration. "So many people revere the czar," I said. "You should have been here when war was declared. Ordinary people filled the streets, marching in support of the czar, holding photographs of him high above their heads."

Carter shook his head. "They might revere him, but they hate his wife and his advisers. Maybe nothing will happen today, but that's not the last of it. Some of the workers in the big factories have gone on strike, and they're calling for a general strike tomorrow." He paused. "Let's stop for a minute. I want to see what happens. If this is it, we may not be able to go skating after all."

The crowd on the bridge turned around and went back the other way, still singing. The Cossacks moved away.

I hadn't realized how tense I was until I saw the crowd leave.

There wasn't going to be a clash, not then, but Carter was right. That wouldn't be the end of it. We'd have to brace ourselves for what might come. I couldn't pretend to believe my stepfather any longer. Things would not get back to the way they'd been before.

And if ordinary people did get hurt, I decided I'd talk to Dr. Rushailo about opening up the hospital for as many as we could treat. I told myself I couldn't get overwhelmed with fear. The doctor never did. She took everything as it came, and I wanted to be the same way.

But Miles still wasn't safe. I didn't believe Carter and his friends really had any idea of when something would happen. Miles still needed to leave. We walked on, and I turned the conversation to what I wanted to know. "How did you get to Russia? My brothers are going back to the United States for a visit, but we haven't traveled for years. I don't even really know where to begin. You said something about the Americans in the hotels being too scared to travel because of the German subs." Everyone had been horrified when the British ship the *Lusitania* had been sunk two years earlier, but American passenger ships hadn't been targeted. "Why are they so scared? They must know something I don't."

"You didn't hear? Just a couple of weeks ago, the Germans announced they were going back to unrestricted sub warfare. Nothing is safe now, so if your brothers want to go the States, they'll be far better off going east, crossing the border into Manchuria and then getting to Japan so they can sail from there."

That meant weeks more of travel, including a very long train ride all the way across Russia. But since there was no other good choice, that was the way they would have to go. Having only one option meant fewer decisions to be made.

We reached the skating area, which held no grand duchesses but plenty of skaters. I couldn't wait to get on the ice. I wanted to skate and not think about anything else for just a little while.

Carter was a good skater. It was fantastic racing around trying to see who could go the fastest. There wasn't a cloud in the sky, and the sun made the snow so bright it almost hurt my eyes.

When we stopped to catch our breath, Carter said, "You wouldn't even know there was a war on here."

"Except there used to be a stand with an orchestra right next to the ice, and food stalls where you could buy oranges and other lovely treats. I haven't seen any oranges this winter at all." One lone stand had survived, selling tea, roasted nuts, and sunflower seeds.

"Even without oranges and bands, this is really something," Carter said. "People told me that Russia was going to get in my blood and I wouldn't want to come home. I didn't believe them, but now I'm starting to understand. I'm not sure I'm ever going to want to leave."

"Yes," I said. "I feel that way too."

"So how long are you staying in Russia?" Carter asked. "I'd think a girl like you would want to travel. See family back home and such. Unless there is some special fellow here." I heard the question in his voice.

"There's no special fellow," I said, though I didn't meet his eyes. "I don't want to travel right now. I'm staying here and eventually going to medical school. I hope I can work with the doctor at the hospital someday."

"Wow! That's going to add to my story." He got a small notebook out of his pocket and asked a few more questions. "Tell me about your mother," he said. "Everyone I've talked to mentions how beautiful she was and how smart, but nothing about her background. Where did she grow up?"

I didn't want to admit I didn't know. She'd always said the past wasn't important and refused to talk about it. I didn't even know if she still had family in the United States. The other foreign women married to Russians didn't like that she wouldn't give them enough information to trace her whole history. It was one reason the boys and I had never been invited to dancing classes and other social activities of that segment of Russian society.

I knew another countess who had grown up in America, so I told Carter some bits using that woman's background, except I changed the state where that woman had been born from Iowa to Indiana and said my mother's maiden name had been Smith. He'd never figure out that was a lie.

"Let's skate some more," I said. "I'll need to get to the hospital later, so I can't stay much longer."

We skated another half hour. I began to think of all the things I had to do, and that made the second time not as much fun. Carter looked disappointed when I called a halt, and I had to promise I'd come skating another time, though I dreaded to think of the reaction from the twins if Carter showed up at the house again.

As we walked away, I noticed that the sky was clouding up. "It's going to snow again," I said. "And it will start soon." I'd lived in Petrograd long enough to be able to predict when snow would start by the color of the clouds.

Carter adjusted his hat, not noticing that practically every Russian we met appeared a bit taken aback by the size of it. "Before I came, I was worried when I heard how much snow fell here, but no one seems to mind it, or the cold. That's another amazing thing about this city. Okay, only a few more questions. Your stepfather is a real count, isn't he? As well as a general?"

I wasn't surprised at the question. Americans were always thrilled with the abundance of princes, counts, and barons that filled the upper reaches of Russian society. "Yes, he's a count and a general, but there are lots of counts in Russia."

"Well, I've never met one. Do you think he'd give me an interview?"

"About what? He's been retired from the military for years."

"About what he thinks of the czar and things like that. His family is very interesting. Is he in contact with his daughter?"

I wasn't paying that much attention to Carter. I was more interested in the crowds on the streets. They had gotten much bigger. "Of course," I said. "You saw them."

"No, I mean his eldest daughter. The one who is in prison."

I stopped walking, barely noticing that someone behind me walked right into me. "Prison? My stepfather has only two daughters, my little sisters."

"No, he has another one, who is now in prison in Siberia for the assassination of a government official. She belonged to a radical group, the Socialist Revolutionary Party. It was a group that advocated assassinations as a method to get changes made. Everyone here calls all revolutionaries nihilists, but that's wrong. There are several different factions, and they all believe different things."

I stood there, trying to make sense of what he'd just said. "You're mistaken. It must be someone else."

"No, I'm sure. I checked it out from old newspaper clippings. The daughter of General Feodor Ivanovich Cherkassky is in prison for murder. Her name is Maria. There can't be more than one Russian general by that name." He paused, as if waiting for me to say something. I didn't. "You look shocked. I guess you had no idea."

I shook my head, still trying to comprehend what he'd just said. He took hold of my elbow. "Let's get something to eat and we can talk more," he said. "I've been wanting to try the patisserie on the corner near my hotel. It's called Pekar's or something like that. Do you know it? It will be warm and the window is full of pastries. We could both use something to eat."

I must have nodded because I found myself walking next to him, his hand still on my elbow. All the while I sifted through my memories to see if there had ever been any mention of a daughter. I couldn't remember anything like that. How terrible for Papa to have to keep such a secret. And I knew he had to feel such shame at it. He was so proud of his service to the empire and proud of his family name. I supposed I should have been angry that no one had told me, but I suspected that that had been my mother's decision. If she had decided Papa should put it in the past and not tell us, then he'd have gone along with that.

I realized that meant I had a stepsister, of a sort, and she'd be an actual half sister to Stepan and the twins. Right there, I vowed they'd never know if I could help it. They didn't need to know they had a murderer in the family. None of us needed a murderer in the family.

I didn't even notice we were at the café until we were ready to be seated. Carter asked, "Shall I order for both of us?"

Again I nodded. When the waiter brought our order, I finally found my voice. "I never knew. Please don't put that in your story. It has nothing to do with the hospital."

"So you never even had a clue about the daughter? Who I suppose would be your stepsister?"

"No." I was amazed Archer and Zarja had been able to keep the secret. They had to have known the girl since they'd been with my stepfather for so many years. How could someone be erased from a family?

I stood up. "I need to pick up my little sisters." I wanted to be home and I wanted to talk to Zarja.

Later, when I remembered the next few minutes, it was as if time slowed down. I heard glass shattering and then what felt like needles piercing my face. Something landed on our table, flattening a piece of cake in front of Carter and making the table rock. The tea sloshed out of the glasses and I realized that the thing sitting on the cake was a brick. I heard shouts and turned to look back at the street. Through the broken window, I saw a man with his arm raised, holding another brick. Carter was still staring at the destruction to his cake as if he couldn't believe it. I moved around the table and took hold of his arm.

"Get down!" I yelled as I dropped to the floor, trying to pull him after me. I wasn't strong enough, and he didn't move. A brick hit the table next to us, and somehow that made Carter fall off his chair, landing on me and knocking the wind out of me.

Chapter Eleven

I GASPED, TRYING to get some air back in my lungs, pushing at Carter to get him off me. I tried to breathe again and the air came back. I pushed harder until Carter rolled off. Grabbing a chair, I pulled myself up into a sitting position.

"Golly! We're right in the middle of it!" Carter said, sounding weirdly happy. "This is sure something!"

"We'd better move back in case he throws another brick." I had to shout because everyone else in the café had begun to shout too. Police whistles blared. I began to crawl away from the table toward the back of the café. When I had gone as far as I could, I looked over my shoulder. Carter was on his feet, scribbling furiously in his little notebook. No more bricks had been thrown, but scores of people came crowding in. A few ran to the back and took some of the cakes out of the display case, cramming them into their mouths. Some policemen rushed in and grabbed the people who were trying to eat, dragging them back out into the street.

I stood up, taking hold of a chair because my legs felt wobbly. Carter was talking to a man who still sat at a table. He didn't notice me when I reached him.

"Carter, we need to get out of here, and I need to go get my little sisters."

He nodded, still scribbling. "Yes," he said.

I repeated myself, but since he didn't make any move to leave, I said goodbye, though I wasn't sure he heard, and made my way through the crowd to the street. Mounted police units had joined the Cossack soldiers and were ordering everyone off the streets. People scurried to get away from them. The mounted police were far more frightening than the foot police. They too wore black uniforms, but their helmets topped with black horsetails, and the black horses they rode made them seem like something out of a nightmare. As soon as I was clear of the crowd, I ran.

I wasn't thinking of anything except getting to my sisters. When I reached the grand duke's house, the footman opened the door, giving a start when he saw me. I realized that my hair was falling down. I also realized I'd lost my skates.

"I'm here to get my little sisters," I gasped, trying to catch my breath.

"They're not here. The nursemaid took them back to your house about an hour ago. Anna Andreevna has developed a high fever."

Anna's flushed face. I should have known. The twins looked the same way right before they came down with a fever. I hoped whatever she had wasn't contagious.

Later, I didn't remember walking home. When I went into the house, Dmitri was coming down the stairs. He saw me and nearly dropped the book he was carrying. "You're hurt!" he said. "What happened?"

"I'm not hurt." I brushed back my hair. More of it had come down.

"Your face," he said, gesturing to his own. "You've got scratches, and some of them are bleeding a little."

I reached up and touched my cheek, feeling darts of pain. I'd forgotten that something had hit my face when the window broke.

"Bits of glass hit me. We were at Pekar's, the American journalist and I. Someone hurled a brick through the window." My legs got wobbly again. I didn't understand why—when I was safe at home, they shouldn't be wobbling.

"Why don't you come into the sitting room?" Dmitri said. "And I'll go get Zarja. She can help with your face." He took hold of my hand very gently. I let him lead me into the sitting room.

Zarja ended up having to pick several bits of glass out of my face. I didn't know why I hadn't felt them before, because they certainly hurt like fire once she began to remove them. No wonder the footman at Anna's house had looked at me so strangely.

After Zarja was finished, she insisted I drink some tea. She fixed a glass and then handed it to me. "I have to get back to making dinner. You just sit there until you feel better."

"I will." My hand shook. I put my other hand up to steady the glass. As soon as she was out of the room, I set the glass back down.

Dmitri was pacing around, which was uncomfortable to watch, since he was in obvious pain with each step. "Where is this journalist?" he asked.

"I suppose he's still there interviewing people."

"He didn't see you home?" Dmitri stopped pacing. He sounded angry.

"I didn't need him to do that, and he wanted to do his job."

Dmitri muttered something I couldn't make out and then started pacing again. "What's the situation on the streets? Is it getting worse?"

"Yes, or at least there are more and more people out. I never expected anyone to attack a café, though. It's not like there was that much food in there."

He stopped his pacing and sat down next to me. "They didn't just attack it for the food. It's rumored that Russians who are secretly working to promote the German cause go there to meet."

I'd heard about the pro-German Russians. They were the faction that wanted Russia to sign a peace treaty with Germany and concede lands to the Germans as a way to end the fighting. I couldn't believe they sat in Pekar's over tea and cakes planning ways to bring down the government, not caring what that meant for everyone who lived in Russia. Not caring about giving away parts of Russia. Not caring that the Germans might turn on us, deciding they wanted the whole of Russia. If Dmitri hadn't been there, I would have cursed them and cursed the war.

I closed my eyes, wanting not to think about any of it for a little while. I heard Dmitri get back up.

"Where are you going?" I blurted out. I didn't want him to leave.

"I thought you had fallen asleep. You should rest."

I forced myself to sit up. I knew we couldn't stay there all day in the little cocoon of safety, just him and me, even if I gave in to the sleep that was trying to creep over me. "No, I need to get ready to go to the hospital."

"I'll walk with you," Dmitri said.

I wanted to say yes, but I didn't want him to think I was scared to go out again. "No, thank you. I'll be fine."

"I know you will, but I want to." He took a step toward me and his leg gave way. I jumped up and tried to catch him, but I wasn't strong enough, and we both went down. Dmitri cried out. I moved away, afraid I was somehow in the way and making the pain worse.

He sat up and pounded on the floor, his face twisted in frustration. "I'm so sorry," he said. "I can't do anything with this cursed leg."

"You're doing more than enough, sticking it out here. And you know your leg will get better." I got up, wanting to offer him a hand but afraid it would make his frustration worse.

He pulled himself up. "Perhaps I won't walk with you. I'll only slow you down."

"Do you like to skate?" I asked. "I mean, would you like to skate when you're better?"

He frowned, and I realized I'd probably confused him by suddenly talking about skating. "I only said I'd go with Carter because I wanted to be outside," I added. "It's not like . . . it's not like I wanted to skate with Carter in particular, but I do like it."

His face relaxed, and I thought maybe he understood what I was trying to say, even though I hadn't said it very well.

"I do like to skate," he said. "Very much." He paused. "Charlotte Danielovna, would you like to go skating with me sometime?"

"I'd love to," I said. "But I'll warn you. I like to skate fast—very, very fast."

He smiled. "So do I. I think we'd be well matched."

Before I left, I tried to find Miles to tell him my plans, but both he and Hap had gone out on errands for Zarja. I decided I could talk to them that night, and we'd tell Papa at the same time. I'd take a few days off from the hospital to get the arrangements worked out. When I set off for the hospital a little while later, I was warm with the thought of someday skating with Dmitri. The incident at the café already seemed like it was in the distant past. I'd read that that happened to some people—once you were safe after a horrible event, your mind worked to convince you it was long ago.

As I walked, I saw that the streets had emptied out of almost everyone except soldiers and the police.

On the way there I passed a group of new conscripts, peasants ordered into the city to train to fight. Soldiers with bayonets walked along on either side, "escorting" them to make sure they didn't run away. The men carried teakettles and small trunks or bags of their possessions. Some were even younger than Peet, and none appeared eager.

I knew from Ivan that in the early days of the war, men and boys had jumped to join up, but that had changed as the war dragged on. Once they were actually at the front, the incompetence of the leaders led to thousands and thousands of deaths. The ones who did survive were faced with shortages of ammunition, food, and even boots. I'd seen many former soldiers hobbling around Petrograd because their toes had been amputated from frostbite. The truth of the situation spread until no one wanted to join up voluntarily any longer.

My mood darkened at the thought, and by the time I got to the hospital, I wished I could have stayed home. I had to explain multiple times, to the nurses and the patients, what had happened to my face. I tried to act as if it were just a random act, especially for the patients.

All of them were worried about their families and concerned that the situation was only going to get worse. I noticed we had nine empty beds, and when I asked Galina, she said some women had insisted on going home, and no new patients had arrived.

The afternoon dragged on, and I got home late again. Hap was the only one in the sitting room.

"Where is everyone?" I asked.

He didn't look up from his drawing. "Stepan went to bed and

Dmitri said he had to go out. Papa went to some dinner. Yermak drove him."

"And Miles?"

Hap didn't answer.

I twisted my fingers together, trying to keep my voice even. "Hap, tell me."

He threw down his pencil. "Don't yell at me. He wouldn't let me go with him."

"Why didn't you stop him?" I heard myself yelling but I couldn't stop it.

"What am I supposed to do? Sit on him to keep him here? Or run after him out in the streets?"

I'd just assumed Miles would be more careful once he knew the baron was suspicious. I couldn't believe I'd been so wrong. I pushed down the panic that was threatening to overwhelm me. "Do you know where he went?"

"No, but whatever he's doing, I'm sure he is with Peet. Do you want me to go look for him?"

"No, I'll do it. Stay here." I didn't want Hap involved at all.

I grabbed my coat and ran back outside, ignoring Osip's questions. It was snowing heavily and there were no droshkies, but I managed to flag down a delivery cart after the driver saw me waving money. I told him the address of the theater, thinking Celeste would be in the office there and she might know something.

When I got to the theater, there was a sign on the door that it was closed for the night due to an electrical problem. I went into the apartment building next, but Hugo wasn't in his usual place. I felt a prickle of unease. The door to his room stood open, so I peeked in. He was lying on the camp cot, struggling to sit up.

"I heard the door." His voice was wheezy. "Just give me a minute."

"It's all right. It's Charlotte Mason," I said. "You don't have to get up. I was just worried when I didn't see you at the door."

He got up anyway, adjusting his coat as he shuffled out into the hall. "The Tamms are all out," he said.

"Are you sure? I think my brother might be here."

He shook his head. "No, not tonight. They went to see a performance at another theater since they couldn't open. You should go home." His eyes shifted to the front door. "Go home," he repeated. "Go now."

There was something wrong. Hugo didn't sound like himself.

"Was my brother here earlier?"

Hugo shook his head again. He still wouldn't look at me.

Something was definitely wrong. "You know my brother's health isn't good. I need to find him and take him home. Are you absolutely sure you haven't seen him tonight?"

Hugo glanced again at the door and then back at me. "They're in a different apartment, he and Peet. Number twenty-eight. You should take him home right now. The ones in twenty-eight, they're not your kind of people."

I ran up the stairs, dread filling me. Anger, too. Anger at Miles for putting himself in such danger. At the door to the apartment I could hear several voices all talking at once, but I couldn't make out if one of them was Miles. I had to knock several times until someone pulled open the door.

"Victor, you're late," a young man with a scruffy beard said. He took a step back when he realized I wasn't Victor and then came out in the hall, pulling the door closed behind him. "Who are you?"

"My brother might be here. I need to talk to him." My words were tumbling over themselves. I almost said Miles's name, and then

I remembered he'd claimed they didn't use real names. I pointed at my hair. "He looks like me. Red hair."

He put his hand back on the doorknob. "He left."

I grabbed hold of the edge of the door. "Wait. Hugo downstairs said he was here."

"He was here, but he wouldn't stop coughing." The man rolled his eyes as if it were Miles's fault. "He and the boy he was with left a while ago." He yanked the door free of my hand as he went back into the apartment and shut it in my face.

I hoped they'd gone to the Tamms' apartment but when I knocked there, no one answered. "Miles? Peet? It's Charlotte. I need to see you." Still no answer, and I couldn't hear anyone inside the apartment. I pounded on the door in frustration. I had no idea where else they might be.

Voices came from the bottom of the stairs.

"Stand aside!" someone ordered, and then I heard boots clomping up the stairs. I caught a glimpse of a policeman with several other men behind him. My heart jumped, but I made myself walk away from the Tamms' door, down the hallway as if on my way to my own apartment, trying not to panic.

"You, girl! Stop!" A man yelled.

It was time to panic. I ran. I heard more yelling but I kept running until I came to the back stairs. I almost went down the stairs and then decided it would be smarter to go up. I pushed myself to go faster and faster until I reached the top floor, gasping for breath as I came out of the stairwell. I listened. There was no sound coming from below, so I moved out into the hallway.

I'd never been on that floor before, but Celeste had said it contained some small single rooms for rent. The hallway was dark and narrow, and there was a strong smell of cabbage and onions. I heard a few voices behind the doors but saw no one.

I went back to the stairwell and waited, hardly daring to breathe, hoping no one would come up the stairs.

I don't know how long I stood there, but when no sounds had come for a long time, I decided I'd go back down one flight and see if I could tell what was happening. I crept down the stairs as quietly as I could and saw that that floor was empty too. I kept going until I came to the second floor. Still no one, but as I looked down the hall I saw that the door to 28 was open and a single shoe lay in the hall. There were no voices.

I made myself walk toward the apartment even though I knew there would be no one inside. It was too quiet. I'd heard that after a police raid, they took everyone to the prison at the Peter and Paul Fortress until they could determine if you were guilty or innocent, though once they had you there, you were almost always guilty.

As I got closer, the only sound I heard was the bubbling of a samovar. I put my hand on the door frame to steady myself and then looked inside. There was no one there. The room was in chaos. Some of the furniture had been tipped over and the drawers to a chest had been taken out and flung on the floor.

My stomach turned over when I saw splatters of blood on the carpet. If Miles and Peet hadn't left early, it might have been their blood. I had to find where they'd gone.

I went downstairs to find Hugo asleep on his bed, snoring loudly. There was a half-filled bottle of vodka on the floor next to him. I understood then, even though I didn't want to believe it. It was the only explanation. Hugo had tipped off the police. Someone like him would not have been able to get hold of a bottle of vodka himself. The czar had outlawed alcohol at the beginning of the war, though of course wealthy people still had access to it. Hugo wasn't wealthy. Someone had given him the bottle. He'd told the police about the people in number 28 and they'd given him the bottle as payment.

The full force of what had happened hit me. The men who had been arrested would be interrogated, and they'd be tortured until they revealed everything they knew. It would be a miracle if no one described Miles and Peet well enough that they'd be identified. Miles and Hap didn't have a week to get ready to leave. They needed to go as soon as we could get them out of the city.

I ran out of the building and down the street, nearly crying with relief when I found a droshky for hire a few blocks away. All the way home I was making and discarding plans, trying to think of the best way for them to leave the city. When the droshky pulled up in front of our door, I got out and paid the driver and then turned around to go inside, but stopped when I saw someone coming toward me. Even if he hadn't had the cane, I would have known it was Dmitri.

As he reached me, an automobile came down the street, the headlights so bright I couldn't really see the vehicle behind them. I assumed it would go past us, but it stopped right in front of the door, and a man got out. It was the baron.

Chapter Twelve

I SHRANK BACK as if I could disappear.

"Don't you want to see him?" Dmitri asked in a low voice.

"No, I never want to see him." Whatever reason the baron had for visiting us, it couldn't be good.

The man walked toward us slowly, as if he were out for a stroll. "Good evening, Count Lieven," the baron said to Dmitri when he got close enough, ignoring me. "I've been concerned that I haven't heard from you. Please accept my condolences."

"Thank you." Dmitri's voice was cool.

"You're a count?" I asked him. My brain was so befuddled by everything that I couldn't think. I felt like I should have known he was a count.

"As of yesterday. My great-uncle in Paris died," Dmitri said.

I remembered then Papa talking about the great-uncle and how after the man's own grandson had died, Dmitri became his heir. I hadn't thought about it at the time, but I realized that meant Dmitri would inherit not only property and money, but the title as well.

"It's very late, Baron," Dmitri said. "If you are here to see the general, I'd suggest you shouldn't disturb him. He hasn't been feeling well."

I didn't know what he meant by that. Had Papa had another spell that I didn't know about?

"No, I didn't come to see the general," the baron replied. "I came to see if Miss Mason was home. I rather thought she might be out or just arriving back here. Getting back from a meeting, perhaps?"

"No," I managed to choke out. I hated that the baron made me so nervous. I tried to think of a place to say I'd been. "I was at the Tamm Theater," I said and then realized I shouldn't have picked that place. If he checked, he'd find out there had been no performance.

The baron gave that same self-satisfied smile I'd seen before. "Oh, and then did you stop in apartment twenty-eight in the building next to the Tamm Theater? I heard a report of a young woman with red hair who got away when the police raided a nest of radicals just a short while ago."

"She wasn't there," Dmitri said. "She was with me. We didn't stay for the whole performance at the Tamm." He put his arm around me. I was so startled, I almost pulled away from him.

The baron noticed my reaction. He looked back and forth between us. I realized my hair had completely fallen down at some point. I could only imagine what the baron was thinking. Dmitri pulled me closer, and I tried to relax as if I was used to it, leaning into him a little.

"Where did you go when you left there?" the baron asked.

"It's none of your business," I snapped.

"It's all right, Lottie," Dmitri said smoothly. "No reason he can't know. We were at the Crooked Mirror with some of my university friends."

I tried not to show my surprise. The Crooked Mirror was a midnight cabaret in a cellar under a gaming club. I'd never been, though Raisa and I and some of our other friends had always wanted to go.

No parent would have approved, and we hadn't been able to convince anyone's older brothers or cousins to take us.

The baron tipped his head as he examined my face. I was glad the glow from the streetlights was so weak.

"So if I visit the club to ask questions, they'll confirm you were there with Miss Mason?" the baron said to Dmitri.

"Yes, though they won't know her name." Dmitri sounded bored with the whole conversation. "This was her first time there, and I didn't bother to introduce her to the staff. It was as crowded as usual. Now, is there anything else? I'm sure the general's daughter would like to go inside."

I don't know if Dmitri's new title had anything to do with the baron's reaction, but I was relieved when he didn't press us any more about our activities.

"I'll say good night then, though I may visit you again tomorrow." The baron nodded and got back into the automobile.

I shivered. Dmitri tightened his arm around me. We waited until the baron drove off to move. Osip must have been watching out the window, because he opened the door before we'd gone up the first step.

"Is everything all right?" he asked.

"Yes, is Miles home?" I asked.

"He arrived about fifteen minutes ago. He was coughing quite a bit." I could hear the worry in Osip's words.

"I'll check on him," I said. If Miles was asleep, I decided I'd let him sleep for a few hours before I woke him up to tell him what had happened. He and Hap couldn't leave in the middle of the night anyway. We'd have to get some money and papers and all sorts of things.

"May I speak to you for a moment first?" Dmitri asked me. He was back to his formal voice.

"Yes." I was aware that Osip was watching us and I felt awkward for some reason. "We could go in the sitting room, I suppose."

Dmitri followed me in and shut the door.

"I'm sorry about your great-uncle," I said as I sat down on the sofa closest to the fire. I found it odd to think of Dmitri as a count.

Dmitri took off his coat and sat down next to me, sighing with what must have been relief at getting the pressure off his leg. "Thank you. It wasn't unexpected. He'd been ill a long time. I'm surprised the baron knew. I only received the news this morning."

"If the baron checks out the cabaret, will they tell him you were there with a girl?" I asked.

"Yes," he said. I felt a twinge of something—not jealousy, of course, but something.

"She didn't have red hair, though." He made a motion like he was going to touch mine, but then drew his hand away as if it had been burned.

I didn't want to move. I didn't think he did either.

He sighed again and shifted away from me a little. "I was with a whole group of people," he said. "None of the staff will remember everyone. There were several girls there."

So maybe that meant he wasn't *with* the girl; she was just part of the group.

There were more questions I wanted to ask, but I couldn't think of the right way to ask them. Then I remembered what he'd said outside. "You mentioned that my stepfather wasn't feeling well. Did you see him today? What's wrong with him?"

"The boys wanted to show him their new experiments with the glasses, and he watched them but seemed a bit unsteady. Archer insisted he rest. It wasn't anything serious. I said that so the baron would go away. I didn't mean to worry you."

"It's all right. I do worry about him. What did you want to talk about?"

"I thought . . . I thought . . ." He paused. It was odd to hear him hesitating. "I thought you and the baron . . . Like I said, he's a very dangerous man. I'm relieved to know you don't like him."

"Like him? I loathe him! Why would you think I liked him?"

"I saw you at the grand duke's party and you were sitting very close to him, and then the way you smiled at him when he came to the house . . ." He searched my face as if he wasn't sure I was telling the truth. "And then . . . well, never mind."

"I was only pretending because I didn't want him to know I was scared." So Dmitri had noticed me smiling at the baron? I felt a little twinge of warmth inside me.

Dmitri leaned closer to me. I realized I was holding my breath. When he spoke again, his voice was soft. "But I want you to know, Charlotte Danielovna, you can trust me. I promise."

I liked the way he said my name, the Russian way. It sounded so much nicer coming from his lips.

"Thank you," I whispered.

Dmitri made that same motion again, as if he was going to touch my hair, but again he drew his hand away and got to his feet, grasping his cane tightly. "Good night," he said.

"Wait." I had just remembered something. "Why did the baron say he was surprised he hadn't heard from you?"

Dmitri didn't speak for such a long time that I felt a little twinge of unease, suddenly afraid of what he was going to say. He sat back down, looking at his cane as if it held the answer. "I haven't found the right time to tell you the real reason I'm here."

I couldn't speak. I knew he was going to tell me what I'd feared from the beginning.

When he looked up at me, his expression was so serious that dread filled me, and I wished I hadn't asked.

"You need to know," he said. "I'm sorry I didn't tell you before. The baron wants me to report to him about your household. He has this ludicrous idea that you are involved with revolutionaries, so he asked me to take the tutoring position to see if I could find out anything. Or at least that's what he told me. I thought he wanted me to spy on you because he was afraid you were seeing another man and he wanted you for himself. There are all kinds of rumors about the man, and it seemed like something he would do."

I felt like someone had tried to knock me to the floor. "You've been spying on us!" I knew my voice would carry out to the hall, but I didn't care. I jumped up, wanting to get away from him. I'd finally thought I could trust him, but now I knew I couldn't trust anyone. First Raisa and then Dmitri. "You acted as if you liked me! You acted as if you cared!"

Dmitri got to his feet. "Charlotte, listen to me. I do care. I do like you. I only agreed to come here because I didn't want the baron to find someone else who might say anything about you just to please him."

"Why would you care about that? You didn't even know us." My head was spinning. I didn't care if he answered my question. I just wanted to get away from him. I moved toward the door.

"I knew Pavel," he said.

I stopped and turned back, not sure I'd really heard him say those words.

"Pavel." I managed the one word but couldn't get any more out.

"Yes. Pavel was a good friend. From what he said about you and your family, I knew that the baron's interest in you would be dangerous, whatever his reason." Dmitri clenched the cane and swayed a little. "It was the least I could do for a friend. I'm sorry I came into your house under a false pretext, but I thought it was something I had to do. I know you must be furious. I'll pack my things and leave tomorrow."

"No, don't go." I needed time to think, and I realized I couldn't imagine the thought of the house without Dmitri. "You haven't reported anything to the baron?"

"No. I was planning to see him tomorrow to tell him he's on the wrong track. Something he said about your mother made me think there is a personal aspect to his dislike of your family, but I have no idea what that is."

I didn't either, though if the baron had wanted some relationship with my mother and she'd turned him down, the baron was the kind of man who would feel so affronted he'd assume the worst of her. She'd laughed about such men, and there had been many.

Pavel. I didn't want to speak about Pavel, not right then, but I had to ask one question. "Were you . . . were you with Pavel when he died? I never heard anything except that he'd been killed."

"No. I was sent with a team to look at a bridge we were trying to repair. The attack on Pavel's group came out of nowhere. It was all over very fast. I'm sorry."

"Thank you," I managed to whisper. No matter how good I'd become at pushing thoughts of Pavel away, I still couldn't keep away visions of how much pain he might have suffered. It haunted me.

I don't know why, but everything spilled out of me then, everything about Miles and the flyers and the raid on the apartment.

Dmitri was so quiet when I finished, I was afraid I'd been wrong to tell him. He'd said he'd agreed to take the tutoring job to prove the baron wrong, and I'd just proved that someone in our family was actually acting against the czar.

Dmitri sighed. "I suspected something like that. Miles is in very serious danger now. If the baron comes here to arrest him, nothing I say will make a difference. We need to get Miles out of Petrograd."

Hearing those words made me want to fling my arms around Dmitri. He really was on our side. "I know. I was already planning on sending Miles and Hap to the United States, but we'll just have to move their departure up. I need to work out the details."

"Yes, details." Dmitri tapped his cane up and down on the floor. "They'll need to get permission to travel, and if Miles's name is on a list of suspected agitators, he won't get the approval," he said. "That's a problem."

I hadn't thought of that. Dmitri was right. Everyone in Russia held an internal passport, and a person had to get permission from the police to travel from one city to another. The policy had been put in place a long time ago to prevent people from leaving town without paying their debts, and it made travel much more difficult. The police didn't bother checking the peasants' movements in their carts and sleighs, but anyone who looked like they could afford the fee for the stamp was at risk if they traveled without it, especially by train.

"They'll have to try to get permission," I said. "If they go right away in the morning, the police stations won't have updated lists, will they? It has to take hours or even days to distribute those."

"Maybe. At least get Hap to go into the station first," Dmitri suggested. "If the last name of Mason is on a list, they'll double-check his first name, and that way he'll know if it's safe for Miles to try to get the stamp."

"Yes! That's a good idea." If it was safe, Hap could make up some story about his brother being late and then go outside and get Miles. "They can go to the train station right after that. I'll wake them up early in the morning and tell them the plan," I said, a yawn nearly swallowing my words. I felt like I hadn't slept for days.

"I'll go see the baron early tomorrow morning," Dmitri said. "If he knows about Miles, he's likely to tell me."

Dmitri's face had gone very pale, and I could see he was exhausted too. He gave a weak smile. "At least now I can stop pretending I'm actually teaching Hap and Miles anything. People who told me your brothers were incorrigible had no idea exactly what that meant."

"You've taught them how to drop glasses without breaking them," I said, wanting to draw out a few more moments. We couldn't do anything about Miles until morning, and I didn't know when I'd get the chance to have time alone with Dmitri again. "That has to count for something."

"Yes, I suppose that's true." Dmitri leaned back against the wall as if he wasn't in any hurry either. "I'll cherish that accomplishment. And they've taught me some card tricks, which I suppose may be useful someday. I may regret that I turned down the opportunity to learn how to saw a person in half." He shook his head. "You have quite a family, Charlotte Danielovna. And I mean that in a good way. Tell me one thing: Do you really know how to juggle while riding a horse and a unicycle? Pavel never mentioned that little detail about you."

I could feel the heat rising in my face. "I can, or at least I used to be able to. It's not something I've practiced for a long time."

He smiled. "Actually, there is a second thing I want to know. Why did you want to run away and join the circus? I can't imagine you ever wanting to leave your family."

I couldn't believe he remembered what Stepan had said when I introduced him to the boys. "I didn't want to leave them. Stepan doesn't have the story right. It was all before we even came to Russia and met him. I wanted my mother, Hap, and Miles to run away with me. Her second husband was awful and I hated him. We'd been to see a circus in Paris and I was obsessed with it, the sparkly costumes and the horses and everything. Running away to join it seemed the perfect solution." I realized how much I was babbling and forced myself to stop talking. "I'm sorry. That was a long answer to your question. It was all very silly." I couldn't help myself. I yawned again.

"You're tired," he said. "And I really have to say good night before I fall down right here and sleep, which would ruin Archer's good opinion of me."

"Good night." I tried to drag my gaze away from his face, from his eyes. I couldn't believe I'd ever confused him for Pavel. A twinge of guilt or regret or something made me finally look away. I felt my face flush. Did Dmitri think I'd acted as if I'd forgotten Pavel? I wanted to explain to him how it had been, how I'd cried for a boy I hadn't really known.

"Good night," he said.

The moment was gone. Maybe it was for the best. Only days earlier I'd told myself I didn't want to get close to another boy. I didn't want that hurt again.

We didn't speak again as we went upstairs, not wanting to wake anyone up. I went into Miles's room to find him asleep on top of the covers and still dressed. His breathing sounded almost normal. I took an extra blanket out of the chest at the end of his bed and covered him up.

I tried to think what to do next. Telling Papa had to be at the top of the list. I went to his room and knocked on the door. When he didn't answer, I knocked again, surprised he hadn't heard the first knock because he was such a light sleeper. I opened the door to look in.

He wasn't there, and his bed hadn't been slept in. I looked all around the room as if he'd be somewhere standing about, but of course he wasn't. I ran back downstairs to see Osip dozing in the room by the door, which meant someone in the family was still out; otherwise the footman would be asleep in his own room. Osip had to be waiting for Papa, though I had no idea where my stepfather would be at such a late hour. I went back to the sitting room, intending to stay awake until he came home.

I sat down by the fire and didn't realize I'd fallen asleep until the next morning, when I woke up with an aching head and a throat so dry it was painful. I drank some cold tea from the samovar. I knew I had to move, to make up for the time I'd wasted sleeping. When I went to find Papa, Osip told me he'd come home late but had already left again.

I wanted to stamp my foot, angry at myself that I'd slept through his coming and going. "Do you know where he went?"

"No. He seemed like he was going somewhere important, you might say, because he was in a serious mood. He didn't joke with me like he usually does." Osip's eyes flickered over me, and I'm sure he noticed I hadn't combed my hair and that I was still wearing the clothes I'd had on the day before. "What's wrong?" he asked.

"It's complicated. If anyone comes to the door asking for Miles, would you say he's not here? It's important. If the baron comes here, say . . . say . . . I don't know what you should say." I felt tears welling up. All of a sudden, it was too much.

Osip patted my arm and smiled. "Don't worry, little sister. I will say you've all taken ill with some horrible disease the doctor can't diagnose and the baron should come in to make sure I'm telling the truth, even though the doctor also said everyone who comes into contact with you might die. And then I will get very close to him and cough in his face. Is that good enough?"

Osip had been around my brothers too long. "I don't know what we'd do without you," I said. "Thank you. That would be perfect. If my stepfather comes back, tell him I need to see him right away. It's urgent."

I found Hap and Miles eating breakfast. Miles looked so calm I wanted to shriek at him like a banshee for acting as if he'd never even thought of going out to more meetings with revolutionaries. When I told him what had happened at number 28 after he'd left, he finally seemed to understand the danger he was in.

"What do I do?" he asked, his face ashen.

"You and Hap need to leave the country as soon as we can get everything organized. I'm going to the bank this morning to get you some money. You can go to Grandmother's house in Philadelphia and then . . . and then . . ." I hadn't thought beyond that. I couldn't picture them in the United States. I felt my eyes starting to water. I was not going to cry.

Miles didn't say a word as he got up and went to the window.

Hap continued to eat, nodding his head. "I won't mind visiting the United States." He stuffed a large piece of bread in his mouth.

The sight of him sitting there so unconcerned that his entire life was about to be upended should have annoyed me, but instead it made me feel better. They'd be all right. Hap would be there. His easygoing nature would help on a long, difficult trip.

Miles turned back to face me. "Hap doesn't need to go with me. I'll be fine by myself. I don't need a nursemaid."

Once again I stopped myself from shrieking at him, this time by actually biting my lip. "We don't have time to argue about this. It's not that you need a nursemaid. If someone comes looking for you, we can say both of you have gone because you're going to school in the United States. It will be more believable that you are both traveling."

That argument worked. Miles sat back down and rubbed his face with his hands, his expression grim. He seemed years older, and I realized what he was thinking. I knew he loved Russia as much as I did, and I'd just told him he had to leave as soon as he could.

I sat down beside him and put my hand over his, intending to say he wouldn't be gone forever, but he looked over at me and gave a slight shake of his head. "Let's talk about details," he said.

I knew how he felt. I'd play along. "The first problem is the passports," I said. I explained about Dmitri's ideas on the passport approvals. "I told Dmitri everything. And we can trust him."

"What about Peet?" Miles asked.

I'd forgotten about Peet. He'd be in as much danger as Miles. I closed my eyes. It was always one more thing. I could feel the tears trying to spill out again.

"Lottie? Are you all right?" Hap asked.

I don't know why, but I thought of our mother. I could hear her voice after she'd found me crying at my father's funeral. *We'll be sad, but we'll always go on. You're strong like me. Bad things happen that you can't control, but we strong ones face up to them and keep going.*

I knew I had no choice. I had to be all right. I had to keep going. I could take care of one more thing.

I opened my eyes. "Hap, you have to go see the Tamms. I don't have time. I'll write a note—no, I shouldn't put something in writing. Tell them the situation is bad and Peet needs to get away too. They can send him to Estonia. I know they still have family there. They'll have heard about the raid on the apartment by now, and if Peet hasn't told them he was there, you tell them. And then come home and pack, but don't pack much. We can send most of your things later."

"Got it," Hap said. "Elder Red, here we come, ready or not." He punched Miles on the arm.

The faintest of smiles crossed Miles's face. They'd be all right, the two of them together.

Chapter Thirteen

I GRABBED A piece of bread and ate it as I went upstairs to change my clothes.

When I came back down, Osip wasn't at the door, but he appeared as I was opening it to leave.

"Wait, Lottie! You shouldn't go out now," he said, hurrying toward me. "It's not safe. Vladislav says there is going to be a general strike and everyone will be out on the streets."

"Don't worry. I'm sure it won't be any worse than yesterday," I said as I pulled on my gloves.

He moved so that he was in front of the door, as if he wasn't going to let me out. "It could be much worse. The workers at one of the munitions factories are already on strike, and there is a rumor that the government is mounting machine guns on rooftops to fire on any crowds."

The words *machine guns* gave me pause. That had to be mere rumor. "I don't believe they'd do that," I said. "The people just want to get out and protest. I *have* to go out. I won't be gone for long, and I'll avoid the crowds. You remember what I told you about the baron? We're in real danger from him. I need to do something to make us safer." I didn't want to tell Osip about our plans. If the baron came to the house, it would be better for Osip not to know what was going on. "If the baron or anyone else comes who wants to know where Miles is, say he isn't home."

Osip nodded and sighed, then moved away from the door.

No one was out on our block, but that wasn't so unusual. The air was frigid even for Petrograd, the type of cold that Miles had labeled *dagger breath* because it hurt so much to breathe in.

When I got to the end of the block and turned the corner, a gust of wind stirred up the snow and blew it into my face. I blinked and brushed it off my eyelashes so I could see. I blinked a few more times until I could understand what I was seeing, or rather what I wasn't seeing. This street was empty too, and that was unusual. I felt a little prickle on the back of my neck that wasn't due to the cold. There was a tram, but it wasn't moving, and the windows were covered with snow. As I got closer, I saw that some of the windows had been smashed.

The prickling spread down my back. Snow was drifting across the sidewalks. Petrograd normally had so many street cleaners; they were out every day clearing off enough of the new snow to get around, and packing down the lower layers enough for the sleighs to operate. From the depth of the snow in front of me, no one had cleared them for many hours.

The city seemed abandoned. I shivered, feeling the cold cutting into me. A voice in my head told me to turn around and go home, back to the warmth, where it was safe.

I made myself go on, slogging through the snow, watching and hoping for some sign that the city hadn't emptied out overnight.

I heard an odd thumping noise behind me and whirled around, nearly falling as my foot came down on something solid underneath the snow, unbalancing me. A company of Cossacks came down the street, the thumping sound the horses' hooves muffled by the snow.

I moved out of the way, and they passed by as if they hadn't seen me, except for one young man at the end, who turned to look at me as he rode past.

The sight of people should have made me feel better, but the looks on the men's faces only made me more anxious. It was getting harder to make myself take in the cold air. I felt dizzy, so I stopped and tried to adjust my scarf around my mouth, forcing myself to breathe.

I made myself go on, walking until I heard sounds coming from the next block: voices and sleigh bells and what sounded like the normal shouts of the izvoschiks. I hurried up, eager to be among people again. The air seemed warmer, and I thought maybe the sun was trying to come out from under the clouds.

The noise grew, and as I turned the next corner, I saw why. The streets were packed, full of people wearing red armbands or carrying sticks with bits of red fabric tied to the ends of them. Placards had been placed everywhere, warning people not to gather in groups larger than three or they'd be fired upon. From the size of the crowds I saw, the signs were being completely ignored. At several different street corners, men stood on crates giving speeches to the people gathered around them.

There was an energy in the crowds I'd never seen before. I felt excitement running through me, but fear, too. This was a different city.

I stopped to listen to a slight man with wire-framed glasses, his voice loud and deep for such a small person. "This is the time to be brave!" he shouted. "The government doesn't care about us, so it has to go. We can do better! Let your voices be heard!" He pumped his fist in the air, and the people around me cheered.

I didn't cheer. My mind was in too much of a whirl. Was Raisa out in the crowd somewhere? I looked around for her and then caught myself. "Focus, focus," I whispered to myself. I had to think about my family first.

As I got closer to the bank, the number of mounted troops patrolling the streets grew. They weren't giving orders, but people parted anyway when they rode through.

There was no line in front of the bakery. The door had a CLOSED sign on it and there were no lights on, but a group of women stood in front of it, shouting as if the baker was inside. One woman pounded on the door while the rest chanted, "Give us bread!"

The bank was closed. I stood there in front of the door, staring at it, trying to think what to do next. Panic began to rise up. The boys had to have money. As I was trying to work out who I could borrow some from, I remembered the lockbox at the hospital. It had rubles in it. We kept some for emergencies. I pushed my way through the crowds, trying to remember how much was in it. If there wasn't enough, I'd have to see if Papa had any on hand. I remembered his words at the grand duke's party: *Tell Sasha I'll pay him tomorrow.* I hoped that didn't mean there wasn't any at home, either.

A policeman rode up and shouted at me. "Get off the street!" I didn't know why he was focusing on me. There were people everywhere. He shouted at me again, calling me *redhead* in Russian. That explained it. He thought I was a troublemaker because of my hair. I pretended I was going into a building, but came right back out as soon as he rode off.

On Mikhail Street the crowds were just as big and seemed to be made up mostly of women. A large group of them linked arms, pushing their way down the street and forcing the policemen to the side, all the while singing and chanting. "No more food shortages! No more war!"

I'd thought the Cossack troops would joke with them again, but all of a sudden the troops charged the women. They scattered out of the way and then cheered as if it were all part of a game.

I didn't feel like it was a game. If someone stumbled, they'd be trampled.

"Charlotte! Charlotte Mason!"

I recognized Carter's voice, and I looked around until I saw him waving his arm frantically at me. He had on his ridiculous hat, and he towered over the crowd around him.

The newsman made his way to me, his eyes wide and a big smile plastered on his face. "Isn't this something! Patrick and I have been out all morning." He waved in the direction he'd come from but I didn't see whoever Patrick was. The crowd was too thick.

I felt jittery with nerves and a little sick to my stomach. The authorities wouldn't let this continue, but if people refused to get off the streets, I had no idea what the troops would do.

"Patrick is getting some great photographs. It's really happening. These people aren't going to back down now. The crowd is too fired up. Watch out there, fellow!" Carter said to a man who jostled me. Since he spoke in English, the man ignored him.

Carter waved his arms around, nearly knocking his own hat off. "I only hope I can get this story out. I tried to file one yesterday about the ugly mood in the city, but the woman at the telegraph office told me not to waste my money. The censors aren't letting any real news out. They don't want the Germans to know how bad the situation is."

His news shook me. If the censors were blocking information, the situation must be very bad. I didn't know what to do. I didn't know what that meant for us.

He looked down at me as if he'd just realized who he was talking to. "Say, what are you doing out in this crowd anyway? The streets certainly aren't going to be safe for the next few days."

"I'm on my way to the hospital. I should keep going."

"Oh, right. I'll see you later. Wait, would you like to go to the ballet with me sometime? I've never been to one, but everyone says since I'm here, I have to go." He didn't seem to realize it was completely bizarre to be talking about going to a performance in the midst of what actually seemed like the start of a revolution.

"Maybe," I said. "We can talk later at a better time." He didn't reply, too busy listening to a new chant the crowd had taken up.

When I finally reached the hospital, Galina stopped me before I could get to the office. "Any news?" she said. "I've heard all kinds of rumors, and we've had more patients leave early when their husbands came to get them. There are only three here now. Is the czar coming back to the city?"

"I didn't know he wasn't here already." Papa hadn't said anything, and he was my only source of news about the czar.

"He's at the front with the troops. A nurse who was there told me. She says she thinks the czar and his men have no idea what's happening here."

"I haven't heard anything," I said. "When I see my stepfather, I'll ask him. He's sure to know."

I went into the office and took off my coat. Galina came in as I was taking the lockbox out of the cupboard. She had a greenish cast to her face as if she was about to throw up.

"Are you coming down with something?" I asked.

"There are more visitors," she said, her voice shaky, which was not something I'd heard before.

I sighed. "Which husband is it now?"

She shook her head, but before she could speak, two men pushed their way around her.

They were policemen. My heart began to pound so loud I thought they'd be able to hear it.

One of them was Irina Igorneeva's husband. I remembered from her chart that his last name was Blok. The other was bigger, with a walrus mustache and a large, crooked nose.

"I believe you are Charlotte Danielovna Masonaya?" Blok said in an official-sounding voice.

I put the lockbox back in the cupboard, hoping they hadn't noticed what it was. "Yes. What can I do for you?" I thought I managed to keep my voice from wavering, though my jaw was clenched so tightly it hurt.

"We are here to inspect the facilities," he announced. "We've had reports of black-market activities. Show us to your food storerooms."

I should have foreseen it. I should have realized a toad like Blok would find a way to take revenge for having to give way to a girl.

I thought of my mother and what she'd do in such a situation. "There must be some mistake," I said. "We are a hospital, and the food we have stored here is for our patients."

"Show us," he ordered.

I hesitated, wondering if I could refuse. The other man chuckled. "I know what you are thinking, but you should realize people don't say no to us, not even foreigners. If you don't like this, complain to your embassy later, but now do what we say."

"Yes," Blok added. "We can find reasons to arrest everyone who works here if you refuse."

I knew they probably would, just out of spite. I couldn't let them arrest the nurses. "This way," I said, and led them to the kitchen in the back, my mind racing.

The cook, Tanya, dropped a spoon when she saw the policemen and then grabbed the ends of her apron, clenching them between her hands. She was Galina's grandmother, a tiny elderly woman who, when she wasn't cooking, loved sitting in a chair in the nursery rocking the babies.

"It's all right, Tanya." I tried to smile. "These men won't be here long." She picked up the spoon and held it in front of her as if it would be some kind of protection. I hated to see the fear on her face.

"In here." I pointed to the pantry. It was only about a third full, and I hoped that the other policeman would see that it was a normal amount for a small hospital.

"Where did you get all this food?" Blok demanded.

I clasped my hands together and tried to sound as if I were one of my former teachers patiently lecturing something to us ignorant students. "We buy it at locations all over the city. Some of this we have had for a long time, since before there were so many shortages. My mother, who founded the hospital, believed that we should keep a stock of basic supplies on hand all the time because we never know how many patients we are going to have in any given week. Patients need good food to recover their strength and go home to their families."

Blok slapped his hand down on one of the empty shelves. "Hoarding food is unpatriotic. You should be ashamed. Our men at the front go hungry while you let women feast on all this."

"They aren't feasting!" I realized I had raised my voice, so when I spoke again, I tried to go back to sounding calm and reasonable. "And many of these women are the wives of our soldiers. I'm sure the soldiers wouldn't want their families going hungry. We send bundles of food home with each patient when she is released, so she can feed her other children."

"Be quiet!" Blok moved so he was only inches from me. "You can talk and talk, but it doesn't change the situation." He turned to the other man. "I think we should arrest her, don't you?"

He was trying to scare me. I sucked in a breath, weighing what to say. The wrong thing might make the situation worse.

"Perhaps," the other policeman said as he walked over to one of the sugar tins and opened it up. He dipped his fingers in and brought up a pinch of sugar, which he put in his mouth.

"This is not illegal!" I said. "The patrons of the hospital are well-respected and well-known supporters of the czar. They will tell you we run the hospital according to the rules." I didn't want to draw my stepfather into this, even though I suspected they already knew all about him.

"Can you prove where you got all this?" the other man asked.

I'd thought about writing up some fake receipts before, but I hadn't carried through with the plan. We did have some legitimate receipts, since we still bought what we could from local merchants, but they weren't enough to account for all the food.

I decided to try to bluff my way around the question. "I can give you some boxes of our paperwork. We don't have a bookkeeper at the moment so they aren't very well organized, but if you want to go through them, you are more than welcome to."

"Dealing on the black market is quite a serious offense," Blok said. "You could be put in prison for many years. It would be a shame for a young girl like you to waste the best years of her life." He paused. I clasped my hands together so they wouldn't shake, though they were slick with sweat. I didn't know if it was better to stay silent or keep talking. A terrible feeling was growing in me that it wouldn't matter what I did.

The corners of Blok's mouth turned up into a smirk. "Though

perhaps we can find a way to overlook this. Of course, if we do, you'll have to swear to never do this again. We could see that all this food gets donated to a worthier cause. The hospitals for our soldiers always need food."

I realized what he was saying. They wanted it for themselves. They'd take it, claiming it would go to another hospital, but it wouldn't. It would go to the police.

I wished I could wipe the smirks off their faces. My fear disappeared, replaced by anger. How low could a person sink to take food from a hospital? I decided I wasn't going to make it easy for them. "Every hospital needs food," I said. "If you know of one that has a shortage, then of course we will let our supplies go to them. I'm afraid you'll have to arrange a way to get it moved, though. We have very little help here besides the nurses, and they must stay with the patients. You saw yourself, the cook is an elderly woman."

I'd hoped they'd both leave temporarily to get a cart or something so we could at least hide some of the food. If we were clever, they wouldn't be able to tell anything was missing.

"Fine," the other man said. "We'll arrange to transport it immediately. You stay here and help load it up. Blok will stay to oversee the transfer."

I gritted my teeth together. "I need to get back to work," I said. "Perhaps the policeman would like some tea while he waits. There is tea in our little sitting room, and it's the warmest room in the building." If I could get him up there, we could get back into the storeroom without him seeing and move some of the food into a hiding place.

Blok rubbed his hands together. "Yes, I will have tea." I took him to the sitting room and motioned at the samovar, not trusting myself to speak, and then hurried back to the kitchen.

I explained to Tanya what I was going to do and asked her to find some hiding place while I went into the pantry. I took a large piece of cheese and one of the baskets of eggs, trying to figure out how much I could take before they'd notice.

Tanya cried out. I whirled around and ran right into Blok.

"Foolish girl." He snorted and then added, "I knew what you were going to do. You aren't so clever."

"These are for the patients' lunch and dinner," I said. "You have to leave us enough to feed them today until we can get more food."

"You'll have to find another way to manage, or they can go without." He grabbed the basket of eggs out of my hand but it tipped. One fell out and broke, spattering both of us. I wished I could throw the rest at him.

I heard a sharp, loud sound from the front of the building, and then another and another from the square. Blok's face went pale. He dropped the basket and ran toward the front of the building. More sounds, a clattering type of noise, and I realized it was gunfire. My mouth went dry. Tanya wailed. "In here," I said, grabbing her and shoving her into the pantry. "Stay here where it's safe."

I ran to the front to find the nurses crowded around the windows, clutching one another. Blok was at a window by himself. I moved so I could see people running in all directions. I took hold of Galina's hand. "What's happening?" I whispered. She didn't answer.

The sound of gunfire continued and then the screaming started. As more people left the square, a grim sight emerged. Several bodies lay in the snow: men, women, and even children.

No one said a word. The horror of it turned to a numb feeling inside me. I knew it was real, but my mind wanted it not to be. I closed my eyes but couldn't get rid of the scene. I didn't realize I was crushing Galina's hand until she made a whimpering sound.

"Look!" One of the nurses pointed at a building across the square. "There's the gun."

I opened my eyes to see two policemen crouched on the roof of the building and aiming a machine gun down at the square. It looked like they were trying to put more ammunition in, but as they worked on it, a group of men burst out of a door onto the roof and ran toward the gunners. The men all had red armbands on and were dressed as ordinary workmen. The gunner tried to swing the weapon around to aim at them, but the other men were too fast for him.

Some of them ripped the gun off its stand and then surrounded the two. I thought they were going to drag them off, but then the men picked up both policemen and carried them over to the edge of the building. The policemen struggled.

"No!" someone gasped.

The men threw the policemen over. They screamed all the way down.

I turned away, bile rising in my throat.

"Get out of my way." I heard Blok's voice. It had gone high and shaky. He was trying to get around the nurses to go back toward the kitchen.

"Coward!" I yelled. "Why are you sneaking out the back? The front door is right there. Let's see you go out it. Be a brave man and walk around the bodies of children. Let the revolutionaries see you."

He rushed over toward me and raised his hand as if he was going to slap me.

Galina stepped in front of him. "Go," she ordered, grabbing hold of his wrist.

He shoved her out of the way and ran toward the kitchen.

"He won't be back," one of the other nurses said. "Now that a revolution has started, the police will pay for what they've done."

"Look!" someone cried.

We went back to the windows. Black smoke billowed from the building across the square as the group of men who had been on the roof emerged from the door. The people who had run away when the shooting began flooded back into the square, cheering the men on.

"They want to make sure the police don't regroup there," Galina said. "But that's not going to be enough." She pointed to one of the streets that led to the square. Policemen were pulling another machine gun mounted on a wagon toward it. Other policemen were running into the square from all directions, their weapons drawn.

I spotted Carter and the photographer on the opposite side of the square. Carter stood in plain view, writing in his notebook as if there weren't bullets flying around. He made a perfect target with his height and his hat. The photographer had had the sense to plant himself behind a parked automobile, though he was still visible as he leaned on the hood. I couldn't understand why they wanted to be in the middle of such violence. I prayed both men would survive the day.

More shots sounded, and then we heard sharp thuds against the building. Bits of stone shot in all directions away from us.

"Get away from the windows!" Galina yelled, grabbing a nurse's arm and pulling her back.

"Why are they shooting at us?" someone cried.

"They're just shooting in all directions to get people out of the square," I said, though I didn't know if that was true. Everything was happening too fast.

When the crowd scattered again, we saw the people who had been hit. The injured tried to crawl away. The dead lay still, but the gunfire continued.

"There's someone trying to get inside." A nurse pointed out the window to the right. I looked out to see a woman dragging herself across the snow toward the hospital, blood staining the snow behind her.

Galina and I both headed toward the door.

I hadn't realized Tanya had come in from the pantry until I heard her voice. "Galina, no! You can't go out there," she cried. "You'll be cut down too. They don't care who you are."

"It's only a few feet," Galina said. "Lottie and I are quick. We can get out and get her back inside fast as can be." She went over to the armoire where we kept some of the coats and grabbed two, tossing one to me. "Put this on and stay low."

The woman was unconscious by the time we reached her. We tried dragging her by her arms but she was too heavy. "Help!" Galina yelled as two men ran by us. They ignored her. The gunfire continued. I tried to shut out the noise.

"Get her feet!" I shouted. "Maybe it will be easier to move her that way."

"I can help," a voice said. It sounded like Dmitri, but I didn't understand why he'd be here. I looked up and saw it was really him.

Between the three of us we managed to get her inside, and once we had the door shut behind us, the other nurses took over.

"What are you doing here?" I asked Dmitri. The expression on his face was so grim, I felt sick. Something had to be very wrong. "Is my stepfather ill?"

He motioned for me to move away from the others. "It's not the general. It's Stepan. He's missing. He was very upset because he overheard Archer talking about how we were all going to be slaughtered by the end of the day. I tried to convince him it wasn't true, but he wanted to go out and see what was really happening."

"How could you let him leave?" I didn't wait for an answer. I ran to get my own coat.

Dmitri followed me. "Wait, Charlotte. I didn't know he was going to leave. He said he wanted to go to his room. It was only later when Hap went looking for him that we realized he was gone."

"What did Osip say? Surely he wouldn't let him leave."

"Osip didn't see him, but Hap said his coat is gone too. No one saw him leave."

I felt like my breath was being squeezed out of me. Stepan was too young to be out on the streets in all the chaos.

"I came here because I thought you might know where he would go," Dmitri said.

I heard gunfire again, and then one of the windows shattered, bits of glass flying everywhere. Dmitri reached for me but I was already on the floor. More bullets hit the outside of the building.

He flattened himself beside me.

"We have to move the patients. They could be hit," I said as I got to my knees and crawled toward the ward. I should have been terrified, but a calm had settled over me. I knew I had to stay focused to help the patients and find Stepan.

Dmitri followed me. The other nurses were already there. We moved the two patients and their babies to a different room, one at the back of the house on the second floor.

When everyone was settled, I spent a few minutes talking to Galina and explained what had happened. "It's all right," she said. "You go. We can manage. Be careful."

I went back to Dmitri. "Stepan doesn't go off by himself. Did you ask Hap and Miles if they had any ideas?"

"Yes, they didn't have a clue. In fact, they were both astounded he'd go out by himself."

I remembered about the train and the plans for the boys to leave town. With everything that had happened, I'd completely forgotten the whole reason I'd come to the hospital. "Are Miles and Hap still home?"

"Yes, the trains have been shut down today."

At least they were safe for the moment. "We can go out the back," I said.

While I was watching Dmitri put on his gloves, I realized he didn't have his cane with him. He hadn't had it at all, and he'd been moving around much better, though he was still limping. The nurse in me worried he should still have it in case he needed it.

"We need a plan before we leave the building," he said. "What about your friends who own the theater? Would he go to the Tamms?"

"I don't think so. He hasn't been there as much as the older boys." He'd always been jealous that Hap and Miles wanted to go there without him.

"Well, what about his friends? Would he go to one of their houses?"

I tried to think of where he might be and what friends he would visit until an awful realization hit me: Stepan didn't have any friends. Even though he would have been old enough to start school the year before, we'd kept him home because he'd been so shaken by my mother's death. He was so quiet, so overshadowed by the other boys, I hadn't even considered that none of us had made an effort to arrange for him to meet other boys his age.

"I can't think of anyone's house he'd go to," I said. "He may just be out in the crowds."

"All right. We'll find him." I heard the determination in Dmitri's words, but I knew it was going to be a nearly impossible task. It would be dark soon. The winter days were short, and we'd have a much harder time when night fell.

I heard Tanya scream, and then came the sound of a man shouting at her. I recognized the voice.

Blok.

He'd come back.

Chapter Fourteen

DMITRI AND I ran to the kitchen. Dmitri was first, and when he reached it, he stopped so suddenly I ran into him. It wasn't just Blok. The room was filled with policemen. Tanya huddled in one corner, weeping.

"Get out of here!" I screamed. Pure rage welled up in me. I tried to shove one toward the door but he pushed me away without even looking at me. The rest ignored me, and I realized they were all drenched with sweat and breathing heavily.

"Up to the roof!" one of them shouted to the others. Two of them carried a machine gun.

I ran to block the entrance to the back stairs. "This is a hospital! We have patients here."

Another one shoved me out of the way. Dmitri took hold of me.

"Stop!" Dmitri said to the men. "You don't have authorization to take over this building."

"We don't have time for authorization. There's a mob out there." He motioned to Dmitri's uniform. "You should be out with your regiment helping us, but if you'd rather hide here with your girlfriend, just stay out of our way."

He spat on the floor, and then some of the men moved up the stairs. Two ran toward the front of the building and another took up a position at the back door with his gun raised. I wanted to throw pots and pans at them or do something, anything, but Dmitri wouldn't let go of me.

"No! No!" I couldn't stop yelling.

"Charlotte, it won't do any good. There are too many of them," Tanya said.

I heard more glass shattering at the front of the house.

Galina ran in. "There are people in front of the house throwing rocks and trying to open the door," she yelled. She saw the policeman at the back door and her eyes went wide.

"They know the police are in here," Dmitri said. "They're trying to get at them."

The policeman at the back door swore. "They're not getting me!" he cried.

"Charlotte, one of them has a torch," Galina whispered.

Horror rose in me, and my throat tightened so much I had a hard time getting the words out. "They're going to try to burn the building down to get to the police. We have to get the patients out of here." I tried to block out the image of the hospital in flames.

Galina hesitated for only a few seconds. "Yes," she said. "Yes." Her voice was back to its normal tone, one that sounded like a nurse. "We'll split the nurses up so that someone is with each mother and baby while we take them to their homes. The woman caught in the gunfire can go with one of us until it's safe to get her to her own home."

I'd already forgotten about the woman we'd brought in. "How is she?"

"She's all right. She can walk, at least. One bullet went right through her arm. Another grazed her face, which was why there was so much blood, but it's just a minor injury."

I looked over at Dmitri. I could see the strain on his face. He nodded.

As soon as we told the other nurses, they began to help the patients get dressed. Galina directed everything, reassuring the women everything would be all right.

I didn't tell the policeman's wife that her husband was in the building or about the attacks on the police.

"Take me to my sister's, please," one of the other women said. "It's closer and she'll be there with my children." A sob escaped her. She was a frail woman named Lena and I feared she'd break down, but she clamped her mouth shut and pulled on a coat a nurse gave her.

I could only imagine how much fear the patients felt, still weak and with fragile newborns to protect.

I heard more sounds of glass shattering, but we acted as if we hadn't heard. All the nurses were calm, and I knew that the others had blocked out the chaos swirling around us because we had a job to do. It was one of the first things I had learned in nursing training: to focus on the task at hand, ignoring everything else.

I didn't notice that Dmitri had left the room until I glanced over to see him coming back in when we were almost ready to go. He made a motion with his head like he wanted Galina and me to go out in the hall.

"The back door is still clear," he said. "The policeman scared off people trying to come in that way. I think they are concentrating on getting in the front because there are more windows. Once we're outside, no one will hurt a group of women with nurses as long as they realize who you are. I've told the policeman what we are doing so he won't stand in our way."

"All right. We're almost ready," Galina said. "Charlotte, you and your friend take Lena Arkhipova and her baby to her sister's house. It will be safe for you to leave her there so you can look for your little brother. We'll take the others to their homes and stay with them as long as necessary."

The worst part was going down the stairs. When one of the policemen fired his gun through the broken window and someone outside screamed, Lena Arkhipova nearly collapsed. Dmitri carried her the rest of the way down. I had her baby, a little girl who was sleeping through it all. The other babies were all crying.

"Hurry," Galina said to the other women. "This way. Don't look. We're going out the back."

The back courtyard was empty. Galina went first. Lena Arkhipova was in such a state that Dmitri continued to carry her. We split up at the street, Dmitri and me going one way with Lena Arkhipova and her baby, the others going in the opposite direction.

"Godspeed," Galina said to me. I nodded my head, not able to find any words.

"Ready?" Dmitri asked me.

"Ready," I said. The sooner we got the woman and baby to safety, the sooner I could look for Stepan.

We skirted the edge of the building until we were close to the front and then turned to go around the square. It was full of people shouting, but no one paid attention to us. Dmitri was still carrying the patient, and he was struggling, limping a little.

"Wait," I said. I touched the woman's face. "Lena, do you think you can walk? We can get to your sister's more quickly if you can."

She nodded, and Dmitri set her on her feet, keeping an arm around her for support. As we walked away, I looked back to see that the front door of the hospital had shattered. A crowd surged into the building through the door and the broken windows. There were shots but they didn't stop. The man with the torch went inside.

All my mother's work, everyone's work—Dr. Rushailo's, Galina's, the other nurses', Tanya's—it would be all gone.

"There won't be anything left, will there?" I murmured.

"I don't know," Dmitri said. "Don't think about that now."

The baby began to cry. I hugged her to me. *Focus on the task at hand.*

It was only a few blocks to the sister's house. We got them settled in and tried reassuring everyone they'd be safe if they stayed inside. I finally had to tell them I needed to look for my little brother so they would let us leave.

When we got back outside, we were surrounded by soldiers. There were hundreds more than there had been even a few hours earlier.

"I didn't know there were that many troops in the city." I didn't understand why the policemen were the ones firing on the crowds while the soldiers didn't seem to know what to do.

"Better follow behind me," Dmitri said. "Fourteen thousand Cossack troops were brought in overnight to bolster the army reserves already here. The authorities knew there was going to be trouble and the guard units stationed here wouldn't be able to handle it. Most of the troops already in the city don't even want to be soldiers. They're just reservists. I don't know if any of them will fire on our own people. I hope not."

"How do you know all this?"

"My friends in the regiment have told me." He shouldered his way through a clump of soldiers. I stuck close behind.

As we walked, I peered into the face of every small boy we passed.

There were too many who had on coats similar to what Stepan wore, and since they were all bundled up with hats and scarves, it was nearly impossible to tell them apart unless I got close enough.

An image of Stepan popped into my head. I remembered his serious little face the first day we'd barreled into the house and his life. He'd just turned three. His mother, Papa's second wife, had died when he was a baby, so he'd been brought up by a very old nanny. I remembered how in those first days he'd go hide in the attic at times, overwhelmed by the boys shouting and running up and down the halls when they weren't sliding down the banisters.

Shouts came from a nearby street, and then the sound of a machine gun. We flattened ourselves against the nearest building. An automobile sped by, packed full of men. One was even lying on the running board beneath the doors, shooting off the machine gun he held.

Another rattle of a machine gun in the opposite direction made me jerk back, banging my head on the stone wall of the building behind us. The pain radiated forward and I saw black dots in front of my eyes. Even after the burst stopped, the sound continued to echo in my head.

We continued on, though it grew more difficult. Sleighs and automobiles had been turned over in the streets, blocking the way. We saw people carrying the injured away, and we heard more gunshots in the distance.

Dmitri flagged down a soldier running by. "What's happening? Where are all the troops?"

"The Pavlovsky Regiment has mutinied!" the man yelled. The whites of his eyes were showing, and he was only wearing one boot. "They're joining the revolution! If my regiment is next, I'm going to

be there when they do. Those officers will see who is in charge now."
He ran on, trying to rip off his shoulder epaulets as he went.

I looked down to see a trail of blood drops zigzagging down the
street in front of us. I heard a strange buzzing and it took me a
moment to realize that the sound was inside my own head. A bad
taste filled my mouth and I thought I was going to retch. I reached
down and picked up a handful of snow and wiped it on my face. The
cold helped. I shouldn't have been so shaken by drops of blood. I'd
seen plenty of blood before.

"Charlotte? Are you all right?"

"I just felt strange for a bit," I said. "Let's keep going."

As we got close to the Krestovsky Prison, the crowds grew much
bigger and the shouting was louder. When I'd gone by the prison
in the past, I hurried, not wanting to look at a place of such mis-
ery, especially because the dirty red brick of the buildings always
reminded me of dried blood.

As we came even with it, the crowd around us began to cheer. I
asked a woman what was happening.

"Soldiers have gone in to let all the prisoners out!" she yelled.

We saw prisoners stagger out, both men and women, all wearing ragged prison uniforms and supporting one another. Some were
shielding their eyes as if they were blinded, even though it was nearly
dark.

Two men barely managing to support each other had tears
streaming down their cheeks. All the prisoners were very thin, and
many had white hair, though they didn't look that old.

"I didn't know there were so many," a man next to me said.

"Hundreds of political prisoners were rounded up after the rebel-
lion in 1905," a woman said. "They've been in there ever since."

Twelve years. Twelve years for speaking against the czar.

"Everyone is going to be free!" someone else in the crowd yelled.

"You fool!" the woman yelled back at him. "They're letting out criminals, too! Murderers and rapists and thieves. You think the streets are dangerous now. Just wait!"

Some in the crowd ran into the prison and soon reemerged carrying stacks of paper. They threw them in a pile on the ground and lit them on fire. More and more stacks were brought out and added until the pile grew into a giant bonfire. With each flare of the flames, the crowd cheered.

"They're destroying the records," Dmitri said. "Very clever. No one will be able to try to round the prisoners back up if the authorities regain control."

"Even if they tried, they might not have a place to put them. Look." I pointed to one of the upper windows of the district court building next to the prison. Smoke was creeping out the edges of it. As we watched, more smoke came from an adjoining window, and then the next one filled too, down the line.

More prisoners trickled out of the building, these in far worse shape than the ones who had come before. My breath caught when I saw Raisa emerge holding up a man I knew must be her father, but whom I didn't recognize. The man she was supporting was completely bald and small and so bent up, he looked like a collection of bones someone had put a prison uniform on.

I realized I was swaying on my feet, feeling so light-headed I had to grab Dmitri's arm.

"Are you all right?"

"Yes," I said. "I need to go help someone."

Before I could take a step, other people rushed forward, and Raisa and her father were soon surrounded. I reminded myself that I had to concentrate on finding Stepan. I could see Raisa later. "We should keep going," I said.

I took a few steps and then stopped. "Wait. I have an idea. Stepan might have gone to the imperial stables. Papa takes him there once in a while because Stepan loves the horses and we don't have any left at the dacha. They were all taken by the army. Stepan has made friends with some of the stablemen and knows a lot of the horses by name."

Dmitri sighed. "If he's there, I don't know if we'll find him on a day like today. I'm sure the place is in an uproar."

He was right. The imperial stables were huge. With six thousand horses, the place was as big as the Hermitage, and I didn't know which section of the stables Papa took him to.

I tried to think of another plan. "Let's stop at home first. Maybe he's returned, or if he hasn't, Papa might be home and he would know where we can look."

When we reached home, Osip wasn't at the door, but I didn't bother looking for him. If Stepan had returned, Miles and Hap would know. They were both in the schoolroom.

"Stepan's not here," Hap said as soon as we went in.

"What's happening out there?" Miles asked. "It's maddening not to know."

"I'm not sure. It's chaos," I said. "Is Papa home?" I didn't want him out on the streets.

"No," Hap said. "He's been gone all day."

I hoped my stepfather was with friends who would watch out for him. "We're going to the imperial stables to look for Stepan. I can't think of anywhere else he might be."

"I'll go," Hap said. "I can move faster than Dmitri with that leg of his." He held up his hand. "Lottie, I know you're going to say it's too dangerous." That was exactly what I'd been about to say. "So don't say it," Hap continued. "I'm tired of you treating me like a child. You don't have to be the martyr who takes care of everything."

I was shocked to hear him speak like that. It wasn't fair. I wasn't trying to be a martyr. I just wanted everyone to be safe.

I heard the twins running down the hall, chattering away to each other in the baby language they'd made up. They had mostly given it up over a year ago, so I didn't know why they'd gone back to it. I looked out. Polina was running after them, calling their names.

When they burst through the door, they flung themselves at me, wrapping their arms around my legs.

"Lottie! Lottie! Come see. Stepan is in the attic and he won't let us in!"

I should have thought of the attic. I ran up the flights of stairs, the others clattering behind me. When I got to the door I tried to open it, but it was locked. I knocked. "Stepan, are you in there? I need to talk to you."

There was no reply. I put my ear to the door. I could hear someone moving around.

"Stepan, please let me in," I said. "I'm not going to make you come out. You can stay in there as long as you want. Just unlock the door."

Archer had a key, but I didn't want to ask him for it. I didn't know how Stepan had gotten in. Papa had ordered it kept locked after Miles had opened some of the trunks.

I heard footsteps moving to the door. I motioned everyone back. "We're not all going to pile in there," I whispered.

My words didn't have much effect. As soon as Stepan opened the door, the twins rushed in. "Stepan! Stepan! We thought you were lost!"

Stepan glanced at me and then looked at the floor. In that brief instance, I saw that his eyes were red. He'd been crying.

"Why are you up here?" Miles asked. "We were worried about you."

"We need a hiding place from the Germans." Stepan burst into tears. "If a revolution happens, the Germans will win the war. That's what Archer says."

"Hey, Stepan, don't cry," Hap said. The twins surrounded Stepan. Nika hugged him and Sophie patted him on the arm.

I could scarcely control my anger at Archer. Everything was bad enough. We didn't need him to make things worse.

I glanced over at the door. Dmitri hadn't come all the way into the room. At first I thought the expression on his face was from pain, because even from across the room I could see he was breathing heavily, but then I realized from the way his mouth was set that it was anger.

I was about to urge everyone to go back downstairs when Miles opened a trunk. He pulled out a picture in an old-fashioned frame. "Who's this?" he asked. I was close enough to see that it was Papa with his first wife and a girl who looked to be about thirteen or fourteen. I recognized the wife because there was a small portrait of her in the library.

The girl had to be the other daughter.

I took the picture from him and put it back in the trunk, trying to signal to him not to ask more questions. "I don't know," I said. "It's not important." We didn't need a lost relative at that moment, or at any moment, especially not one who was a murderer. "Let's go downstairs now. It's cold up here. Stepan, why don't you come down and have some tea? You can come back up here later if you want."

We moved to the schoolroom, all of us, including Polina and the twins. Somehow it felt like we all needed to be in one place. Every once in a while I thought I caught faint sounds of gunfire, but I couldn't be sure.

At least the twins were completely unaware that anything was wrong. They were delighted to be allowed to play in a room that was usually off-limits, and had soon set up their own little school area. Dmitri stood at the window, looking out, though there was nothing to see except the back courtyard.

I couldn't sit still, but the room was so cluttered it was hard to move around. "I'll be back in a minute," I said. "I want to talk to Zarja."

Dmitri followed me out in the hall. "I know it's not my place, but I'll talk to Archer if you like. He's got to stop this nonsense about the Germans."

"Is it really nonsense?" I asked, searching his face.

"Yes," he said. "If I thought your family was in any danger, I'd tell you. Don't you know that?"

"Yes." I almost hugged him, but I stopped myself, knowing I had to keep my feelings for him under control. "Thank you for the offer, but I'll talk to Archer. He likes Stepan, so when he hears he's been scaring him so much, I'm sure he'll stop."

I went down to the kitchen to find Zarja making soup.

"Where's Archer?" I asked.

"He's taken to his bed. He isn't feeling well. I'm worried, Lottie. He's never sick."

She was right. I didn't remember Archer ever taking ill. "Should we call a doctor?" I asked.

"The fool won't let me! I don't like the look of him but I'm not sure what's wrong. He's got a blue touch to his mouth, which is never a good sign."

I sat down on a stool, feeling a little odd, and I realized that the back of my head was hurting where I'd hit it on the wall of the building. The pain increased, as if it had stored itself up until I got home to take effect.

"If he's not better soon, I'll get a doctor or send Hap out for one," I said.

"Yes, that's a fine idea. Ha! I'd like to see Archer try to boss a doctor around." She put a ladleful of soup in a bowl. "This will help him feel better."

When I went back to the schoolroom, Dmitri was the only one who noticed me. He was back by the window, but he turned around when I came in and went over to him.

He spoke in a low voice. "Now that we've found Stepan, I need to go see what's happening. We've been waiting a long time for this."

His voice wasn't quiet enough. "Who's 'we'?" Miles asked. "You said 'we've been waiting a long time.'"

"The political group I belong to, the Constitutional Democratic Party," Dmitri said. "It looks like we might finally have the chance to make Russia into something better, and I want to be a part of it."

I gaped at him. I hadn't even given a thought to Dmitri's views, which had been stupid of me. Of course he'd have a side he supported. Every Russian did. I hadn't heard of the particular political party he mentioned, but since it seemed like there were dozens, it wasn't surprising I didn't know it. I wished he'd told me about it. It was a whole side of him I didn't know.

"Is that something men in the Horse Guard belong to?" Stepan asked. "Can I join too?"

Dmitri smiled down at him. "You can join, but it has nothing to do with the Horse Guard. All my friends from the university belong to it."

All my friends from the university. Another side of him I didn't know. How many more were there?

"Osip belongs to it too," Dmitri added. "But don't tell Archer. He wouldn't be pleased with a footman he considered a radical."

"Good for Osip," Miles said. "If I had known, I would have gotten him to help me instead of lying to him about where I was going and what I was doing."

Osip. I'd have never guessed Osip was part of a group. Everyone seemed to have a secret life I didn't know about.

I sat down in a chair, about to lose my ability to act as if I could handle anything that happened. The day had been too much and my head was pounding. "Is that where you've been going at night?" I asked Dmitri. "To meetings?"

"Yes, mostly. We meet in different places. We didn't realize this would all happen so fast. I'm not sure what is going to happen next. It will depend on what the czar does."

Papa's voice came from the hall. "Where is everyone?" he called.

Relief washed through me. With us all together, some of the tension eased.

He came in, and everyone talked at once. He hugged the twins, who were clinging to his legs. "Everything is fine, my little chickabiddies! I'm fine!"

When I looked at him more closely, I didn't believe that. He was stooped over like he was too tired to stand up straight. His eyelids drooped down so that his eyes were only half open.

"Let's let Papa talk," I said, "after he sits down."

Once he was settled and I'd brought him some tea, he motioned for all of us to listen. "I've been meeting with some people to discuss the situation. The unrest is widespread, but the czar has been notified and I'm sure he is on his way back to the city. Once he arrives, everything will get back to normal. We just have to stay calm in the meantime."

This brought on some sharp questions from Miles. While the two were talking, Dmitri drew me aside. "I'm going now. I won't be gone long."

"Will you . . . will you check on the hospital?" All the time we'd been looking for Stepan, I'd been thinking about it. I should have tried to stop the man with the torch. I should have done something. I didn't want to think about what I'd do if the place was gone.

"I'll check," he said.

"Do you think anything will change when the czar gets back?" I asked. I couldn't see the city going back to the way it had been before.

He shook his head. "I don't think the czar's return is going to accomplish what the general thinks it will."

I wanted to ask Dmitri not to go, but I held myself back. "All right. We'll be fine here."

"I know you will." He smiled and leaned in close to me. "Do you know what you are?"

I shook my head, confused.

"You are the flame that keeps this house warm, Charlotte Daniel-ovna, the flame that keeps me warm. I'll be back as soon as I can."

He walked out of the room, leaving me feeling as if the sudden warmth inside me were an actual fire that had been lit.

It was so late by then we were all drooping with tiredness. After everyone went to bed, I sat in my room for a while and then went back downstairs, deciding I'd wait up for Dmitri so Osip wouldn't have to.

I took Osip's place in the chair. I dozed off, and sometime much later a soft knocking woke me up. I stumbled to the door, surprising Dmitri when I opened it.

"You should be getting some sleep," he said. "You didn't need to wait up."

"I wanted to know what's happening." I rubbed my eyes.

"The hospital has been badly damaged, but it's still there," he said. "Looters have been in, so there isn't much furniture left."

I think I only heard the "it's still there" part. I put my arms around him and hugged him. He held me tight. "Thank you," I said. We could put it back the way it was. I didn't care how long it took, but we'd make it work again. "What about the rest of the city?"

I let go of him, and Dmitri took off his coat, brushing the snow from his hair. "Every police station has been attacked," he said. "They are all in flames or already burned out, and any policeman the mob could find has been killed. A few tried to escape dressed as women, but they were caught. People are saying most of the known members of the Okhrana are either dead or in hiding."

I couldn't take in his words, so I made him repeat what he'd said and asked how he knew. After he explained, I wrapped my arms around myself, remembering the image of the men being thrown off the building. I should have felt a tremendous relief that the Okhrana were gone and Miles and I were both out of danger, but the suddenness and the sheer violence of it all made me feel twisted up inside, as if no feeling was the right feeling.

A giant yawn overtook him. "I'm sorry. I may fall asleep standing right here."

He did look exhausted. I couldn't keep him up no matter how much I wanted to be with him. We went upstairs as quietly as we could, and when we came to my room, we stopped outside my door. Dmitri was very close to me, and I felt a little tingle run up my arms.

"Good night," I said.

He closed his eyes for a moment, and when he opened them, he leaned in and spoke in my ear, whispering, "Good night, Charlotte Danielovna. Sleep well."

As he walked away, I leaned against the doorway to steady myself, the warmth running through me again. When I went to bed, sleep did not come easily.

The next morning I woke up to find that Papa and Dmitri had both gone out. Papa came back just as I was getting ready to try to make my way to the hospital to see the situation for myself. Osip opened the door for him, and he shuffled in, looking as if he had aged ten years overnight. Osip and I helped him off with his coat.

"What's wrong?" I asked.

He wiped his eyes. "The czar has abdicated for himself and his son. He was trying to come back to the city, but a mob pulled up the train tracks so he couldn't get here. His brother is next in line but I'm sure he will abdicate too. He doesn't want the job. The Duma is to be given power again and be the ones in charge of the provisional government. But I'm afraid the Duma won't succeed. Too many officials who can't agree on anything."

I saw that his hands were shaking. I put my arm in his.

"Romanovs have ruled Russia for three hundred years, and now it's all over. Just like that." He slumped over and would have fallen if Osip hadn't caught him.

I got a better hold on him, trying to keep my voice steady but fearing he was going to have another spell. "Let's get you to your room."

"No, Lottie. Osip, will you help me into the library? I need to go to the library. I must record this day."

Osip looked over at me, and I nodded. I understood why my stepfather felt he had to write it down. He worshipped the czar—not the man himself, but the idea of him—and the thought of a country without a czar must have made him feel like the world had turned upside down.

It made *me* feel like the world was upside down. I got the same twisted-up feeling inside again and felt sick. We'd wanted things to change, but talking about it was far different from the reality.

We settled him in his chair and then he nodded at us. "I'd like to be alone."

As we left the room, I heard him say, "Only God knows what will become of us now."

Chapter Fifteen

I WAITED A little while and then checked on Papa, who did seem better after he'd had some tea. Osip promised to keep a close eye on him, so I decided I could take a quick look at the hospital.

The streets were crowded again, though most people just seemed confused by all that had happened. There was no further news of the czar, and the troops had disappeared. I heard some distant gunfire, but since no one else seemed concerned, I tried to ignore it too.

When I came into the square, it was a relief to see the hospital, but as I got closer, I began to see the damage. The door was completely gone, and all the windows on the lower level had been smashed. Dmitri had said it was badly damaged. Somehow I hadn't taken in what those words meant.

When I went in, it felt like the place had been abandoned months ago, not hours. Snow was already drifting in through the windows. I walked through the nearly empty rooms, glass crunching beneath my boots. The fire damage was confined to the nurses' sitting room. The settee had burned, leaving a charred frame behind and damage to the floor and the wall.

A dull feeling came over me, like I was shriveling up from the cold and the emptiness. All the time we'd spent there, my mother and I, and a shell was all that remained. I didn't even feel like crying. I didn't feel anything.

"Charlotte?" It was Dr. Rushailo's voice. She came into the room and gave me a hug. "I heard the news. Galina came to see me."

It was good to hear her voice, the brisk no-nonsense tone that never faltered.

"I'm sorry," she said, surveying the damage. "I've seen many things in my life, but I'm still astounded at the things people do to each other. I'll never understand." She sighed. "Your mother put her soul into this place."

I brushed away a tear. "She did," I whispered.

The doctor patted my back. "You know she never let a setback stop her. This is a setback—a big one, to be sure, but one we can overcome. We can reopen the hospital later when things calm down or even wait until after you finish medical school. It's going to take a lot of work and quite a bit of money to get the place back into operation, but it can be done if we have the will."

I couldn't imagine so far in the future any longer. I had a hard time picturing what the next week would be like, much less years in the future.

"What about the other nurses?" I asked. It hit me that without the hospital I didn't know when I'd see everyone again. They were almost like a second family.

"Don't worry about them. There is plenty of demand for nurses. They can all find jobs today if they want. Galina and Tanya are going to stay with me for the time being. I need a housekeeper, and Galina can help me deliver the babies."

"That's good." I tried to sound positive, to match her tone.

She went over to one of the windows and examined the frame. "Now, do you want me to find someone to board up the windows and the door until they can be replaced? We don't need any more water damage in here. I know someone in my neighborhood who will do the work."

"Yes, thank you!" The snow coming in was burying the place, like it was covering up all that we'd done.

"All right." She patted my back again. "I have to go, and you shouldn't stay here. It's too cold and the streets aren't safe. We'll talk soon. Think about what you want to do."

I went home. I didn't want to think about it right then.

Over the next few days it felt like we were in some sort of limbo. The hours were taken up with trying to find food to buy and helping Zarja and Polina.

Dmitri was at first elated about the new provisional government, but within days his mood changed.

"There is so much bickering going on, I don't know if the government will last," he told me. "Everyone wants power and they don't want to share. It's as if they can't understand that one group holding all the power led to the need for a revolution in the first place."

"What happens if the government doesn't last? You don't mean the czar will come back?"

He shook his head. "No, I don't think so, though some would like that. I don't know what will happen. But be careful when you go out. Things could change at any time."

People had raided all the food-storage depots, and for a few days the streets were safer—until all that food ran out and the looting began in earnest. No one took the place of the hated policemen, which was both a blessing and a curse.

I tried to see Raisa. I wanted to tell her about Dmitri, but she was so busy helping her father restart his newspaper that we never had a chance to really talk, grabbing a quick visit here and there. I was glad she was so occupied with the newspaper that she no longer seemed to be interested in Miles.

The seventh day after the hospital burned, I came home from the shops to see a group of men pounding on the door of the house next to ours—General Stackleberg's—while they screamed to be let in.

No one opened the door. I realized one of them was Vladislav, but he was dressed as a workman, not a footman.

He began cursing and kicking at the door. Each of the men had a turn. The door was big and thick like ours, and I didn't think they'd be able to kick it in, but they seemed overtaken with a rage that I didn't understand.

I didn't know what to do. I heard Osip's voice from behind me. "Lottie, Lottie, come inside!"

Another man took out a gun and aimed it at the door handle. I froze at the sight of the gun. He shot the door, and the wood around it splintered. I let out a scream, but they didn't act like they heard me.

They went back to kicking it until more and more of the wood broke. A shot came from inside the house, and one of the men staggered back, blood dripping from his shoulder. That enraged the rest of them, and they rushed inside, shouting. I grabbed hold of the railing on the steps. They had to be stopped but I didn't know how.

More shouts and then another shot and then, to my horror, they dragged the general out and down the steps. He was older than Papa and much more frail, though he tried to struggle. His glasses fell off and someone stepped on them.

"Stop!" I yelled. They ignored me. When they reached the bottom, they let go of him and he fell to the ground. Before I could react, Vladislav aimed a revolver at the general and pulled the trigger.

Bile rose in my throat and the scene wavered in front of me like I was seeing things underwater. I thought I was going to faint, so I put my head down on the railing.

I heard them cheering. "Let's go get those guns!" one of them yelled, and they ran back inside.

I knew the general was dead, but I couldn't just leave him there. I had taken a few shaky steps toward him when Osip came out the door and down the steps.

"Get inside!" he said, taking me by the arm and pulling me back. "You can't do anything now." He shut and locked the door behind us.

"He's dead," I said. "We have to do something."

"We can't. Those men will kill you if you get in their way. Lottie, don't you understand? They might come here next."

I felt like I'd been punched. "Where's Papa? Is he here? What about Dmitri?'

"No, they are both out. Someone came to pick up your stepfather and I don't know where the tutor went." I saw he was shaking. "I don't know what to do. We should get Mr. Archer or Yermak."

"No, no." Archer still wasn't feeling well, and from what little I knew, I suspected that the bluish look to him meant there was something wrong with his heart, though he refused to let the doctor see him. I didn't want to get Yermak, either. He would just roar at the men and put himself in danger.

"We can act as if no one is here," Osip suggested.

"They'll break the door down if we don't open it for them," I said. "What is Vladislav doing with them?"

"He left his job and joined up with a group of friends. They aren't really revolutionaries—they just want weapons and money and liquor."

"They were yelling about weapons." Papa had a few guns in the house. I knew then what we had to do. "It's probably better to let them have what they want," I said, though the thought of them and their fury was terrifying. "They'll take them anyway, but if we let them in, they can take them and then go away before anyone is hurt."

We could handle this, I told myself. We had to. "When they get here, I'll show them where the guns are," I said. "Can you go to the end of the block and watch for my stepfather? If you see him or Dmitri, tell them to go away until it's safe. Go out the back and warn Zarja before you go. Have her tell the others to stay upstairs."

I didn't want to be near those men, but I didn't want any of the others near them either. It would be safer for me to let them in than anyone else. I prayed that neither Dmitri nor my stepfather would come home while they were here.

After Osip went downstairs, I waited a long time, hoping maybe I'd been wrong and they'd gotten all they wanted at the other house. I was just about to open the door and peek out when someone pounded on it.

"Open this door!"

I took a deep breath and made myself call out, "Just a moment."

When I opened it, I held on to the handle so tightly my fingers hurt. "Please don't be so loud," I said. "My little sisters are taking a nap. If they see you here, they'll be frightened."

The man who had shot at the general's door was in front. His face was badly scarred and he was very thin. He looked at me, his eyes narrowed.

"We want weapons. Are there guns in the house?" he asked.

"Yes," Vladislav snarled. "I told you already there is a general here too."

"There are weapons," I said. "But not many. My stepfather is very elderly and got rid of most of his guns a long time ago. You can have what's still here." I pretended to be exasperated. "I don't know why he keeps such old pieces of junk around anyway."

I knew Papa had a pistol in his desk drawer in the library and an old rifle hung on the wall behind his desk, so I took the men in and showed them both.

The leader examined the pistol. "This is a good weapon," he said, frowning. "It's not junk at all and it's been kept up. Are you sure there aren't more here?"

My mouth was so dry, I had to swallow a few times before I could answer. "I'm sure. It's just my stepfather and me and my little brothers and sisters, and I can assure you none of us hunt."

Vladislav took the rifle off the wall. Another man went over to a small table that had a bottle of vodka on it and a decanter of whiskey. "Take that, too," I said. "My stepfather drinks too much." I heard a noise out in the hall and my breath stopped. I was afraid Stepan or one of the other boys had come down. "I really need to check on my sisters. I don't want them to get out of bed and come looking for me."

"All right," the leader said. He motioned to the other men. "Get that alcohol and let's go. I'm ready to celebrate." He raised his gun in the air and the other men cheered again. I followed them back out in the hall to see Archer marching toward them.

"You now!" he yelled at the man. "What are you doing? That's the general's pistol! You can't have that!"

"Archer! It's all right! I gave it to them."

"You—you—" he sputtered as he reached up and tried to wrest the pistol from the man's hand.

Vladislav came forward, and I yelled again. He raised the butt of the rifle. I grabbed at it but I missed. The man hit Archer on the forehead with the weapon. Archer's eyes went wide and he opened his mouth, but no sound came out. He collapsed to the floor.

I dropped down to him, only dimly aware the men were leaving. "Archer! Archer!" He didn't open his eyes. I put my hand on his heart. I couldn't feel a beat. His face went gray.

I leaned back on my heels, crouching there. I didn't even realize I was crying until Zarja found us. At the sound of her scream, I managed to get up and put my arms around her as I tried to make her understand what had happened.

"Old fool!" she said. "Old fool! Why didn't he let them have the guns?"

"He thought he was doing his job," I said. "It was important to him." I wiped my tears and tried to pull myself together. We had to do something before the twins or Stepan saw him.

I went up and got Hap, who found Yermak. The two of them moved Archer into his bedroom and then went for the doctor. Zarja sat in Archer's room, rocking herself and whispering prayers. I left her there and made myself go upstairs to tell the others. It turned into a nightmare because I wasn't able to hold myself together after all. After their initial shock, Miles and Hap did better, saying the right things to the younger ones while I stood at the window watching for Papa and Dmitri, but really only seeing that last look on Archer's face.

When Papa came home and heard what had happened, I feared his heart would fail him too, but he surprised me by taking charge of everything. Over the next few days it was Zarja who fared the worst, coming and going throughout the house without a word. I didn't know what to say or do to make her feel better. I helped Osip, which took my mind off things, but none of us seemed to be able to believe Archer was gone.

We had the funeral at one of the English churches, though we were the only ones in attendance. I sat through the service thinking of all the years Archer had spent in the house, never seeming to want to return to England, though he complained about all things Russian all the time.

After the funeral, Dmitri and I found ourselves alone in the sitting room. I couldn't stop thinking about Archer. "Why do you think he never went back to England?" I said. "He lived there when he was a young man. You'd think he'd miss his home."

"Maybe he didn't feel like it was his home," Dmitri said. "The general told me Archer had a bad time when he was a young boy, and he was happy to get out of England with the general's wife."

"He told you that?" Papa never spoke of Archer to me.

"I asked him. The general said Archer liked the house. I suspect Archer secretly liked Zarja, too. It's too bad he never told her. He even liked Russia, believe it or not. Did you know he went every week to view the art at the Hermitage?"

I was flabbergasted. I'd had no idea.

"And he liked to listen to you and the boys play music together. Archer told me that, not the general, and not in so many words, but he did give you a roundabout compliment. I think he secretly liked all of you. This was home to him, not England."

Dmitri laced his fingers in mine, and the warmth spread through them and up into me. I sat there very still, not wanting the moment to pass.

"He liked it when you played Bach," Dmitri said. "I'd like to hear you play that too. I've only ever heard you play folk songs."

"I'm very out of practice." I was going to make more excuses, and then I remembered the image I'd had of Dmitri sitting next to me on the piano bench.

"I'm sure you are very good." He got to his feet, pulling me up with him.

I played, though Dmitri sat so close to me, I could hardly keep my mind on the music. Poor Mr. Bach would have been appalled at the jumble I made of his piece.

I got to the end of the page, but Dmitri didn't turn it. I looked over at him. He wasn't paying any attention to the music. He was looking at me. I felt the heat rise in my face.

"Very nice," he said, his eyes fixed on mine. He had such lovely eyes.

Hap burst into the room. "You're making a real hash of that piece, Lottie. You need to get back to practicing."

I jerked away from Dmitri.

"My fault," Dmitri said. "I was distracting her."

"Since you're at the piano," Hap said, "let's practice some of our other music." He went out in the hall and yelled, "Miles! We're practicing."

"Thank you for playing," Dmitri said as he got up from the piano bench. "Next time I really will turn the pages for you."

We played long into the night, and I hoped Archer was somehow listening to us.

When I came downstairs the next morning, Dmitri and Papa were in the hall. "Lottie, there you are! Dmitri Antonovich wants to speak to us," Papa said.

I followed them into the library. Dmitri wouldn't sit down. He stood very straight as if he was at attention.

"What is it?" Papa asked him.

"Sir, I think you should send everyone to your dacha in the country. There's been more rioting, and the streets are too dangerous for Zarja or Lottie or even Hap to go out for food."

"No, Papa," I said, glaring at Dmitri. I wasn't going to be sent to the country like a child. "The others can go. I can't leave you and Zarja here alone." It wouldn't be fair to ask Osip to watch out for them.

Papa sighed. "I feared we'd come to this. I've been thinking the same thing."

"No," I said again. "I'm not going."

I heard a shuffling sound from the hall. I turned around to see Polina standing in the doorway, twisting her hands together. She never came into the library.

"Nika is ill," the girl said. "She has a very high fever and she doesn't want to get out of bed. She's asking for you, Lottie."

I got up and followed her upstairs. It was probably whatever Anna Andreevna had come down with. "What about Sophie?" I asked. When one twin was ill, the other soon followed.

"I sent her down to the kitchen so she'd be out of the way."

Polina and I went into the twins' bedroom. Nika had the covers pulled all the way up to her chin. Her face was pale, except for a bright red spot on each cheek. Her eyes were swollen and red.

"I don't feel good, Lottie." She coughed, a dry cough that made her gag. I helped her sit up and gave her a drink of water. She took one sip and cried out, "That makes my throat hurt more. Can you do something to make my throat hurt not so much, Lottie? That's what nurses do, don't they?"

"I'm sorry, darling. I can take care of you, and we can give you drinks to make your throat feel better, but I can't make the hurt go away all at once. I know it's no fun to be ill, but if you stay in bed, you'll be better soon."

"Would you read to me?"

"Yes, of course. I want to talk to Polina for a few minutes first."

We went back out into the hall and I explained about Anna

Andreevna. "I could send someone to ask what's wrong with her," I said.

She sighed. "You could, but I'm almost certain Nika has measles. If she does, we'll see the spots soon enough. I saw it when my brothers all got it."

Measles. I remembered that Dr. Rushailo had said she'd seen some cases weeks ago. A trickle of fear ran through me.

"Have the rest of you had them?" Polina asked.

"Yes, we all got them a few months after we moved here. Miles and Stepan were very ill with them, but Hap and I had much milder cases. The twins usually recover very quickly from any illnesses," I said, more to reassure myself than her. "They are healthy children, so that's good, but it's almost certain Sophie will come down with them too. If by some miracle she hasn't caught them already, it would be best if we kept Nika isolated."

I tried to sound like I was discussing a case at the hospital, but my legs felt wobbly remembering how close we'd come to losing Stepan when he'd had the measles.

Polina patted my arm as if she knew what I was feeling. "We'll take care of them. I'll go down and talk to Zarja about what we'll need over the next few days. If we can get Nika to drink broth, it will help, though I know she's likely to lose her appetite very soon."

"Yes, I'll sit with her, and when you come back, I'll get the boys to take turns coming in to read to her."

I went back in the room and picked up a book, though Nika had her eyes closed. When I sat down next to her, she opened her eyes a little. "Can we wait until Sophie comes back?" she asked. "She'll want to hear the story too."

"Sophie can't come in right now. We don't want her to get sick too."

Nika closed her eyes again. "Then I don't want to hear a story. It's no fun without Sophie." She fell into a restless sleep, and Polina, the boys, and I took turns sitting with her throughout the day.

I had hoped Sophie was listless that day only because she couldn't see Nika, but by nightfall she'd fallen ill too. Her fever went so high so fast, we sent for the doctor and moved her to a different room so Nika wouldn't be awakened by the noise.

I sent Hap to Dr. Rushailo's house, but she was out on a difficult delivery, so we had to settle for Papa's doctor. "It's not uncommon for children to have high fevers," I told Polina and the boys several times while we waited for the man. "It doesn't mean it's serious." I knew I was saying it more for myself than them, but I couldn't make myself stop.

When the doctor was done examining her, he motioned me and Polina out of the room. "You both know there's not much to be done except wait. Even with the best care, with a case of measles it's all chance and how an individual's body reacts. These two aren't the first to fall ill. One of the grand duke's granddaughters has died, and her nursemaid, too, and I'm afraid that's just the beginning of this particular run."

My throat caught. "Not Anna Andreevna." I hoped he meant another grand duke and another granddaughter.

"Yes, that one. A shame. She was a lively little thing."

I put my hand over my mouth. *Not Anna.*

The doctor jerked his head toward Sophie's room. "If she survives the next two days, she'll probably live. This is a bad time for a measles outbreak, but I fear we haven't seen the worst of it yet."

I felt the tears falling down my cheeks but I didn't bother to wipe them away. As a nurse, I knew children died all the time, but I had always tried to pretend we could keep our family safe—that I could keep them safe.

The next two days went by in a blur. Nika was back up within a day, though she wasn't completely better. I insisted on staying with Sophie at night because I knew she'd be afraid of the dark without Nika. She had terrible fever dreams and would wake screaming that the curtains were on fire or that there were monsters that weren't letting her breathe. Each time, I'd lie next to her until she calmed down and fell back into a restless sleep. I was so tired I moved through the hours in a daze.

The third night I was dozing beside her when I woke to her small voice.

"Lottie, Lottie, is Dmitri still here?" Her voice was raspy.

I took her hand in mine. It was so hot and dry, I almost dropped it. "Of course he is, darling. I'm sure he'll come visit you if you like."

"Yes, please. I like Dmitri." She closed her eyes for a while and I sat there watching her chest rise and fall. I said every prayer I knew, trying not to cry. Our family needed all of us. We wouldn't be the same with a piece missing.

Sometime later, Sophie gave a little start and opened her eyes back up.

"Hello," I said. "Can I get you to take a drink of water?"

She shook her head. "I have an important question." Her voice was so faint, I leaned in close to hear her.

"Yes?"

"Does Dmitri like you more now than he did before, do you think?"

I smiled for her, though it took an effort. "Yes, yes, I think he does like me. But don't worry about that now, darling."

She smiled back. "I'm not worried." Her voice got a little stronger. "The love potions we've been giving him are working. You'll be all right."

"Love potions?" I didn't think I'd understood her. "You've been giving Dmitri love potions?"

"Yes." Her eyes fluttered shut. "Nika and I knew . . ."

Her voice trailed off and my heart stopped.

"Sophie," I whispered.

She didn't answer. I put my hand on her chest, willing it to rise. When it did, I began to pray out loud, willing her to keep breathing.

Polina found me like that. She put her hand on Sophie's forehead. "The fever has gone down," she said, smiling. "I think we've gotten through the worst of it. You should get some sleep. I'll sit with her now."

I stumbled out into the hall and saw that it was daylight, though still very early in the morning. I leaned against the wall, trying to find the energy to walk to my own room.

"Lottie?" It was Dmitri's voice. I turned around and he was right there, and I put my arms around him like it was something I'd always done. He hugged me, brushing my hair. "I'm here . . . I'm here . . . ," he whispered. "Is she . . ."

"Polina thinks she's going to be all right." I burst into tears again and laid my head on his shoulder, the tears refusing to stop. We stayed like that until I realized I was getting his shirt all wet. I also realized he wasn't wearing his uniform tunic.

I moved my head so I could see his face, wiping my eyes. "Why aren't you wearing your uniform?"

"It's gotten too dangerous. So many officers have been killed by mobs that no one is wearing a uniform anymore. The Horse Guard is no more. It's been disbanded."

I let go of him and stepped back.

"I'm sorry," I said. "Do you mind?"

He rubbed his eyes. "I don't know. I didn't want to join, but once I was there, I made some good friends. And it was two years of my life. Let's not talk about it, not now," he said.

He seemed so different in regular clothes, much more like the university student he'd been, but I'd gotten so used to him in uniform, it was disorienting to see him so changed.

"Then I'll tell you Sophie would like to see you when she wakes up," I said. I remembered about the potions and my face flushed.

As if he could read my mind, Dmitri smiled. "Does she want to see me drink another love potion?"

"You . . . you knew?" My face went from flushing to flaming.

"Yes." He pulled me back to him and put his arms around me again. "I cornered Polina after the first one and asked her what was in them. I'm afraid I intimidated the poor girl so much she confessed everything. The bad taste is just some dried herb. If I drink it fast enough, it isn't so terrible."

I choked out a laugh. "I'm sorry! You don't have to keep drinking it."

"I made Polina promise not to tell the twins I knew. They were having such fun with it, I didn't want to spoil it."

"Thank you," I said, leaning my head back on his shoulder. "Thank you."

"You should get some sleep," he whispered. "You're so pale, I'm worried you're going to get ill yourself."

I let him take my hand and walk me to my room. He gave me another hug and then waited until I went in. "I'll be here when you wake up. We'll talk later."

I smiled and lay down on the bed, falling asleep right away.

Chapter Sixteen

I SLEPT FOR hours, and when I woke up, I lay there for a long time, knowing that once I was up I wouldn't have a moment to myself. I had no idea what had been happening outside the house since the twins had fallen ill and I dreaded to know if conditions had gotten worse.

I finally made myself get up. When I went downstairs, Dmitri was waiting for me. He was wearing a serious expression again.

"I'm famished," I said.

"Zarja told me to tell you there is some bread and jam in the dining room."

He followed me in, his expression still serious. He wouldn't sit down.

"Something is wrong, isn't it?" I asked.

"As soon as the twins are well enough to travel, you need to go to the country. All of you, your stepfather too."

This time I didn't get angry at his suggestion. "How bad is it?"

"It's bad. Everyone wants to be in charge but no one is in charge and the city is beginning to fall apart. There have been more food riots, but there's just not enough food. I don't know what's going to happen. Everyone is on edge and more people are still coming into the city. Things are bad all over, but you'd be better off in the country."

I felt a sudden longing for the dacha. Dmitri was right. It would be better in the country. "We'll go soon," I said.

He sat down and took hold of my hand. "I'm going out for a bit, but I'll be back in a few hours. Osip knows how to find me if you need me."

After he left, I decided I had to get out of the house too. I'd been inside for days and I wanted to check on the Tamms. I didn't know if they had found out it was Hugo who had tipped off the Okhrana, and even though the secret police were gone, it seemed like they should know he had betrayed them.

When I reached the Tamms' building, I was surprised to find Celeste in Hugo's room, putting his things in a trunk by the light of a candle. There was no sign of Hugo himself.

"Why is it dark? What's happened?" I asked.

"It's dark because the electricity has been going in and out. Haven't you heard? Most of the workers at the electric plant have abandoned their posts. I'm amazed you haven't had any trouble at your house."

"Not yet." I dreaded that. The twins were scared of the dark. "Where's Hugo?"

She opened a small drawer in the dresser and took out some papers. "Hugo died. He was sick and then he drank a whole bottle of vodka. Stupid man. After what he did, I cannot manage much sorrow." She slammed the drawer shut.

So she knew. I couldn't manage any sorrow either. I told her what had happened when I'd come to the building.

"I'm sorry," she said. "I had my suspicions that Peet was in with a group he shouldn't have been with, but when I talked to him, he lied and swore he wasn't. He didn't say anything about Miles. I would have told you."

I sighed. "It's all right, and it doesn't matter now. They're out of danger. Everything will settle down soon." A piece of paper on top of the dresser fluttered to the floor. I picked it up. It was Hugo's passport. Looking at his photograph, I was once again struck by how much he had resembled Papa. I gave it to Celeste and she put it in the trunk.

"I don't know what I'm going to do with Hugo's things," Celeste said. "It's too hard now to send them back to Estonia to give them to his family."

"I didn't know he was Estonian." I'd never thought about the man's life before he became an actor.

"Yes, he came from the same village as Kalev and was one of the first actors to join Kalev's troupe there. To betray our family like that!" She slammed the lid of the trunk shut. "I'd give all this away if I didn't know his sister was still alive. I don't know if she'll want it, but I'll keep it until I can get it to her. Would you help me carry it upstairs?"

I helped her, and even though she offered me tea, I knew I couldn't stay. It was a long walk home. No one had bothered to try to get the trams running again, and droshkies were still hard to find.

The next day I went to the train station, hoping to find out if they were getting back to having some sort of schedule.

The station was packed and the man in the ticket booth could tell me nothing I needed to know. "I can sell you tickets," he said. "But then you just wait for the first train to arrive. We don't know when anything is coming in."

I turned away in frustration. We couldn't bring the twins here and just wait, at least not until they were much better.

As I turned to leave, I heard my name. It was Carter. With every-thing that had happened, I hadn't thought of him much since I'd seen him the day of the revolution. He pushed his way through the crowd, saying, "Pardon me. Pardon me."

"I didn't expect to see you here," he said when he reached me. "But when I was looking around the crowd, I saw that red hair and it caught my eye right away." He laughed. "You sure can't hide easily."

"What are you doing here?" I asked. "Is something important going to happen? Is that why there is such a big crowd?"

"No, nothing is happening, not today at least. Just too many people who want to leave. I'm here because a newspaperman I know finally managed to get into the country through the Eastern border. He took the train from Siberia to Moscow and now he's coming here. I said I'd meet him and show him around. He missed the big speech, though."

"What big speech?"

"You didn't hear?" he said. "The leader of the Bolsheviks has come back to Russia to take part in the revolution and the new government."

I wasn't sure the government needed more people trying to reor-ganize it. "So why was this one a big speech? There are so many different political groups who are going to take part in the new gov-ernment, and they all seem to be making speeches."

"This one is a man named Lenin. He's been in exile for years, and he's quite a radical. He wants to wipe out all traces of the old ways. His older brother, Alexander, was hanged for attempting to assassi-nate the czar, and Lenin has been planning on how to bring down the czars for years. You should have seen the crowds cheering him when he came out on the balcony of the Kshesinskaya Palace."

Kshesinskaya Palace was the gorgeous mansion of Petrograd's

most famous prima ballerina. Rumors were that as a young woman she had been a favorite of the czar and some of the grand dukes. I didn't understand why a revolutionary would be giving a speech there.

Carter answered my question before I could ask it. "The Bolsheviks took it over after the woman who owned it fled the country. Some dancer. One of my friends who speaks Russian told me this Lenin fellow talks like he wants all the power for himself. Lenin says Russia doesn't need any 'bourgeois democracy,' as he calls it. That's going to make a lot of other people unhappy. This isn't over yet. People have some power now, and they aren't going to like it if he tries to take it away. It may get very ugly before it's all said and done."

I couldn't imagine it getting any uglier than it already was.

"Say, what are you doing here, by the way?" Carter asked. "You don't have any luggage, so you aren't catching a train, are you?"

"I came to see if there was actually some sort of schedule again. We're going to go to my stepfather's dacha in the country."

His expression turned serious. "I'm surprised you aren't thinking of leaving the country altogether. Most of the other foreigners are."

"We aren't leaving. This is our home. Russians aren't running away. We're not going to either."

"Think about it. Like I said, things may get very ugly."

An incoming train whistle blew, cutting off any more conversation. People began to surge toward the tracks. "We still need to talk about the ballet!" Carter called as some people cut between us.

I waved at him, thinking that someday I'd like to read something he wrote.

I almost went home, but since I was so close to the hospital, I decided to check on it. I'd seen a note from Dr. Rushailo that the work boarding up the windows and the front door had been done, and Papa had told me he'd paid the bill. We hadn't talked about how to clean up the mess inside. I'd missed the routine of going to the hospital each day and doing work that seemed important. Maybe I'd overreacted to the destruction. Maybe it wasn't as bad as I thought.

The kitchen door hadn't been damaged, so I went around to the back and reached for the light switch as I came in, hoping the electricity was still on. When the lights blazed on, I almost turned them back off. It *was* as bad as I remembered.

The first time I'd been in, I'd seen that the office had been ransacked and there were papers everywhere. When I went to look at it again, a feeling came over me that I needed to do something, anything, to bring some order back to it.

The desk and the chair were gone as well as the lockbox, but they'd left the file cabinets.

I spent the next several hours doing the best I could to pick up the papers and put the records in order. I knew it probably didn't matter, that Dr. Rushailo could get by without the patient records, but it felt good to work there in the quiet actually accomplishing something. I was glad that the office had no windows, so none of the papers had been damaged by snow coming in.

I lost track of time and stopped only when my stomach rumbled so much I knew I had to eat something, or I'd find it hard to walk home. The pantry was empty except for one jar of apricot jam on the top shelf that someone had apparently overlooked. I opened the jar and ate it with the end of a broken wooden spoon.

When I finished, I looked out the kitchen window and saw that it was snowing heavily. The wind whistled through the boards on the front of the building and I could feel the cold seeping in. It was time to go home. I got my coat from the office and took it into the kitchen. As I was putting it on, the electricity went out.

Definitely time to go home. When I opened the back door, snow that had been building up against it fell inside, and I realized it must have been snowing for hours.

Out in the square, the snow was so heavy I could only see a few feet in front of me. If there was anyone else out, I couldn't see them. All the buildings were dark, and since the streetlights weren't lit, I realized that the power outage covered the whole area. I began to wish I had gone home from the train station instead of coming to the hospital.

Since no one had been clearing the snow from the streets, people had made narrow paths through them, like deer trails in the woods. I told myself it would be just like taking a hike as I headed down one that led in the right direction. All too soon it disappeared. Not enough people had been out on the streets to keep it visible.

I trudged on and on, the cold creeping farther inside me with each step. The snow was falling in big clumps, and I had to keep brushing it from my face. My teeth began to chatter and I pulled the collar of my coat up around my face, but it didn't help. I tried to think how nice it would be when I got home, but I couldn't hold a picture of home in my head. I couldn't think of anything but cold.

I almost turned around to go back, but then decided I had to be closer to home than to the hospital. It was hard work wading through the heavy snow, and eventually it became hard to catch my breath. My chest hurt with each freezing bit of air I took in.

I stopped to rest, but as I looked around, nothing seemed familiar. I didn't recognize any of the buildings, and a dread grew in me that I'd somehow taken a wrong turn. With the heavy snowfall and the darkness, I couldn't see any street signs.

"Hello!" I yelled.

No one answered. I couldn't be lost. The idea was ridiculous. I thought I knew every street in the city. Even more ridiculous was being in one of the most sophisticated cities in the world, but lost in the dark, because too many people were too busy arguing about politics instead of figuring out how to keep the lights on.

My eyes teared up from the cold, and the tears froze on my eyelashes. I forced myself to keep going, hoping I could see a light through a window somewhere to get someone to let me in. There were faint glimmers of candlelight in upper windows, but the shops on the ground level were all shut up and dark. I found one door that I was sure led to apartments above the shops and pounded on it, hoping it would have a dvornik who could let me in. No one answered.

When I turned back to start for home again, a snow-covered figure loomed in front of me. I screamed and backed up against the door.

"Charlotte! It's me, Dmitri. It's all right."

I flung myself at him, wrapping my arms around his neck, startling both of us and nearly knocking him over.

"What are you doing out here?" I asked, taking a step back.

"Looking for you. A curfew has been put in place and the patrols are arresting anyone they see, though the snow has gotten so much heavier I'm not sure they are still out on the streets. I was worried about you. Yermak took your stepfather somewhere hours ago, so I couldn't get him to bring me to find you." He looked more closely at me and then touched my nose. "You're freezing. We've got to get you off the streets. I know somewhere close by. Are you all right to walk a little farther?"

"Yes," I said. "I hope it's close." We didn't speak again as the wind picked up and the snow whirled around us.

I followed him, finding it easier to walk with him blocking some of the wind. We finally stopped in front of a vast house that was completely dark. It was even bigger than my stepfather's house.

Dmitri pulled out a key, and I realized where we were.

"Is this your great-uncle's house?"

"Yes, though I suppose I should say it's my house now."

Dmitri had to push hard on the enormous door, and when it creaked open, I followed him inside to a darkness so complete I couldn't make out anything. I could feel Dmitri's presence more than see him, even though he stood right next to me.

"I'll get a candle," he said. "You should stay here until we can see better."

I heard him move to my right, and a few seconds later a candle flickered and then caught.

He came back to me and held the candle up. I saw him frown. "You don't look like yourself. We need to get you warm. This way."

We walked down a hall past a few rooms. From what little light the candle gave off, I saw large, dark shapes that I thought were probably furniture covered in dust sheets.

"In here."

I followed him into a small room and waited while he set the candle down and lit another. The room was furnished like a combination of a study and a sitting room. Bookshelves lined one wall. A sofa and a couple of comfortable-looking chairs sat in front of the stove, and a small desk in the corner was crowded with pictures and other items.

"It will warm up soon," Dmitri said as he lit the fire.

I was shivering so much I had trouble unbuttoning my coat. Dmitri helped me get it off and then took my hands between his. His hands were so warm, I started to get some feeling back in mine.

"Let's sit," he said, and led me over to the sofa. Once we sat down, he continued to rub my hands. I felt a little dizzy; I didn't know whether it was from tiredness or from being so close to him. He was concentrating on my hands, and I felt awkward, like I should say something.

"This is a nice room," I said, realizing that wasn't much in the way of scintillating conversation. It actually was a nice room, though. It had the feeling of a place where a person would go after a long day, to sit in front of the fire and forget.

Dmitri looked up at me and smiled. My heart did a little skip. "My great-uncle let me have this space to do what I wanted with it, so I put some of the belongings from my parents' house here. I would have shut up the house completely after he went to Paris, but the housekeeper wanted to stay. I stop in every day to make sure she's all right, but I wish I could find someplace else for her."

He stood up and I felt some of the chill come back inside me. "Are you all right if I leave you for a moment?" he asked. "I need to let Tatiana know we're here so she won't think someone is breaking in. It will just take me a minute."

I nodded, and after he left, I sat for a moment and then got back up. I was too curious not to explore, so I took one of the candles and made my way around the room. I went over to the desk and picked up a picture in a silver frame. I knew right away which of the two boys in the family portrait was Dmitri. The other brother had a much wider face and lighter hair. I could see how Dmitri resembled his father, though the man appeared to be taller and broader than Dmitri was now.

Dmitri's mother wasn't what people would consider conventionally pretty. Her face was too long and her nose was big, but she looked interesting. When I studied Dmitri's sister, I saw she was a younger version of Dmitri's mother. I wondered how often Dmitri looked at the picture.

I heard footsteps in the hall, so I set the picture back down. I didn't want Dmitri to think I'd been snooping.

He came back carrying a tray and a blanket draped over one arm. "Tatiana insisted I bring food when I said I had a friend with me. You're probably hungry."

I was and my mouth began to water as I caught the scent of what I thought might be pirozhki. I caught myself before I reached for one. "Does the housekeeper have enough for herself?" I asked. "I don't want her to go hungry because of us."

He chuckled. "Food is the one thing Tatiana does have. She's been here so long she knows all the servants on the block, and they bring her food because she treats their ailments. She's always been good at diagnosing what's wrong with someone, and she won't take payment, so they leave food for her by the kitchen door."

He set the tray down on a table next to the sofa and then gave me the blanket.

"I can share the blanket if you're cold too," I said, though I felt my face flushing at the thought of him that close to me.

"No," he said, a bit too abruptly, like there had been something wrong with my offer.

I felt embarrassed, so I didn't speak as we ate the pirozhki. The little filled pies were delicious, and somehow Tatiana had made the potato filling taste amazing. They might have even been better than Zarja's, though I'd never tell Zarja that. We ate them all, and when we were finished, we watched the fire in silence for a few minutes.

"I'm afraid everyone will be worried that I'm not home yet," I said.

"I told Hap and Miles I was going to meet you. They know not to worry. Hap wanted to come too, but I wouldn't let him."

"Thank you." I meant not only for coming to find me, but also for not bringing Hap. Three would definitely have been a crowd here at this moment.

"How did you know where to look?"

"Osip said you had gone to the train station, but when you weren't there, I thought you'd probably gone to the hospital since it was so close. When you weren't at the hospital either, I started back to your house."

"But I was going the wrong way. I was a long way from the hospital."

He looked at me strangely. "No you weren't. You were only a few blocks from it."

I'd been walking in circles. I couldn't understand how I'd gotten so confused.

The silence grew awkward again. I didn't know why it felt so different between us just because we were alone and in a different house. Dmitri got up and stirred the fire until it flared. He put the poker back on the stand and sat back down, looking at the fire as if trying to see something in it.

I wanted to think of something to say. I spotted a large instrument case in the corner next to a music stand. "Is that a cello? Do you play?" I remembered thinking when I'd first seen him that his hands were those of a pianist, with his long, elegant fingers.

"I used to. I haven't practiced for a long time. My family played together, like yours, though we were a little more serious and there wasn't so much talking and laughing." He smiled.

I realized I was warm enough to take off the blanket. My hair was wet, so I took it down and tried to run my fingers through the tangles. I heard a sound from Dmitri, and when he spoke, his voice was strange. "I can get you a towel to dry it."

"No, I don't need one. It will dry quickly enough. Why didn't you tell us you could play? The boys would love to have you join in."

"I didn't want to intrude. I like watching you all play and I'm not at your level. I kept up with lessons for a few years after, but . . ." He looked away from me.

I hadn't thought through where this conversation would lead. I reached out and put my hand on his arm. "Papa told me what happened to your family. I'm sorry."

He took my hand between his again. The gold ring he wore flashed in the light from the fire. "You've warmed up." He hesitated before he spoke again. "It was years ago. I don't want to think about the past. I was lonely for a long time. Now I'm not lonely anymore." He let go of my hands and raised one of his own as if he was going to touch my face, and then, like the times before, he took it away.

I didn't want this to be like the times before. I reached for his hand and placed it on my cheek. He closed his eyes and then opened them again and smiled, moving closer to me.

"I've thought about asking you to come here, but I knew I shouldn't," he said. His voice was odd again, a little like he couldn't catch his breath. He took his hand away as if his words had reminded him that he was touching me.

"Why shouldn't you?" I asked, even though I thought I knew the answer.

"Because it's not a good idea for us to be alone. Because of the war. Because I don't know what's going to happen."

He reached out again, this time taking a lock of my hair in his hand and wrapping it around his fingers. "You have the most beautiful hair. It's a shame you have to wear it up. Though when you do have it up, I can see your pretty neck."

He brushed my hair off my shoulder. "So stunning, like the color of a firebird," he whispered, and then sighed, taking his hand away. "I wish I'd met you a long time ago."

"I do too. But we're here now in this lovely room. That's enough for me."

He leaned in close. I could feel his breath on me. It was so warm.

"You smell of apricots," he murmured, his lips brushing my ear. "I'm very fond of apricots. They remind me of lazy summer days and the bees buzzing and warm breezes."

I felt like my whole body had suddenly caught fire. His lips touched my neck.

"I see you when you are all covered with snow," he said, "and I think that you have such warmth inside you, it should all melt away in an instant, and that you could take us into summer if you wanted."

I turned to face him and he tangled his fingers in my hair and kissed me. It was as if we really were in summer, surrounded by the heat. I pulled him toward me and forgot about everything except that I wanted to stay like that forever.

When he moved away from me, I reached out for him to bring him back close, but he caught my hand. "We should stop," he said.

"I don't want to," I murmured.

"We really, really should stop." He got up. The warmth drained out of me and out of the room. "Don't look like that, please," he said. "This is exactly why I didn't ask you to come here before."

I sighed and sat up straight, my sense coming back to me. "I know," I said. "But it was lovely." So lovely I'd remember it always. "I want to come back here. Will you bring me?"

He didn't answer for what seemed like a long time. I sat very still. "Yes," he said finally. "Yes, of course."

He sat back down and we began to talk, about nothing really

important, but we talked for a long time, about our families, about school and how we had lived before the war. When I heard someone moving in the hallway, I looked over at a small clock on the table.

"Tatiana is up. It must be close to daylight," Dmitri said. "Do you want her to fix us something to eat or do you want to go home?"

I stood up. "Let's go home." I knew the longer I stayed here, the more I'd never want to leave.

Chapter Seventeen

BY THE TIME we got home, my stomach was rumbling again. "Let's go straight to the kitchen," I said.

"I need to be somewhere," Dmitri said. "I just wanted to make sure you got home all right, but I will be back later."

His lips brushed my forehead before he walked away. I climbed up the stairs to the front door. Osip opened it, jerking his head to one side.

I didn't understand what he was doing until I came in and saw the baron standing by the window. I stared at him, unable to believe he was back. I had thought we were free of him since the Okhrana was gone.

"Ah, good morning, Miss Mason. I see you were out for perhaps an early-morning walk with the count?" The man's eyes went to my hair, which I realized I hadn't put back up.

"Yes," I said. "That's exactly what we were doing."

He smirked, and I wished I could wipe the expression off his face. "What do you want with us?" I asked. "Little pieces of paper calling for revolution hardly matter now."

"I don't want anything with you. Forgive me for my lack of cordiality in greeting you. That was wrong of me, especially now. At this point, it no longer matters what you do, but the general is in great danger of being arrested. We both know he would not survive long in prison."

I didn't understand. "Why would anyone want to arrest him? He's an old man who sits in his library and writes." Why was the baron still tormenting us?

"It's not just him. It's all the known supporters of the czar. The general must go take an oath in front of the Duma to show he believes the czar's time is finished. The czar is under house arrest with his family until it is determined what is to be done with him, but there is fear that some may try to free him in an attempt to reinstall him as ruler. The provisional government must know who is loyal to the new order. They've already arrested several members of the nobility who are not loyal."

This was a new nightmare. I had thought Russia was done with the horror of political prisoners. I had thought the point of the revolution was to move forward.

I knew my stepfather. "You're not going to be able to convince him to speak against the man even if he needs to do it to save himself."

The baron sighed. "He has to speak the oath. He doesn't have to mean it."

"You want him to lie?" I couldn't imagine Papa doing that, either. His code of honor was very strong.

"He has to lie if he wants to survive. Please help me with this. I am not your stepfather's enemy, Miss Mason. I would do anything for him. I owe a debt to him for something he helped me with in the past. I always pay my debts, and this may be the last chance I get."

The last chance I get. The words were chilling and I finally understood that the baron was deadly serious.

"All right. Maybe you can convince him." I took him upstairs to Papa's bedroom and left the two men alone.

A little while later the baron came back down. "I have to go now, but I'll be back at one o'clock to show him where to go."

After the baron left, Zarja told me my stepfather didn't want to see anyone. I explained to the boys what was happening, and a few minutes before one o'clock I was waiting in the hall as he came downstairs, taking each step very slowly and holding on to the railing with one hand. I hadn't seen him in his full military uniform in a long time. It was too tight on him, the buttons straining to keep the coat together. He wore his dress sword and spurs on his boots, which jangled a little with each step. The Cross of St. George glinted on his chest.

"Should you wear that?" I asked. "You'll call attention to yourself." Dmitri had said it was too dangerous for soldiers to wear uniforms, though I realized that taking off the medal wouldn't make him less conspicuous.

"I will wear it," he said. "I was awarded it for service to my country, so I shall wear it. I am still serving my country. I will always serve my country. Whatever this new government asks, I will do."

There was nothing I could say to that.

He noticed I had on my coat. "You don't need to go with me, Lottie."

"I know, but I want to."

"I'm going too." Hap bounded down the stairs as the bell rang and Osip opened the door to admit the baron.

We followed the baron and Papa outside to find a group of elderly men in uniform standing on the sidewalk. There were eight in total. I recognized a few, but Papa appeared to know all of them. He went around and spoke to each one. One didn't seem to understand what was happening. A woman who might have been his daughter held him by the arm.

The baron gave them all red armbands. "After you swear the oath, you will have to register, and you will receive an identity card, which you must carry with you at all times. Are you ready?"

He didn't wait for them to reply as he led them down the street. It was slow going. Some of them couldn't walk well at all. Hap offered his arm to one man, who took it gratefully.

I had been afraid the crowds we passed would jeer, but instead they fell silent and moved aside to let the men through.

"Bless you, little grandfathers," one woman said, and her words ran through the crowd, people saying it all along the way.

We passed a group of men working to pry the imperial-eagle seal off the top of the gate to one of the government buildings. When it came free the crowd cheered and surrounded the man who held it as he carried it to the river and threw it in. Papa shuddered at the sight, but he continued on.

When we reached the Tauride Palace, the baron stopped us. "Only the soldiers should come inside," he said. "The rest of you need to wait out here." He went over to the man who was being helped by the woman. "I'll make sure he comes back out to you," he said to the woman.

We didn't have to wait long for them to return, but when they did, every man's face was so gray, it was as if we were seeing dead men walking toward us. No one spoke as we walked home, and when we got there, Papa let Osip help him take off his coat, and then he went into the library without a word and shut the door.

"What should we do?" Hap asked.

"I don't know," I said. "Let's let him sit for a bit and then maybe Zarja can coax him to drink some tea."

"I'm going to go tell Miles what happened." Hap walked up the stairs slowly, not bounding up as he usually did.

"I'm sorry," Osip said. "The general shouldn't be punished for the czar's crimes."

The front door opened, and a woman walked inside, right past us, until she stood in the middle of the hall. She was dressed in an old-fashioned coat, so long it dragged on the ground.

I was so startled I stood frozen in place.

"Miss! Miss! May I help you?" Osip said, a bewildered look on his face.

The woman was very thin with a lined face and graying hair. Something about her looked familiar, but I couldn't place her. She didn't seem confused, like she didn't know where she was, but I couldn't think of any other reason a person would walk into a stranger's house.

Even though I stood no more than fifteen feet away from her, she didn't acknowledge my presence. Her gaze traveled all around the hall as if she was committing it to memory.

Zarja came into the hall. She must not have seen the woman at first because she spoke to me. "You're back. How is the general?"

"Hello, Zarja," the woman said. "Don't you recognize me?" She gave a harsh laugh. "I've aged a bit, haven't I? Ten years in prison with a little torture thrown in will do that to a person." I recognized her then. Papa's daughter.

Shock ran through me. I hadn't thought about what the release of prisoners would mean, especially for those who had been sent all the way to Siberia. They'd of course come back to their homes instead of staying in Siberia. I hadn't thought what it would mean to have Papa's daughter come home.

"Maria—Maria Feodorovna!" Zarja sputtered. "We didn't know. We didn't expect you."

"No, I'm sure you didn't." The woman took off her coat and handed it to Osip. "I decided to surprise you. Is the general home? I'm sure he'll be delighted to see me."

Delighted to see me. Those words brought me back to myself. Would he be delighted? After what she had done? "He's not feeling very well," I said. "Perhaps you can come back later." I wanted to tell him she was here before he saw her. He'd had enough shocks in the past few weeks.

"No, I'll stay. I'll see him in a little while, but I do want tea first. I assume my mother's sitting room is still a sitting room?" she said to Zarja. "You can bring me something to eat, too."

As if noticing me for the first time, she added, "And you, whoever you are, join me. You're a little too young to be a new wife for the general, so I'm consumed with curiosity about you. Come into the sitting room with me. I want to talk to you."

I followed her in, still befuddled by the shock at her reappearance.

She made herself some tea and sat down, motioning for me to sit too. "Have you ever heard of me? Does my father speak of me?"

I could feel my face getting warm. I didn't want to lie, but there seemed no good way to soften the truth. "He might have spoken of you to my mother, but he didn't bring you up with me or any of the other children."

"'Other children'?" Some of the tea sloshed out of her glass onto her skirt. She ignored the spill.

I explained as best I could. She kept her eyes fixed on me. They were an intense blue, vivid against the paleness of her face. She didn't seem to blink, and I had to keep looking away so I wouldn't stumble over my words. There was something about her that didn't feel quite right. I stopped talking after I told her about the twins and my mother's death.

She drank more tea as we sat there in silence for several minutes. I had so many questions to ask her, but I didn't know how to phrase them. I was still trying to envision this woman as a little girl running through the house. I tried to imagine myself in her position, coming back home after all the years away to find strangers here.

When she spoke again, her voice was high, and I could hear anger in it. "So two wives since I've been gone. And both dead now with me still alive. I'm sure my father would prefer it to be the other way around. A brother and sisters. How odd." She gave another laugh, just as harsh as when she'd spoken to Zarja. "I longed for brothers and sisters when I was a little girl. I was very, very lonely, but of course that little girl died a long time ago."

"I'm sorry," I said.

She held up her hand. "Don't think I'm looking for sympathy. I'm just talking to myself. One resorts to that in solitary confinement." She sighed. "I suppose I shouldn't be surprised my father never speaks of me. I didn't ever receive a letter from him. I thought others might have spoken of me. I was in all the newspapers at the time."

I shook my head. "No, I haven't heard of you, though I'm sure others have," I said. I thought it was strange she wanted people to remember her for her crime.

Another sigh. "I'm sure it's not just you. A whole new generation of young people won't know my deeds. How fast we are forgotten. Would you believe my picture was once on the cover of every news-paper in Russia?"

She didn't seem to expect an answer to that as she set down her glass, took a cigarette out of a bag, and lit it. She inhaled, closing her eyes as a blissful expression appeared on her face.

"Do you know what I did?" she asked.

"I think I heard . . ."

"I killed a man." She paused and stared at me with those unblinking eyes again, like she was waiting for a reaction. I was getting nervous that the woman was more than a little unhinged. We didn't need her in the house, but I couldn't think of a way to get her out of it.

When I didn't speak, she kept talking. "I shot him five times right in front of his Cossack bodyguards. They were so surprised a woman would do such a thing, they just stood there and let me shoot him. I was so nervous, my aim wasn't very good. It took him five days to die." She shrugged. "I think the loathsome ones are hard to kill. Their blood is already so full of poison; they aren't like other people."

The woman was definitely unhinged. I tried to think of what Dr. Rushailo would do if faced with such a person, but nothing came to me. The whole conversation was so bizarre it was almost like I was in a dream. I didn't want her to meet Stepan and the twins.

She stood up. "Now I want to see my father."

I had to stop her. "He's had a long day. Are you sure you couldn't come back?"

She gave that same harsh laugh. "He's had a difficult day? I've had a difficult life."

She got up and walked out of the sitting room. I followed her, asking her to stop, to wait, anything I could think of, but she didn't listen. She went into the library, shutting the door behind her. I heard her say, "Still working on the memoir, I see," and then I heard the door lock.

"Did you tell him?" I asked Osip.

"No, who is that woman? Zarja is storming around cursing. What is going on?"

I explained as we hovered in the hall, counting the minutes she was in there. I didn't have to wait long until she came back out and walked over to me.

"Good, you're still here. My father tells me you somehow manage things in this house. My people are taking it over, but I've consented to let him and his hangers-on stay in the attic. Move any personal items you want to keep by the end of the day tomorrow. We'll move in the day after." She laughed. "Close your mouth. You're gaping at me."

"You're taking over the house?" She'd gone too far.

"That's what I said."

I shook my head. I was really beginning to dislike this woman. "You can't be serious. You can't just show up here and take over the house. Papa would never agree to that. It's his house."

"Papa? Oh, what a sweet name. You have wormed your way into his heart." Her voice was full of hatred. "But he has agreed. He knows he's lucky I'm letting you have the attic after I told him the alternative. I could turn you all out on the streets. That's where most of the worthless nobility are going to end up—there or in prison. They are being arrested by the scores."

She was trying to scare me. "No, not my stepfather. He took an oath of loyalty."

"To whom? The Duma? They're on their way out too. It's time for the aristocrats to pay for spending their whole lives exploiting the people. My people will see to it."

She wasn't making sense. "I don't understand. Who are your people?" Did she mean other released prisoners?

"My comrades. My party, the Socialist Revolutionaries. The people who are going to be in charge now."

My head was spinning. She couldn't just move people into the house. There had to be a way to stop her.

The woman turned to Osip. "We don't need a footman, of course. So ridiculous! Go find yourself a job that is of use to modern Russia." She looked all around the room. "Though not until after we arrive. We'll need you to do some rearranging."

She swept out the door, leaving it open. Snow swirled inside. As Osip moved to close it, I heard a choking sound from the study. I ran in, hearing Osip following close behind me. Papa sat behind his desk, his face red and his hand pulling at his collar.

"Help me get him down on the floor."

I loosened his collar, relieved to see his breathing ease a little.

"Go get Hap and tell him we need a doctor," I said.

We got him up to bed and the doctor came to examine him, though by the time the man arrived, Papa seemed better. Once again the doctor said that Papa had overdone it and he needed to rest. I knew it was more than that.

When Dmitri came home, I pulled him into the sitting room to tell him what had happened.

"Is there a way to stop this woman from taking over the house? Is there anyone in charge I can go to? It will kill Papa to have her and all those people here."

"There's no way to stop it," he said. "It's happening all over the city."

I threw up my hands, anger rushing though me. "He's an old man and he worked hard for years and years. It isn't fair." I wanted to scream.

"I know. But they won't be stopped, and some of them could get violent."

The image of Vladislav clubbing Archer jumped into my mind, and my stomach turned over.

"I've agreed to turn my own house over to my own party," Dmitri said. "I just met with one of the leaders this morning."

"You're letting them have your house?" I couldn't believe it. He'd said he'd take me back there.

"I heard some horror stories this morning. It was better them than a bunch of strangers storming in and taking it over. At least they are going to pay Tatiana and hire someone else to help cook for all of them. It's not ideal, but I couldn't think of a better solution. I wish I'd known about the general's daughter. I would have made my group set aside some rooms for you. I can't even give you my room. I told them I didn't need it."

"That's all right. You thought you had a room here."

He went to the window and looked out, then turned back to me. "No, that's not it. I didn't want to bring it up before, but perhaps now is the time. I'll need to leave soon."

"Why? Where are you going?" I was confused.

"I'm not sure, but I need to leave Petrograd."

I sank back into a chair, my throat closing up. "Leave?" I whispered. It was too much. I couldn't bear it.

He came over and knelt down beside me, taking my hands. "Yes. The provisional government is going to fall. And it's going to fall soon. There are too many factions fighting for power, and Lenin is too powerful for all of them. The general's daughter is going to find out very soon that her group may not have any power at all." He grimaced. "It wasn't supposed to be this way. There are remnants of the army in the south and in the east. I thought I'd try to get to one of them."

"Why? I thought those regiments all wanted to bring the czar back."

"Not all of them. That's Lenin's propaganda. But we'll band together with them to get rid of the Bolsheviks. It's our only hope for Russia and to hold out against the Germans."

I couldn't believe Dmitri wanted to throw himself back into fighting. "What can a few regiments do against the whole German army? You're just giving your life away!" I wanted to grab hold of his shirt and shake him to put some sense in him. They'd be wiped out immediately.

"I don't know what good I can do, but I can't stay in Petrograd. My leg is almost healed. I can't hide away here, as much as I'd like to stay with you." He paused. "But you can't stay here either. We've got to find a way to get you all out of the country, not just to the dacha. I've heard things, unsettling things."

The day before, my automatic response would have been no, we weren't leaving. The last few hours had changed my mind. "What sort of things?" I couldn't imagine how much worse it could get.

"Some of those in power don't want foreigners here. They think you're all part of the old ways, and they want to remake Russia into something completely different. And more and more people are speaking out against the nobility. They want to punish anyone who has held power in the past. I told you I'd let you know when your family was in danger. It's in danger now."

I pulled my hands out of his and clenched them together. I'd tried to pretend things would get better even as they had gotten worse and worse, but it was time to stop pretending.

"You have to leave the country," Dmitri said. "I won't leave until you are safely away, but you have to go. All of you. And you have to go soon. I don't know how much longer the trains will be running and it's still not safe to leave by the western route."

"I know." I got up to go to the window. It felt as if the gray fog that hung over the river were seeping into the house.

Dmitri came to stand beside me. I turned to him and put my arms around his neck, pulling him down so that I could kiss him, wanting not to think for just a little while.

I didn't hear the boys until they were already in the room. It was Miles's voice that brought me back to reality. "Oh," he said.

I pulled away from Dmitri to see both Miles and Hap in the doorway, their mouths wide open.

"We're busy," I told them. "Why don't you go away for a little while longer." It wasn't really a question and they knew it. They were back out the door as fast as they'd come in.

Dmitri gave a bit of a sheepish smile. "I suppose I've just destroyed any sort of authority I might have had over them, not that I had that much anyway."

"Don't worry about it. It's about time they realized I'm not just someone who exists to arrange their lives for them."

"No, you are far more than that, Charlotte Danielovna." He brushed my hair off my face. "I have to go out for a while again, but I'll be back soon."

"I'll talk to Papa. It's going to be hard to convince him to leave."

"If anyone can do it, it will be you." He kissed me once more and then left.

I went up to Papa's room, weighing what to say about the daughter. When I got there, I didn't have to say anything.

"Lottie," he called out. "Lottie, come here. I've made a decision. You and all the children need to leave the country. It's too dangerous at the moment."

His voice was strong and his color back to normal. We had to get *him* out of the country so he wouldn't have any more shocks. "We will," I said, "but you have to come with us." I told him everything Dmitri had said. "It's dangerous for you too. We can all go to the United States until things settle down here."

I could tell he'd never even thought of the idea. Even when my mother was alive, he hadn't liked to travel out of Russia.

"You can take all your papers and work on your memoir while we're gone," I said. "There will be plenty of hours on the trains and the ships."

He leaned back on his pillows and twisted the end of his mustache. I waited, trying to read his expression. He sat up. "Perhaps a trip is not such a bad idea. After all, no one here seems to want my help with anything."

I was relieved it hadn't been as difficult as I feared. "And if the war in Europe ends soon, we can come back through Paris and stop there for a while," I said. "We haven't been to the apartment there in a long time." We'd gone back only once and that had been before the twins were born.

His mouth turned down. "We could go to Paris for a few days, I suppose, but not to the apartment. I sold it."

"You didn't tell me." The news stung. There was nothing special about the place, but we'd been there all together with my mother, and she'd made each trip like an adventure. It was breaking a link to her.

"Yes, I sold all my properties in Europe and moved all my money back to Russian banks at the start of the war. The czar asked us to as a way to show we supported the country and him."

I felt a pinging of unease about Papa selling everything. If Papa had all his money here, why were his gambling debts a problem? We'd need money to get us out of the country, and we'd need money to live on.

He slapped his hand down on the bed "Yes! Let's do it. There's still some life left in me. Let's take a trip!"

But as soon as the elation came onto his face, it disappeared. "It will take quite a bit of organizing. My bones are getting old. I'm not sure I'm meant to leave Russia again."

"Please, Papa, we don't want to leave you behind." I'd keep begging as long as it took.

"All right." He looked around the room. "I suppose a few months away isn't that long."

"It won't be. Papa, we have to get ready to leave as fast as we can. We're going to need money. I'm going to the bank to get what's left from the hospital account, but we're going to need more than that."

He didn't say anything for a few long moments. "I'll go talk to some people," he said. "I'm afraid we're a little short of funds, but we'll manage."

"We'll manage," I said. Nothing was going to stop us from getting everyone to safety.

Chapter Eighteen

IT WAS TOO late to go to the bank that day but when I got to the bank the next morning, there were some of the new Red Militia standing around inside with rifles. They all wore red armbands. A line of people waited to get to the single clerk, so I went to the back of the line.

When I finally got to the front, the clerk stood up.

"We're closed," he said to me. I didn't recognize him. I thought I knew everyone in the bank.

I gripped the edge of the counter. "I need to see the bank manager. It's very important."

"He's not here." The man picked up a stack of papers and turned away.

"No, wait! Where is he? It's important."

The man turned back to me and shrugged. "I think he quit."

I took a deep breath, trying to stay calm. "Then who is in charge? My name is Charlotte Mason. My mother had investments. The manager took care of the funds. I need those now."

He shook his head. "We're out of money. People took out what they had. There is none left. I gave out the last hundred rubles to the man ahead of you. The government has nationalized the banks, and people came to get what they could."

"But you have our money!" My voice rose. We had to have that money. No one was going to take us to the United States for free.

The man frowned. "Young lady, banks aren't stuffed full of everyone's money. That's not the way it works. Once our supply is gone, it's gone unless we get more, and no one is putting money in the bank these days."

I knew that. I'd just never expected them to run out. "What am I supposed to do?" I said. I wanted to reach over the counter and grab his arm until he gave me a solution. "What are we supposed to do?"

I glanced around, hoping to see someone I knew. Another line had formed over by the vault.

"What is that other line? Do they have money over there?" I asked.

"No, people are being allowed to open their safety deposit boxes."

I hadn't thought about my mother's safety deposit box since she died. She'd put my name on it when she was ill, but I hadn't ever looked in it. I knew it had some of her jewelry in it. I didn't know what else.

I ran home to get the key and then went back, praying they wouldn't have closed the bank in the meantime. If the box didn't have something of value in it, I didn't know what we'd do.

When I got back to the bank, I waited a long time in the other line. It moved slowly, and I thought I would scream with impatience. The soldiers only escorted one person into the vault at a time. None of those who went in would answer any questions when they came out. They'd just scurry away, looking from side to side as if they expected someone to rob them. I realized that was a real worry and I began to wish I'd asked Hap to come with me.

Once it was finally my turn, I had almost convinced myself we'd be lucky and the box would be full of money I didn't know about. When I opened it up under the watchful eye of the militiaman, I saw the glittering of both jewels and gold coins, and underneath those, some old papers. My elation was brief.

"The coins are for the state," the man said. "Put them in the basket on the table."

I cursed under my breath.

"What did you say?" The man scowled at me.

"Nothing. I was just clearing my throat." I scooped the coins up, wishing I could slip one or two in my pocket, but he was watching me too closely. Once they were all in the basket, I turned back to the jewels. They were what I remembered, mostly rubies and diamonds, my mother's favorites. I tensed up, expecting the man to demand those too, but he looked at the clock and said, "Hurry up. Take your baubles and go."

I tried not to show my excitement in case he decided he needed another look. The "baubles" would be worth a lot of money. I put them all in the little bag I'd brought and grabbed the papers too and then hurried out, afraid he'd change his mind. I had no idea what the papers were, though I doubted they would be of use to us now. I just didn't want to leave them behind.

I walked home as fast as I could, trying not to look as if I was carrying a fortune in jewels. I put everything in my room until I could pack them and then headed back out to the American embassy. Someone there would have to know the steps we needed to take to get out of the country. Now that we were planning to go, I didn't want to drag it out. I didn't want to stop and think about it.

The streets were full of people again, most of them milling about aimlessly as if waiting for someone to take charge. The main danger came from the automobiles. Groups of men had commandeered any they could find and sped around the city with their guns pointing out the windows, firing randomly.

I wanted to yell at them for their stupidity. Somehow they thought having a gun made them important, when all it really did was make people hate them for turning the streets into danger zones. The city was falling apart, and they were making everything worse. It made me furious, and I stomped along through the snow, not even noticing the cold.

The embassy was overrun with people all wanting the same thing I did. I waited in another long line and when I finally reached the front, I tried to explain to the man at the desk what I was trying to do. I had to speak loudly so he could hear me over the noise in the room.

"Everyone is trying to leave," he said, flipping through a large stack of papers like he was looking for something. "And yes, the train to the east is definitely the safest route now. Once you get to Japan, the embassy there will know more about ships across the Pacific. Of course, you'll need to make sure your passports are up to date, and you'll need the proper Russian stamps to leave the city."

"That's one reason I'm here. My little sisters don't have passports, except for the internal Russian ones. They've never been abroad."

He looked up at me and frowned. "If they've never been abroad, do you mean they were born here?"

"Yes."

"Well, your parents must have been given their birth certificates. It will state their citizenship. Bring that in and we'll issue them passports, though your parents should have done that when they were born. I must say—even though I'm an American, of course—Americans abroad take too much for granted. They assume whatever they need can be produced on demand."

"My stepfather, their father, is Russian, and we didn't think about passports."

He set down the papers and shook his head at me. "If their father is a Russian, then they'll need Russian passports, and I can't help you with that. Now, the line is very long behind you. Move aside, please."

"But my mother was American," I said.

"It doesn't matter. Children born in Russia to Russian fathers are Russian. That's the law here." He craned his neck so he could see around me.

I moved to the side, berating myself for not having realized that and for wasting time standing in line. I knew there would be another long line at the Russian passport office.

But when I reached it, it was closed, and no one could tell me when it would reopen. I rattled the door handle as if that would make the office open. Nothing.

I leaned my face against the door, suddenly overcome with weariness. As I stood there, anger began to spark in me again. We weren't going to be defeated for the lack of a few papers. We weren't going to wait around to see when it might open again. We just weren't.

I knew what we had to do. I'd heard rumors that before the revolution people could get fake passports. Surely they were still being made, and while I had no idea how to go about finding the right people, I could find out. Raisa's father might know. As a newspaperman, he seemed to know everyone.

I headed home, wanting to tell Dmitri everything that had happened.

I'd barely gotten in the door when someone began pounding on it. "Let us in! Arrest warrant for General Feodor Ivanovich Cherkassky."

I was done being afraid. I was too angry to be afraid. They weren't going to get him.

"Where is Papa?" I asked Osip, who stood looking at the door in horror.

"He's . . . he's out, but he should be back anytime."

"Don't open the door unless they try to break it down," I said as I whirled around and ran to the kitchen. Papa often came in the back way to save Yermak a trip all the way down and around the block just to drop him off at the front door. I didn't see Zarja anywhere, but my stepfather was coming through the door.

"There are men here to arrest you!" I cried. "Go back out. Get Yermak to take you somewhere." I pushed him toward the door.

"Lottie, stop. Yermak has taken Zarja out to buy food," Papa said. "Who has come to arrest me?"

"I don't know. Militia, I suppose, but they are banging on the front door."

There was movement out the back window. Two militiamen were headed toward us and one of them was looking right at me. The sight of me had given away that someone was in the house.

I felt a brief flash of panic but I pushed it down. Papa couldn't run fast enough to hide anywhere, and eventually the men would probably search the whole house. I had to think of something else. I grabbed one of Zarja's aprons. "Put this on," I said. "And pretend you only speak French." He got the apron on just as the men began to pound on the back door. I shoved a spoon in his hand. "Stir the soup. Remember, only French."

I hoped he'd understand what we were doing. When I opened the door, I spoke first in English, thinking the men might be confused by a foreigner at the house of a Russian.

"What do you want?" I asked.

The two looked at each other and then at me. One of them spoke to me in Russian, telling me about the arrest warrant. I pretended I didn't understand. I said, "*Nyet Russkiy*," which meant "no Russian." They saw Papa, who stood holding the spoon in the same spot I'd left him. They pushed their way around me and began telling him they were looking for General Cherkassky. He looked over at me.

"He doesn't understand Russian either. *Nyet Russkiy*." I pointed at him. "*Français.*" I doubted they spoke French either but thought they might recognize the word.

They did recognize it, but continued to talk at me in Russian for a while, asking me where the general had gone. I pretended I didn't understand any of it. Papa was miraculously playing the part of a chef, getting down spices and putting pinches of things in the soup.

If I hadn't been so scared, I would have smiled to see him like that. One man came over and smelled the soup, then backed away and shook his head. They continued to poke around the kitchen a bit until they found some bread and some biscuits. They took those and left.

As soon as they were gone, I looked over at my stepfather, afraid he would have another attack of illness at the shock. I was amazed to see him smiling.

"Those devils aren't going to get the better of me!" he said. "I did well, didn't I? All those theater performances your mother dragged me to, I suppose I learned a thing or two."

"You did wonderfully, Papa!" I ran over and hugged him. "You were so brave!"

"Did you forget I am a general?" he said. "We're supposed to be brave."

The twins came running in the kitchen. "Zarja, we're hungry!" Nika shouted. They froze at the sight of Papa wearing an apron, their eyes enormous.

He waved a spoon at them. "Hello, my little chickabiddies. I'm learning to make soup. Would you like some?"

They looked at me and then back at Papa. He laughed like he didn't have a care in the world, and they ran to him. I couldn't believe that what should have been a terrifying encounter was making my stepfather seem twenty years younger. As I stared at him, I realized I could see traces of the soldier he had been.

While Papa was teasing the twins, Zarja and Yermak came through the door.

"Girls, why don't you go back upstairs?" I said, grabbing some pieces of bread for them. "Tell the boys I'm coming up soon, and then later I've got a surprise to tell you about."

Once the twins were gone, I told Zarja and Yermak how Papa had almost been arrested. It was time to tell them our plans. "So you see, we've decided, as much as we don't want to, we need to leave Russia until things settle down again. We're going to the United States on a visit."

"Good," Yermak said. "Get the children away where they will be safe."

"Will you take Zarja and Polina to the country?" I asked Yermak. "And Osip, too, if he wants to go. It's too dangerous for any of you to stay here." I didn't want to leave until I knew they were safe.

"Yes," he said. "That's where they came from and that's where they belong."

Zarja hadn't said a word so far. She'd just stood there with her mouth open, and then her face changed to one of dismay. "But I can't leave the house to those people! What would Mr. Archer think?"

Papa put his hand on her arm. "He'd want you to take care of yourself," he said. "Please go, my old friend. It will be hard for me to leave if you don't."

I knew Zarja was stunned at the thought. "Please, Zarja," I said.

"We're going to try to leave as soon as we can get everything organized. You have to go. Papa, I need to talk to the boys."

I left them, hoping she'd listen to reason. When I told the boys about Papa's near arrest, Stepan turned very pale.

"We're all leaving the country," I said to him, trying to sound like I was excited. "We're going on a trip to the United States until it's safe to come back. We'll all be together. It will be fun, don't you think? A real adventure."

He nodded, still pale, but his face wasn't quite so tense. "And I thought you might like to tell the twins," I said. "Do you think you can explain it to them for me?" I wanted him out of the way so I could talk about the passport problem. He nodded again and ran off, looking happy he got to be the one to bring news.

Once he was out of earshot, I explained to Miles and Hap about the passports, talking so fast I wasn't sure they followed it all. "While I'm working on getting them, you have to help Papa figure out what papers and things he needs." I didn't know what that would be, beyond money, but I hoped he did. "Put any papers he wants to save but can't take with us in the attic. I hope they'll be safe there." I didn't want to think what the house might look like in a year without Archer to manage it. "And you need to pack a bag that's easy to carry."

I wanted to talk to Dmitri before I left the house again, so I decided to pack my own bag while I waited. I gathered what I thought I might need, including my nursing veil. I didn't know how easy it would be to sell the jewels. If we didn't have enough money to get all the way to the United States, I hoped I could at least work as a nurse to earn a little money no matter where we ended up.

I opened the drawer of the dressing table where I'd put my mother's jewels and looked down at them, knowing I couldn't just carry them around in a bag. I'd heard people were constantly being asked to give up anything valuable, and the jewels were certainly valuable. I knew some women sewed jewels into hiding places in their clothes, but I didn't have time for that, and I didn't know how to take the stones out of the settings anyway.

There had to be a way to keep them safe and out of sight. As I pondered the problem, the thought of keeping them out of sight stuck in my head and gave me an idea. I hurried to the schoolroom and began to pull things out of the cupboard. At the bottom of the pile, I found what I wanted: a set of trick boxes we'd used in a magic show to make small items disappear. Each box had a false bottom.

I took them back to my room and fit in as many jewels as I could, bracelets and rings, then closed the false bottom and added some of my own trinkets, a few necklaces and a broach, to the main part of the box. If anyone looked inside, they'd think I'd brought the boxes to hold the trinkets. The necklaces were too big, so those I put in a small evening bag. The boxes and the evening bag went into the bottom of my larger bag.

After that, I began opening the papers I'd taken, on the wild hope they might be records of some secret bank account in Paris or Boston, but they were just old records of my mother's marriage to and divorce from her second husband and the original passport we'd used to come from Paris to Petrograd, with my mother's name at the top and me and the two boys listed underneath. There were also some letters, including one from my father to my mother, which I quickly folded back up. I didn't want to read it right then.

The last paper was an even older passport made out in the name of Martha Winsor. I stared at it, and at the dates, and realized that it was my mother's original passport when she moved from America to France before she'd married my father.

Martha Winsor. Not Lise. I'd always suspected Lise wasn't her real name because it didn't sound American and she was so vague about her early life, but it was odd to have proof of it. I supposed it didn't matter who she had been in an earlier life—she was Lise Mason to me—though I thought someday I'd like to find out more about what made her leave America and change her name. I added a photograph of her to the pile, and then I was done. I wanted to say goodbye to Raisa but I didn't know if I could bear it.

I heard voices, so I went out into the hall to see Celeste coming up the stairs.

"What's wrong?" I asked. She never came to the house. We always went there.

"I wanted to say goodbye," she said. "We're shutting the theater and going back to Estonia. I couldn't leave without seeing you."

After all that had happened, I was so numb I didn't even feel shocked. Everything I loved about Petrograd was being chipped away bit by bit. I told myself I wanted them to be safe too, and that meant they needed to leave the city as well.

"How are you going to get there?" I asked. "I thought it was hard for people to leave."

"The authorities have said Estonians can get exit visas easily, and they are encouraging us to go home because of all the shortages. I think it's because we're foreigners to them, and they don't want us here any longer."

That did shock me. There were so many Estonians in Russia; they were part of the culture. How could they not be wanted?

"We'll come visit you in Estonia," I said, my voice catching. "If you want us to."

"You know you'd always be welcome. You're like a daughter to us." She hugged me. "I'll pray for you," she said. "I have to go. We're trying to leave tonight."

I nodded and put on a smile. "Be safe." I watched her go and the tears started to fall. I let them, until there were none left. Everything was happening too fast and not fast enough.

I went downstairs to wait for Dmitri, trying to think only of the days ahead. I wasn't going to think of anything else, I told myself. When he came in, he looked terrible. We went into the sitting room and he closed the door.

"What is it? Tell me!" I clasped my hands together and squeezed them, bracing myself.

He rubbed his face, and when he spoke his voice was trembling. That scared me more than anything. "There is a new law that was instituted today," he said. "No one in the nobility will be allowed to travel out of the country. They are to stay here and either work for the state or be tried for their crimes against the people. It's bad, Lottie. That means your stepfather can't leave, and technically, neither can Stepan or the twins."

Chapter Nineteen

I SAT DOWN, feeling as if a weight were pushing me into the floor. I couldn't get my breath. It felt like my throat was closing up and all the air in the room had disappeared.

"Lottie! Lottie!" Dmitri was shaking me.

I looked up at him.

"Do you feel faint?" he asked. "You look like you're going to be sick."

I shook my head. "I didn't believe Maria when she said the nobility would be put in prison. I can't believe they aren't letting children leave."

Dmitri sat down beside me and took my hands. "I'd tell you and Hap and Miles to go without them, but I know you won't."

"No, I won't." I stood up. Enough was enough. "I was already planning to find a way to get them fake passports and exit visas." I explained what I'd learned at the embassy. "We're still going to get them fake paperwork. Stepan, too. We'll change their names! No one will know they are part of the nobility. I mean, how important is the name you are born with anyway?" I laughed, feeling almost as giddy as the twins. "Martha, Lise, it's all the same person."

"Are you all right?" Dmitri frowned. "You're not getting a fever, are you?"

"No. And Papa isn't staying behind either. I have an idea. We have to talk to Yermak."

Dmitri followed me down to the kitchen and I explained it all. Yermak went to his room to get what we needed. His clothes were far too big for Papa, but they made Papa look more like an old dvornik who'd once been an actor than an esteemed general of the imperial army.

"Are you sure, Lottie?" Papa asked more than once.

"I'm sure," I said. "It's the only way. It will just be temporary, only until we can figure out our next move."

I convinced Dmitri to stay behind at the house while Papa and I went to the Tamms'.

When we got there, I explained what we wanted, and Celeste dragged out Hugo's trunk and got out his identification papers.

"I don't know if this is going to work," Celeste said. "There will be a record that Hugo died."

"Dmitri says it's chaos right now, and the place where they keep the death certificates is different from where they issue the exit visas. No one is going to check. I know it. Papa looks enough like Hugo that they'll believe these are his papers."

Kalev looked at Papa and then at the picture of Hugo. He whistled. "She's right, Celeste. It's going to work." He put his hand on Papa's shoulder. "Just don't speak much. Your accent isn't Estonian."

"I would like an exit visa," Papa said, sounding as if he'd just arrived from Estonia. He chuckled. "I've listened to many accents over the years," he added in his normal Russian accent.

We all stared at him. I'd never heard Papa do accents before.

"I'd almost forgotten I used to entertain the boys in my regiment by imitating them," he said. "They came from all over, so I had many to choose from. They got so much amusement out of such a little thing. You all look so surprised. Perhaps I should have gone on the stage instead of into the military." He chucked me under the chin. "Close your mouth, Lottie. You're going to catch flies."

I felt like I was looking at a man I'd never met before, or a man with many lives behind him.

"If you want a job in your retirement, you have one waiting for you," Kalev said, still looking stunned. "I'm going to start a new theater when we get home."

"Perhaps I will." Papa shook Kalev's hand and kissed Celeste on the cheek. "Perhaps I will. Thank you."

Papa and I headed to the passport-control office and waited in an enormous line, the longest one yet. The building was filthy and full of people who were just sitting on the floor not doing anything. When it was his turn, Papa set down Hugo's passport and repeated the exact words he'd said at the Tamms'. The man stamped it without even looking up. Papa was about to pick up the paper when I saw what the stamp read.

"No, wait. That's the wrong stamp. He's not going back to Estonia. He's going to America."

"No, we're only issuing those exit visas to Americans and Canadians. Estonians go to Estonia. He can get a stamp in Estonia to go to America. Next!" The man waved at the woman behind us.

I felt panic rising and threatening to spill out. "But why? Why do you care where they go?"

He rolled his eyes at me. "I don't care, but that's the rule. Now move out of the way or I'll call a guard. Next!"

We went outside. I couldn't speak, though I tried several times. It was as if I couldn't put the words in the right order. Papa had gone very pale, and I was afraid he was going to have another attack, but when he saw how upset I was, he put his arm around me.

"Don't worry, Lottie. I'll be fine here. You take the children and go, and when I can leave, I'll meet you somewhere."

"No!" I said so loudly people passing by turned to look at us. "You can't stay here!" I lowered my voice. "You'll be arrested and sent to prison." I pointed at the paper. "Go to Estonia! Once you are there, you can get a different set of papers or something, and then maybe you can get to Paris and from there you can arrange passage to get to America." I tried to keep the panic down. I didn't see how he could do all that by himself, but he had to get out of the country.

He was shaking his head the whole time I was talking, so I added the only thing I could think that might convince him. "Think of what Mama would do. She wouldn't stay here. She'd pretend to be someone else until she got to where she wanted to go."

He stood there, motionless. A few tears ran down his face.

"Papa, please. We're not leaving unless you leave too."

"You're right," he whispered. "She wouldn't give up."

I then did something I wondered if I'd regret later. "Go now to the Tamms. They're leaving tonight. Go with them. Don't come home. It's not safe. The militia could come back at any time."

"But, but, I have to say goodbye to everyone."

I steeled myself. "No, it will only make it harder on the children. We'll meet up as soon as we can. I'll tell them that." I started to cry too. I didn't know if we'd ever see him again. "Please, I don't think I can bear to see you say goodbye to them." The tears turned to sobs.

He hugged me more tightly. "Please don't cry, little Lottie. You're right, it's better this way for all of us. I wouldn't want my little chick-abiddies to see me cry. I'll go now."

I found a droshky for him and watched him go, feeling like our entire life in Russia was going away with him.

When the droshky disappeared around a corner, I leaned back against the wall. All I wanted to do was go home and sleep for days, but I knew in a few hours I wouldn't even have a bed to sleep in. I headed for home, not wanting a droshky, so I could have a little time before telling the others what was happening. I had to keep myself together for all our sakes.

The men from the militia were back, waiting outside the door when I got there. "He's not here," I said. "Wait as long as you like. I don't care." I rang the bell and Hap opened the door.

"We're coming in to wait out of the cold," one of the men said as he tried to follow me inside.

"No, you're not." I slammed the door in his face and locked it.

Dmitri and Miles had come out of the sitting room into the hall. Everyone was staring at me. "Where's Osip?" I asked Hap.

"He's gone. He said he wasn't going to wait around for some woman to order him to move furniture around and then not pay him. I gave him some money, though we didn't have much after Papa gave some to Yermak and Zarja."

"Are they gone too?"

"Yes," Miles said. "Zarja wanted to wait to say goodbye, but Yermak said they had to go. I asked her to take the rabbits with her. We obviously can't take them to the United States."

The rabbits had been the last thing on my mind. I was glad Miles had taken care of them.

"The twins cried when they said goodbye to everyone. Zarja cried too, but not about the rabbits," Hap added. "Was that a good idea to slam the door on that man? Where's Papa?"

I burst into tears. Dmitri put his arms around me and I choked out the story between sobs. At first Hap was angry at me, but after he saw how miserable I was, he finally came over and patted my back. "I'm sorry, Lottie, don't cry anymore. We'll see him again."

"Yes, no more tears. Let's get out of this place before we're kicked out," Miles said. "Dmitri has been telling us about how we're going to get some forged papers for the little ones. We've been trying to figure out how much money we have and how much we'll need. Papa had some laid out on the desk that he was going to take, so we've got that. We'll take the memoir now too. Papa will want it when we see him again. How much do you have?" he asked me.

I wiped my face. Miles was right. No more tears, at least not for the moment. "I've got a better idea about the passports. Meet me in the schoolroom." I ran up to my own room and got the passport that we'd come to Russia on. When I got to the schoolroom, I laid it on the table. "I worked this all out. We can add Stepan and Nika and Sophie to this with some American-sounding names. There's room underneath Hap's name. They have no way to check if it's accurate. We just have to write in the names to match the other handwriting."

I pointed at the precise writing of some long-ago official. "Hap, you have the best handwriting. I'm sure you can match this. Then we'll take it to the American embassy and tell them our mother is dead so we need a new one without her name on it. They don't know us there, or at least the ones who do this sort of thing are usually young and come and go from Russia. Whoever is there now probably knows nothing of Mama and her history."

I'd been talking so fast, I had to stop and take a few breaths. "And finally, we take this to the Russian office and get an exit visa." I sat back so I could see their reactions, thinking I was happy for the first time that the American community had paid no attention to my mother. The fewer Americans who knew us, the better.

Dmitri picked up the paper and smiled. "Yes, that's brilliant, Lot-tie. I suspect the American embassy is in as much chaos as everywhere else, since so many people are trying to leave. Do you think you can do it, Hap? You'll have to write over the old date too."

"Of course!" Hap jumped up and went to look at his collection of drawing supplies. "The ink is faded, so if I mix a little brown into regular ink and dilute it with water, I think I can match it that way. Once I get the ink right, I can practice the writing."

Seeing a plan put into motion made me feel much better. It took more than an hour, but Hap eventually had writing that looked exactly like the old script. We'd decided to use Americanized names for the children because we could convince them it was a game to play for going to the United States.

Stepan was easy. He became Stephan, and we decided to keep Sophie's given name, Sofiya, but just change it to the English spell-ing, though I knew she'd be disappointed she didn't get a new name. Nika's was more difficult. Since we rarely called her by Veronika, we decided we needed something closer to Nika. We had several choices but finally settled on Nickie.

"We'll have to make her name Nicole on the passport though, because Nickie is just a nickname," I said.

We all sat quietly while Hap got ready to do the writing. He dipped a pen in the ink mix and then stopped. "I can't do this with everyone breathing down my neck. Go away."

When we went out in the hall, I realized that the house had been remarkably quiet for a long time. "Where are the twins and Stepan?" I asked, horrified at all they could have gotten up to in the time we'd been talking.

"We came up with a good way to keep them occupied," Miles said. "They brought a kitten over from the next-door stable cat's litter to be a 'friend' for Bobik, but we let them bring it inside for a while and told them they could play in the attic. They'll be busy for hours. The twins are convinced it's a girl and there is going to be a continuous supply of kittens and they asked a lot of questions about how the kittens got born. Poor Dmitri."

I turned to Dmitri. "They asked you?" I felt my face get very red.

"Um, they did." Dmitri's face was a bit red too. "I explained it in a very scientific way. I don't think they understood a word I said."

"Done!" Hap called. "And if I do say so myself, it's perfect."

He was right. I couldn't tell a single difference. "It is perfect. All right, first thing tomorrow, we go get all the papers and stamps we need; then we'll go to the train station and wait for a train going in the right direction." It sounded easy as I said it, but I suspected it was not going to be easy at all.

The rest of the evening was a whirlwind of packing and eating and preparing food to take with us. I was amazed I managed to convince both the twins and Stepan that Papa was just going on a short visit to Estonia before he met up with us. It was better if we all pretended that. The twins cried when I told them they couldn't take the new kitten, and they cried again when we took the kitten out to the carriage house and made it a bed.

"But she will be cold," Sophie said.

"We've made her a nice bed. She lived outside at the neighbor's house, didn't she?" I knew the more time the twins spent with the kitten, the more attached they'd get, and the harder they'd cry when we left. It *was* an adorable little thing, gray and white with a sweet little face. They named it Musya, and it had the cutest meow ever.

By the time everything was ready, I fell into bed. I was glad I was so tired. I knew what tomorrow meant. I'd have to say goodbye to Dmitri. It had been in the back of my mind ever since I'd made the decision to go. There was no other choice. I was strong enough to let him go. I had to be. And I'd be able to remember the time we had together. I'd never think of Russia again without thinking of Dmitri.

I had hoped to leave the house before Maria and her comrades arrived, but they were there very early. She was aggrieved that we weren't going to be living in the attic, and especially aggrieved that Osip wasn't there to help move things. She tried to order Dmitri and Hap around, but they ignored her.

At one point I thought I had lost the twins, only to have Hap tell me they'd gone to say goodbye to Musya. We had so much luggage, Hap went to hire a cart. I was about to send Nika to find Sophie when Sophie came downstairs carrying a basket full of dolls. I looked at the pile of luggage we already had and shook my head.

"We can't take anything else, Sophie, and you don't even play with dolls."

"I do now," Sophie said, hugging the basket to her. Her lower lip trembled. I heard Hap shout that the cart was here.

"All right, but you take one and Nika take one. We don't need the basket."

"We do!" Sophie said. "It's their bed and they'll be sad if we leave any behind."

Hap came through the door. "Let's go," he said. "I had to pay that fellow a lot of money."

"Please, Lottie!" Nika begged.

"All right, bring the basket and let's go." At least they weren't begging to take the kitten along.

I thought I'd cry again when I shut the door behind us for the last time, but I was too keyed up about trying to get all the documents we needed. I knew I'd have time later to be sad.

I didn't look back as we drove away, afraid I'd break down if I did. *Cities don't disappear*, I told myself. *It will still be here when we come back.*

It was chaos at the embassy, as Dmitri had predicted. The person behind the desk was not the same as on my earlier visit. This time it was a much younger man who seemed completely frazzled. When I told him what we wanted, he blanched. "I don't know how to do that," he said. "I haven't had a case where there was a change in the head of the family. Where's your father?" He looked between me and Hap and Miles. "I can certainly see you three at least have the same father." Pointing at Stepan, he started to say something, but Miles held his hand up.

"Both our father and our mother are dead," Miles said. "We're orphans. Look, all you have to do is fill out a new passport paper and leave off our mother's name. Then you can get back to helping other people." At that point Nika was leaning on the desk staring intently at the man. I knew she had noticed his nose because it was very thin, but the man didn't know that that was the reason she was staring at him. I'm sure he found it a bit unnerving to be stared down by her.

The man sighed. "I suppose since you are all here it will be all right. When I take it back for the consul to sign, he'll come talk to you if there is a problem." He counted heads and then pointed at Dmitri. "Who's he?"

"He's a friend." I put my arm around Stepan's shoulders. "The rest of us are the Masons."

I felt Stepan tense up as if the man was somehow going to know I was lying, but instead he pulled a blank passport paper out of the drawer. "Who is the eldest?" he asked.

"I am," I said.

"No, who is the eldest male?" he asked, giving an exasperated sigh. "I need a name for the person who is the head of the family."

"My mother was allowed to be the head of the family when we came to Russia," I said. "And she wasn't a man."

"She was a married, or rather divorced, woman. In that situation she would be the head of a family." He looked down at the original form. "Which one of you is Miles?"

"I am," Miles said. "Can you hurry? We have places to go."

I wished Miles hadn't said that. The man put down his pen. "You do, do you? I'm so sorry to inconvenience you."

"It's just that we are trying to catch a train," I said.

The man crossed his arms. I was afraid he was going to find a reason to change his mind.

"You have a nice nose," Nika blurted out. "I've never seen one like that."

A look of bewilderment crossed the man's face and then he smiled. "What did you say, little girl?"

"I said you have a nice nose. A lot of people have ugly noses. My sister Lottie went skating with a boy who had a very ugly nose. I didn't like him, but I think I like you."

A baby began to cry in the line behind us. "What's the problem?" a man called.

"Nothing, sir," the man said, uncrossing his arms and picking up his pen again. I held my breath while we waited for him to get the consul to sign it, but when he came back, he just handed it to Miles. "Have a good journey," he said, smiling again at Nika.

The man at the exit-visa office was not the same one who had stamped Papa's papers, but this one didn't look up at us either. He gave us the stamps we needed.

We climbed back in the cart and Hap shouted, "Yahoo!" drawing stares from everyone.

"Better not call attention to yourself," Dmitri warned. He'd been very quiet all morning. He took my hand and held it all the way to the station. I didn't want to think about the next few hours.

When we got there, the booking hall and the platforms were packed with people camped out surrounded by their luggage. I thought we had a lot, but other people had brought trunks painted with flowers that must have been used as blanket chests, old suitcases tied up with ropes, rolled-up mattresses, even samovars and a gramophone.

Hap surveyed the crowd. "Let's get all the luggage close to the train, and then we can get the tickets." He led the way, weaving in and around groups.

I was relieved the twins seemed intimidated by the crowds and stayed close without me needing to constantly check on them.

Miles and I went to buy the tickets. I knew we'd have to show the passport paper with the exit visa to get them and I was worried there would be a problem, but once again, the man just glanced at it and then slid the tickets across to Miles. Miles put the paper and the tickets in his pocket. I thought about telling him not to lose them, but then I realized he'd know not to lose them. He didn't need me nagging him.

Once everyone was in one place, all we had to do was wait. Dmitri and I moved a few feet away, though there was no illusion of privacy. I was very aware that everyone else was staring at us.

"I wish . . . I wish . . . ," I murmured, vowing to myself that I would not cry again.

"I know," he said, and then kissed me for all too short a time.

The train whistle blew. "Oh, lovebirds!" Hap called out. "We need to go."

Dmitri started to say something. I put my fingers up to his lips. "Don't," I said. "It will only make it harder."

It was a rush to find a place on the train, and I was afraid the twins would be trampled, but between Dmitri and Hap we got them aboard safely and found a corner at the front of one third-class car. I dreaded the thought that we'd have to change trains in Moscow and move the luggage again. Dmitri gave me one more kiss, and when the whistle blew, he got off the train.

"Look ahead, look ahead," I whispered to myself.

"Miles and I are going to try to find a better spot in a different car," Hap said.

I didn't stop them, though I was sure every other car was just as packed as this one.

Stepan pulled out one of his Dymkovo toys from his pocket and then another, lining them up on one of the food baskets. The twins sat down next to each other, whispering. The few words I caught were the baby language again. I wasn't paying too much attention to them. I struggled to pick out Dmitri in the crowd, expecting to see him walking away from the train.

Nika started to sing. "Come on, Sophie, sing too," she said after a couple of lines. Sophie joined in. I had no idea why they were singing, but as long as they were happy, they could sing as much as they wanted.

I peered out the window, thinking I would see Dmitri walking away, but instead he stood right by the car, looking up at me.

I got up. "Stay right here, you three. Don't move! Promise." Stepan didn't answer but Sophie nodded her head.

I jumped back off the train and threw my arms around Dmitri. "I wanted a few more minutes." He hugged me so tight I could hardly breathe, but I didn't care.

He murmured my name and then the train whistle blew again. I broke away from him and ran back to the train, not daring to look back. I knew we were leaving too many things unsaid.

When I got back to our spot, it was empty. I stared at it as if the younger children had somehow turned invisible.

Hap came through the door at the end of the car. "Lottie, there you are. Help us move all this. We found a better place two cars in front of us. Miles and Stepan are saving it for us."

"Where are the twins?" I said.

"I thought they were with you."

"They were. I told them to stay right here. I got off to . . . to say goodbye to Dmitri." I glanced all around the car. I didn't see them anywhere. "Nika! Sophie!" I called out, trying not to panic.

"They can't have gone far," Hap said.

I moved down the aisle. "Did anyone see my sisters? Two little girls. Twins."

An old woman who was trying to knit looked up. "The little girls with the pretty hair? Their kitten jumped out of its basket and ran down the aisle. We all tried to catch it but it was a quick little thing. It got out the door at the other end of the car. They went to get it."

I shook my head. "My sisters don't have a kitten."

"The little blond twins. Yes, they had a cat. It was dressed up in doll clothes. Cute little thing."

I wanted to scream. Instead I pounded my fist on the side of the car and then got back off the train. Hap followed me. I should have known. They hadn't cried when they left the kitten.

"They can't have gone far," the woman called.

Dmitri was still there. Somehow he understood my babbling. "We'll find them," he said. "Better split up."

We fanned out in the crowd. I'd have thought the twins would be easy to spot with their blond hair and the two together, but there were little blond children all over the station.

"Charlotte! Hap! I've got them," Dmitri yelled. "I've got them! Get to the train and I'll hand them up to you."

I heard the whistle again. I knew Dmitri couldn't bring both of them, so when I saw him, I pushed my way through the crowd to meet them. Dmitri picked up Nika and I got Sophie, who was clutching the kitten. We ran as best we could, though we couldn't go very fast. I saw Hap jump up onto the step as the train began to pull away.

"Hurry!" Hap called. I stumbled, nearly falling down. Dmitri turned back.

The train picked up speed. We weren't going to make it. Hap made a motion like he was going to jump off.

"No!" I yelled. "We'll take a later train and meet you in Moscow! Stay with Miles and Stepan."

I set Sophie down. Dmitri let go of Nika. We watched the train pull away. Both twins began to cry.

"We had to bring her!" Sophie said. "She's too little to catch mice by herself."

I couldn't bring myself to speak. Miles had the passport with the exit visa and the tickets. We had nothing. We were stuck. The twins kept babbling and crying but I ignored them.

Dmitri put his arm around me. "We'll think of something," he murmured.

"Yes," I said, though I wasn't so sure.

Chapter Twenty

AS I STARED down the tracks, I heard a voice. "Dmitri! Dmitri Antonovich!"

I looked around to see a young man with a wispy beard and wire-framed glasses trying to get to us while he called out Dmitri's name.

When he finally made it through the crowds, he put his hand on Dmitri's shoulder. "I'm glad I saw you. I thought you were going to leave a week ago."

"Some things came up," Dmitri said. "Charlotte, this is a friend of mine from the university, Evgeni Kurnetsov. Evgeni, this is Charlotte Mason. And these are her sisters, Nika and Sophie." The twins had fallen silent after realizing exactly how much trouble they'd put us in. It was a good choice because I was still so angry I didn't want to speak to them.

"You must be the girl with all the brothers," Evgeni said. "I've heard all about you."

"You have?" At any other time I would have loved to know what Dmitri had told his friends about me. Dmitri looked uncomfortable for some reason, as if he hadn't wanted to introduce me to his friend.

"What are you doing here?" Dmitri asked.

"An old friend of my parents is coming to stay with her daughter, and her daughter is ill, so they recruited me to meet her and help her navigate the crowds. What time is your train?" he asked Dmitri. "I am so glad you managed to get an exit visa. They came looking for you again today. For some reason you are high on their list."

"What? They? Who came looking for you?" I asked Dmitri.

"The Red Militia," Evgeni said. "I heard they were after your stepfather, too, Charlotte. We tried to convince them that Count Lieven had died in Paris and they couldn't arrest a dead man in a different country, but somehow they learned there was a new Count Lieven. So how did you get an exit visa?" he asked Dmitri.

Dmitri didn't respond for a few moments. "I don't have one," he said finally. "I was here to see Charlotte and her family off, but we ran into some problems. I'll get one later."

I was still taking in what Evgeni had said. Why hadn't I realized that since Dmitri was now a count, he'd be on an arrest list just like Papa? They were looking for him too and he hadn't said anything.

"Oh, I think I see the woman," Evgeni said. "Nice to meet you, Charlotte. Dmitri, if you need help, come see me. I don't know what I can do, but I'll try to think of something." He disappeared into the crowd.

"You stayed for me and now you can't get out?" I said, feeling like I was going to throw up. I wrapped my arms around myself so I could stay upright. "How could you?"

"I didn't plan it," Dmitri replied. "I didn't know they were going to go against the nobility like they did."

"What were you going to do once we left on the train?" I asked the question calmly but I wanted to scream instead. If they found him, they'd beat him just like the police had beaten Samuel, and then he'd be in prison, and then . . . and then . . .

"I haven't made a plan yet, but I will," Dmitri said. "Let's concentrate on getting you some new papers. I think you can go back and explain to someone at the embassy what happened. There's no reason for them not to give you replacement documents."

Sophie was tugging on my sleeve. "Why can't Dmitri leave? Why doesn't he come with us?"

"He is going to come with us," I said. "I'm not leaving this city without him." I turned to face him. "If you think I'm going to go and leave you to the mercy of these men, you don't know me at all."

"Charlotte, there is nothing you can do," he said.

"Oh yes, there is. I mean it. We are not leaving the city without you. We've fooled the people at the embassy before. We'll do it again. You can leave here using Miles's name when we get that document."

Dmitri sighed. "If the same man is there when we go in, he's going to remember Miles, and Miles and I look nothing alike. Charlotte, I know you want to help, but that idea won't work. If they discover what we're trying to do, none of you will get out. You have to go without me."

"It will work," I insisted. "We'll put a hat and a scarf on you and say you're sick and you've lost your voice. I'll do the talking."

"You do look kind of like Miles," Sophie said. "You're taller, but if you acted sick and sat on a bench, nobody would know. Miles has to sit down a lot."

"Why don't you paint your hair red?" Nika suggested. "Then you'd look a lot more like Miles than you do now."

I stared at Nika and then picked her up and swung her around. "That's brilliant!"

"Paint my hair? Are you serious? That's not going to work," Dmitri said.

I set Nika down, excitement racing through me. "Just wait. You'll be surprised at what we can do." I didn't let him offer up any more objections. "We'll go to my friend Raisa's house. She'll help us. There might be some old paints there, and if there aren't, I can go find some. Once your hair is painted, we'll go back to the embassy, get the paperwork, and get on the next train. With any luck, we'll be gone by nightfall."

Nika and Sophie jumped up and down, giggling. I knew they were happy I was no longer angry at them.

"Don't argue," I said to Dmitri. "You won't win."

"I don't know where you get these ideas," Dmitri said, "but I suppose I'm willing to try. I know I won't get you out of here any other way."

We headed to Raisa's house. With every step that took us farther from the train station and away from the safety of the crowd, the more nervous I got, sure someone would stop us or recognize Dmitri.

When we reached Raisa's house, she was just getting home. "Charlotte," she cried, hugging me and then looking at Dmitri and the twins and the kitten in the basket.

"Can we go inside?" I asked. "We need to get off the street."

Once inside I tried to figure out how to explain about Dmitri, but it was so complicated I stuck with something simple. "I wish I had more time to talk, but the situation isn't good right now. My friend Dmitri needs to get out of Petrograd with us as soon as possible. We need to try to make him look like one of our family, so Nika came up with the brilliant idea that we could paint his hair red and then he'd look more like a Mason. And while we do, we need someplace where no one will look for him. That's why we came here. Do you have some old watercolors or other paints we could use?"

Raisa put her hand to her head. "I understood the part about painting your friend's hair to look like you, but the rest is a bit of a jumble. Promise me that once I bring you the paints, you'll explain it all again."

I nodded, relieved to be safe, at least temporarily. As I had hoped, Raisa did have some old paints, and I set to work on Dmitri's hair. Raisa helped me mix the paint, and we managed a shade of red, though it wasn't nearly as vivid as Miles's hair. I hoped a hat and a scarf would help the illusion. I told myself it was just like a magic trick. We'd have to convince the audience and use a little distraction if necessary.

I looked at the clock. "We need to hurry if we are going to get to the embassy before it closes," I said. I gave Raisa a quick hug.

"Write to me," she said.

We nearly ran all the way but we were too late. I could see people inside but the door was locked and no one would open it even after knocking.

"Do we have to wait until tomorrow to get on the train?" Sophie said.

"No, I'm done waiting," I said. Every hour we stayed in the city, Dmitri would be in more and more danger. "We're going to get some help. We need to go to the Hotel de France." I remembered Carter telling me he was sleeping on the billiard table at his hotel. I hoped he'd still be there.

It ended up that I didn't need to find Carter. He found us. As we approached the hotel, I heard a voice from down the street and then saw Carter jogging toward me, followed by his photographer friend. "Charlotte, Charlotte!" he cried, as if there were some way we hadn't seen him.

When he reached us he was all out of breath, so before he could start talking, I explained what we needed, introducing Dmitri as Count Lieven. Both Carter and the photographer, whose name I thought I remembered was Patrick, acted as if they were a bit in awe at meeting a count. That was exactly what I had hoped.

"Our escape will make a wonderful story for you," I said to Carter. "And all you have to do is get us into the embassy. We'll do the rest."

"I don't know," Carter said slowly. "It would make a wonderful story, but journalists aren't supposed to help make stories. We just report on them."

I couldn't believe he was having an attack of ethics. "You're not making the story. You're just going to get us inside." I was not going to give up.

He looked at Dmitri as if he were some sort of specimen. Dmitri scowled.

"I suppose that's true, and golly, what a story it is," Carter said. "Young Russian Count disguises himself to escape certain arrest, helped by beautiful American girl."

"What about us?" Nika asked. "Do we get to be in the story too?"

I grabbed her by the shoulders and pulled her in front of me. "And children caught up in the politics of war, being forced to escape the only country they've ever known."

"With a kitten!" Sophie said, pulling the kitten out of the basket. It squeaked in protest.

Carter laughed. "With a kitten. I'll do it." He slapped his knee. "I can't pass this up."

"Wonderful!" I said. "Once we get the documents, you can interview us at the train station while we wait."

Dmitri's scowl deepened. "Do you have to use my name?"

"Yes!" Carter said. "It wouldn't be newspaper-worthy if I didn't. It has to have facts!"

"It's all right." I didn't want a disagreement to ruin things. "The story won't be published for a while, right? Carter, you said you had trouble getting information out. And it will be published in St. Louis. That's a long way away," I said to Dmitri. I wanted to add *and no one you know will read it* but I was afraid Carter would be insulted.

"I'll get the story out one way or the other. And Patrick here can get some pictures."

I thought Dmitri might refuse that, but he didn't say anything, though I knew he wasn't happy. We walked to the embassy while Carter peppered us with questions.

When we arrived, Carter knocked on the door so loudly that someone finally answered. The man who opened the door immediately began to tell us to go away and stop knocking, but Carter interrupted him.

"Say, I know you." Carter grabbed the man's hand and pumped it up and down. "I'm Carter Jenkins. We met a few weeks ago. I'm Walter Jenkins's cousin. Is he here? It's important."

The man looked over at us and at the photographer. "These are my friends," Carter said. "We do need to see Walter pretty badly."

The man opened the door wider. I saw that Dmitri had pulled up the scarf around his mouth and had his hat pulled down low. Enough of the orange hair showed to make him sort of believable as a brother.

I hoped Walter Jenkins was not the young man we'd seen before, and when a slightly older man appeared, I breathed a sigh of relief. Carter introduced all of us, remembering to refer to Dmitri as Miles and explaining why Dmitri couldn't talk. "I'll let Charlotte tell you what she needs." Dmitri hunched over and coughed a few times.

I launched into our story. When I was finished, Walter looked at me doubtfully. "This is very, very irregular," he said. "I'm not sure I have the authority to do this, and the consul is not here. Can you come back tomorrow?"

"No!" I knew my voice was trembling but I couldn't help it.

"Please help us. Everything has gone so wrong, and I need to get my little sisters out of the country as soon as I can. I don't know if there will be any more trains after today. Please. We don't have any other choices."

The begging worked, probably helped by the woebegone faces of the twins.

The man gave several more reasons why he shouldn't but then said, "All right, I'll do it, but don't tell anyone else. Just this once." He sighed. "I'll explain to the consul tomorrow and hope I don't get fired. Everything is in such an uproar. We're doing the best we can to get Americans out of the country. You certainly qualify as Americans who need to get out of the country."

Once we had the paper in hand, I clung to it. I knew if it got lost, we couldn't go back a third time.

"What are you going to do about the exit visa?" Carter asked. "Do you know someone who can help you get it?"

"I'm going to forge the stamp mark," I said. "I looked at the one on our other passport. It's just black ink, and now that I know what it looks like, I can draw the same stamp. No one looks at them that closely. Can we go back to your hotel so I can use a pen there?"

"This story is getting better and better," Carter said. "Come on. Patrick, you'll have to get a picture of her forging the stamp." Patrick nodded. He had said nothing the whole time.

"You'll get your cousin in trouble if you write the story," Dmitri pointed out.

Carter stopped in his tracks. "Hmm . . . that is a problem." He snapped his fingers. "I won't say which documents are forged and where you got them. That will work out fine."

I hid a smile. Poor Dmitri. Foiled again. He'd just have to accept that his name was going to be in a newspaper.

By the time we got back to the train station, I was nearly asleep on my feet, and we'd had to carry Sophie, Nika, and the kitten basket the last several blocks. They were all fast asleep. We finally had a rare bit of luck when two trains came in close together near daylight, both returning to Moscow, and we were able to get on the second one, which wasn't as crowded as I feared. As it left, I waved out the window to Carter and Patrick, feeling a little strange that I was leaving and they were staying behind.

Dmitri fell asleep right away, but I spent the trip looking out the window trying to memorize everything. I'd seen it before on all the train trips to the dacha, but I'd never paid much attention This trip I felt like I shouldn't close my eyes for one second or I'd miss something I needed to remember.

By the time we pulled into the station in Moscow, both the twins and the kitten were famished. I hoped that Miles and Hap still had some of our supplies or we would have to buy food.

"There's Miles!" Sophie cried. "Look, he's got on his fortune-telling robe."

I peered out the window to see my brother standing there in the long silk robe. Hap and Stepan stood next to him, all our baggage piled at their feet. I noticed that people had left space around them.

We climbed off the train. "Why are you dressed like that?" I said to Miles. "You're drawing too much attention to yourself. And I can't believe you used space in your bag for a fortune-telling robe."

He grinned at us, looking better than he had in days. "I spent a long time practicing my fortune-telling and I'm not giving it up. Who knows, maybe I'll really join the circus once we get to America. I'd like to see what Elder Red would say about that."

Only Miles. I shook my head. Our grandmother was going to

be in for enough of a shock as it was with the addition of some extra small children and Dmitri.

"Now, are you going to tell us why Dmitri Antonovich is here and why he has red hair?" Miles asked. "I hate to say it, Dmitri, but red does not suit you."

I'd forgotten they didn't know. After I explained, Hap and Miles nodded. "Good job. You're going to like America, Dmitri," Hap said. "Though I'll have to add a name to our original paperwork because we can't have two Mileses. Dmitri, you get to choose a new name."

Dmitri started to say something and then stopped.

"Later," I said. I turned away, not wanting to see the look in Dmitri's eyes.

"Okay. See what we got!" Hap pulled part of the cloth off a basket to reveal a loaf of bread and some hard-boiled eggs.

"How did you manage that?" I didn't see anyone selling food.

Miles sighed. "Lottie, you usually are a little sharper. I've been telling fortunes, of course. That's really why I brought the robe. You're not the only practical one. No one pays me very much, but I've told quite a lot of them. People pay to hear about all the riches they will earn and all the romances they will have. We collected enough money and then went for a walk outside the station to find the food. It cost a lot, but I thought we needed to stock up."

"I told him he shouldn't be taking money from people who can't afford it," Stepan said.

"Giving them a little hope is a good thing," Miles said. "I'm not going to feel bad."

I put my hand on Stepan's shoulder. "That's a good thought, and you can remind Miles of that in the future." I almost said *Papa would be proud*, but I was afraid that would upset him.

"We should try to move forward," Hap said. "The trains have

been fairly frequent, but you still have to be quick to get on one going east before it fills up."

We didn't make the first train that arrived because there were too many people in front of us, but once that train left, we were much closer to the front of the platform.

We had first-class tickets, but when the next train pulled in, there were no blue carriages, which meant no first class. We tried to climb into a second-class one, but they were all packed, and the people inside yelled at us to go away.

"Third class it is," Dmitri said. "We're getting on this car one way or another. Hap, stay close to me, and everyone else, keep right behind us."

A man in a uniform made us show him our tickets and then we pushed our way through into a car that was almost full, squeezing in wherever we could find. I was surprised when people got up and moved away from us, giving us enough room to sit all together. One man even left the car, muttering about the bad luck that our red hair would bring to it.

"See," I whispered to Dmitri. "You might get used to having red hair if it gets you better seats on trains."

He ran his fingers through his hair, and some of the red paint flaked off. "I think I'd prefer just to let you get us the seats."

I looked around, knowing we'd be in the same car for a long time, days and days. It had the typical woodstove at the opposite end, but the stove wasn't lit and there was no wood stacked beside it. It was almost as cold inside the car as it was outside.

"Once a lot of people are in here it will warm up," I said, trying to sound optimistic.

"It's too dark," Sophie said. "Why aren't there any lights?"

"The dynamo must not be working," Dmitri said. "But in daylight we'll be able to see just fine." The car smelled of sunflower seeds, and the floor was covered with their shells. It was clear no one had cleaned the place for a long time.

Other people kept coming into the carriage, eventually taking up all available space on the floor and even crawling beneath our feet under the benches. In ordinary times the people under the seats were the ones without tickets, called "hares," and the paying passengers cooperated to hide their presence by placing their luggage and bundles of bedding to block the conductor's view. If the conductor was in the mood to look for them, he'd pull out the items and order the hares off the train.

When we'd first come to Russia and Papa had translated the signs for us, we'd been excited, thinking Russia must be full of rabbits if they were even hopping on trains. It had been a disappointment to learn the truth.

Now no one was bothering to hide since there didn't seem to be conductors. I felt odd knowing someone was beneath my seat and tried hard not to move my feet backward so I wouldn't accidentally kick them. I got out the bag with the necklaces in it and put the passport inside, then hung the whole thing around my neck, buttoning it up underneath my shirt. I felt better having the paper close to me.

The train wouldn't start for another three hours, but we were afraid to stand up and stretch our legs in case someone else took our seats. Once we were finally underway, I lost track of time, lulled into sleep by the rhythmic noise of the wheels. We made spaces in front of our feet for the twins and Stepan, and they slept curled up, the kitten alternating which child it slept on. Every time we stopped, I'd wake up, hoping no more people would crowd into our car. It was a useless hope, because they just kept piling in.

I fell asleep again, dreaming I was somewhere out in the woods with the snow falling, lovely flakes drifting down, and Dmitri was there, his hand reaching up to brush the snow off my face.

I woke suddenly to find the train coming to a screeching stop. It was daylight, but I had no idea what time it was. Hap stuck his head out the window.

"There's a big group of soldiers surrounding the engine," he said. I looked out in time to see a couple of them climb up into it. The rest of the soldiers spread out, getting into the cars.

I took hold of Dmitri's hand. "They're not after me," he said. "We're a long way from Petrograd now."

When four men tried to get in our car, a man near the front yelled at them. "There's no room! Get off!"

"We'll find room," one of them said, shoving the man out of the way. "Now stop complaining or we'll throw you off. That will make room for us."

I relaxed a little, knowing they just wanted a ride.

Finally after a few more stops the train got so full, there was no room for people to even push their way in through the doors. Thuds sounded from the roof of the carriage as people clambered up the sides of the train to perch there. I didn't know how they'd stand the cold. It was cold inside the carriage even with all the bodies.

"When are we going to get there, Lottie?" The twins asked and repeated this several times every day. My answer was always the same.

"Soon. It's a long, long way."

They did keep occupied much of the time with the kitten, talking to it in their baby language. I was relieved the little animal seemed content to stay with them and ate whatever we fed it, mostly bread softened in water and bits of hard-boiled eggs. I did not want to go on another chase.

Miles said very little, and I finally realized he was getting a fever. He looked terrible and he had no energy. He sat slumped against Hap, not reading or writing, but just either staring off into space or closing his eyes as if he were sleeping, though I knew he wasn't.

Hap and I took turns coaxing him to eat and drink with what little we could buy at the stations. We weren't always successful. The twins and Stepan were always hungry, so the rest of us cut back on what we ate to try to keep them filled up. My stomach felt like it rumbled day and night.

I watched out the window during the day, though there wasn't much to see. I was surprised to see Cossack troops on the move, looking as if they were maintaining some sort of order as they rode.

"Where do you think they're going?" I asked Dmitri.

"I've been talking to some of the other passengers. One man said he's heard a few of the generals have gone east and are putting together new regiments to fight the Bolsheviks. The Reds may hold the west, but there are people determined not to let them take over all of Russia."

"Do you really think they'll be successful?" Miles asked. "They don't have any supply lines or anything."

"I don't know," Dmitri said. "But they have to try." He was quiet for a long time after that.

At the next station, two men dressed in makeshift police uniforms got on. "Bag inspection!" they called. "Open your bags."

"Why are you inspecting bags?" Dmitri asked. "I've never heard of that before."

The man frowned. "It's not for the likes of you to question authority. Who are you?"

"He's my brother," I said, trying to make my Russian sound bad.

"We're Americans." I hoped they wouldn't notice Dmitri's perfect Russian.

That seemed to mollify the man. "Americans, you say? Good you are leaving the country. It's for Russians now. We're inspecting bags because some people have been trying to blow up the train bridges. They've thrown small bombs out the windows as the train is going over. It's our job to keep the line open. Now show us your luggage."

They went through everyone's things, and I was glad I still had the bag with the necklaces in it around my neck. When they found the boxes, they immediately opened them and poured out the trinkets I had put inside, stuffing them into their pockets. Dmitri made a move as if to protest, but I put my hand on his arm, holding my breath that they wouldn't shake the boxes to hear the hidden jewels rattling around. They didn't, and soon tossed the boxes back at me.

"Thank you for your contribution to the Railway Safety Fund," one of the men said, chuckling. I bit my tongue and stayed quiet.

The next time soldiers stopped the train, Hap looked out the window and then drew his head back in so quickly he bumped it. "Bad news," he said. "They're making the people in the cars in front of us get off so they can get on."

I looked out the window. We were in the middle of nowhere, and snow was thick on the ground.

"We are not getting off this train," I said.

Chapter Twenty-One

I GOT UP and climbed on a bench and raised my voice to get the other passengers' attention. After I explained what was happening, I called out, "Do you want to get kicked off this train?"

Several people called out, "No!"

"Then pull the shades and listen to me. We only have a few minutes. I'm going outside to tell those soldiers they can't come in here because everyone is ill. You're going to have to help me. Do some moaning and groaning, and if anyone does board to check, act sick." I reached into my bag until I found my nursing veil and put it on. "My brother will tell you when to make noise," I said pointing to Hap. "Don't let them overdo it," I told him as I went out the door.

I left the door cracked open and then climbed down the steps, waiting for the men to approach. When they got close enough, I called, "Do you have a doctor with you?"

They ignored my question. The one leading them was so covered in dirt, I could hardly make out his features. "Move aside," he yelled. "We're boarding this car."

I clenched my hands to act like I was worried. "Thank goodness! So you are doctors! We've got several cases of typhus in this car. I had everyone who was feeling ill move back here, though I'm afraid some of the others in the front cars will fall ill too."

The soldier in front took a step back, bumping into the men behind him.

"I don't believe you," one of the others said.

Nika began to wail, very loudly, and others joined in. Miles coughed. He didn't have to act. His cough was unmistakably consumptive.

The men began to argue among themselves about what to do. The noise from inside rose and I was afraid it was becoming too fake, when it began to drop off again. What followed was almost a perfect orchestra of moans and groans with just the right pauses.

After one particularly pathetic cry from Nika, the men moved away, walking back up the side of the train, pounding on the train cars and shouting, "Typhus! Typhus! Get off the train."

The soldiers who had already boarded jumped off until they were all gathered in one spot. Some of them kept pointing back at me, so I stood in the same spot, hoping no one would be brave enough to actually check. After what seemed like a very long time, the men moved off and the train chugged forward. Dmitri came out and helped me back up onto the landing outside the car.

Once I got inside, I hugged Hap. "Brilliant!" I said. "It was perfect!" He grinned.

As the days went on, our moment of triumph faded. Miles was no better, and I spent the next night listening to him cough while the other passengers grumbled about the noise. The day after, he was a little better and I slept for several hours after Dmitri promised he'd wake me if I was needed.

More days passed and we stopped at a station that actually had food, though we spent far too much money on it. Dmitri rinsed his hair under a pump and most of the paint came out, leaving only a few faint tinges of red. He hadn't had a chance to shave, and with each day he looked less and less like a count from Petrograd and more like an adventurer of some sort. I liked the look except I didn't like the scratchiness of his face when I leaned my head against him as we dozed.

When Miles pointed out we had to be getting close to the border, the twins and Stepan grew so excited they could hardly sit still, wanting to be the first to spot the crossing. I finally told them it would be at least another day and they settled down, keeping themselves amused with talking about the ship we'd take to America.

That night, when everyone around us was asleep, Dmitri kissed me until I thought I was going to just melt into him. I clung to him, wanting the night to go on and on. At some point I fell asleep and dreamed we were back in our house and people were pounding on the doors and breaking the windows. I tried to scream for them to go away, but they wouldn't stop.

"Lottie, Lottie." I woke up to find Dmitri shaking me gently. "You're having a bad dream," he said. He put his arms back around me. "Go back to sleep now."

I may have imagined it, but as I drifted off I thought he was singing to me, so softly it was almost a whisper. *Fly, my horses, at the gallop / to my dear, you know the way! / Fly, my horses, fly at the gallop / to my dear one's house, you know the way.*

Early the next morning, I was almost awake when I heard a terrible screeching sound, so loud it made my ears hurt, and then all of a sudden the car was tipping and everything and everyone was tumbling. Sophie was right next to me, so I grabbed her as she cried out. I was so groggy with sleep I didn't understand what was happening until the car tipped all the way over on its side, Stepan landed on both of us with a thud, and my head hit the wall. I heard screams and cries and Nika calling for me.

"We've derailed!" someone shouted. I saw Dmitri's face in front of mine. He had a cut on his forehead and blood was pouring out, dripping down on me. "I've got Nika," he said. "Are you all right?" He lifted Stepan off me. Stepan wasn't crying, but his face was so white I thought he might faint.

I remembered to breathe. "I'm all right, I think. Where are Miles and Hap?" I looked around and felt the panic rising in me. Why didn't I see them?

"Here," Hap called, already shifting baggage around and reaching out a hand to help Miles up. Miles didn't look hurt from what I could see, but then he turned to one side and threw up.

"Where's Musya?" Nika cried.

"She's here," Dmitri said. "Still in her basket." The kitten had its claws dug into the wicker like it never intended to let go. It looked up at us and blinked its eyes.

Sophie sobbed in relief and grabbed the basket.

I managed to stand up. "We need to get out of here so I can put a bandage on your head," I said to Dmitri. Dmitri put his hand to his forehead as if just realizing he was bleeding.

Hap moved over to the door and helped people climb through, encouraging them to move along so everyone could get out. I took along one of the bags, which had an extra petticoat of mine. I could tear it up and use it for bandages.

Once we were outside, I stood still, trying to understand what I was seeing. It was as if we were looking at a battle scene.

"We're lucky we didn't have a working stove," Dmitri said grimly. Two of the cars ahead of us were on fire, and there were people being helped off who I could see had been burned. The panic bubbled up again but I pushed it down. I was a nurse. I could help them. I had to concentrate on the task at hand.

I ripped off a piece of the petticoat and handed it to Dmitri. "Hold this to your head," I said. "I have to help the others."

I moved among the people, trying to help those who were hurt, but besides bandaging there wasn't much I could do except urge people to keep the injured victims warm so they wouldn't go into shock. I was relieved to find that another nurse had been aboard, and she and I set a woman's broken arm. Some of the men took charge of the dead, putting them close to the engine and covering them with donated blankets. I didn't want to know how many there were.

I kept repeating to myself, *Keep to the task at hand*, though some of the burns were so horrific it was hard to keep my voice calm when I tried to comfort the victims.

I finally took a break to check on the others and found them back in the tipped-over car. Some of the other passengers had rearranged their belongings and were sitting on what was now the floor, huddled together to keep warm. I saw tracks in the snow as if some had started to walk to safety but then turned back.

"We can't just wait here," I said to Dmitri. "Some of the injured need to get to a hospital."

"Someone is going to have to come clear the tracks of the damaged cars or no trains are going to get through," Dmitri said. He looked over at Sophie and Nika and Stepan, who were playing with the kitten. He lowered his voice. "The engineer is among the dead, but some men set off for help. They said the next station is only a few miles ahead."

Shouts came from outside. Hap jumped up and moved to the door. "It's Cossacks," he called.

My heart skipped a beat. "That might be a problem," I said,

trying to stay calm. The Cossacks had always been a mystery to me, sometimes bloodthirsty and violent in carrying out the czar's orders, especially during the pogroms, and sometimes acting as the most disciplined of soldiers. I had no idea where their loyalties lay with the czar imprisoned.

"No, I think they've come to help," Hap said. "They're carrying supplies."

There were dozens of them, and they were indeed there to help, lighting campfires and sharing food. I went back to helping the wounded and didn't realize how many hours had passed until I heard the sound of a train chugging toward us.

The passengers took up a cheer. I watched the train draw closer and saw men leaning out the windows. They were all in uniform, and they were all wearing red bands.

Dmitri came up beside me.

"I didn't know the Bolsheviks had moved this far east," I said.

"It's probably mostly political prisoners who were freed from the Siberian prisons. Word has spread and they're organizing everywhere. And I'm sure some of them are former army who deserted months ago to go home."

I wrapped my arm in his. "It doesn't matter. They won't be looking for any aristocrats from Petrograd, and you look like a regular person now anyway."

The train came to a stop and the soldiers poured out of it. The passengers fell silent. The leader, who had red bands around both arms, moved among the crowd, followed by two men who acted as if they were his bodyguards.

My hands began to sweat. I didn't like the looks of them. The leader stopped a man, and though I couldn't hear what he said, the passenger got out a paper and handed it to him. The other soldiers had spread out and were walking around looking at everyone. I knew they were trying to determine who might have money or valuables.

"Why are they asking for papers?" a woman next to us said.

One man walked right up to us and stood too close. He stared at Dmitri. "You look familiar," he said, spitting out a sunflower seed shell. "What's your name, comrade?"

I saw Dmitri's jaw clench. "I don't speak Russian," Dmitri said in English.

The man peered at him. "I swear I know you."

Dmitri looked back at him as if he hadn't understood.

"You remind me of a lieutenant I had in the west. One of the stinking officers who thought they were better than us and could give us orders."

Dmitri stayed motionless. The man pointed a finger at him. "Don't you move. I want to talk to the captain about you."

The others had gathered around us. Nika grabbed Dmitri's hand. "Do you know that man?" she asked.

"He was part of a group trying to rebuild a bridge," Dmitri said. "I was assigned to oversee it. He didn't like that I knew more than him about bridges. Stay here, all of you."

"Where are you going?" I asked, dread filling me.

"I need to get away. Hap hasn't added me to one of the passports and there isn't time now. I'll only put you in danger if that soldier recognizes me."

I heard a man cry out in pain and looked to see someone doubled over, clutching his stomach. The leader stood over him with his fist clenched, as if he had just punched him.

Another woman screamed as a different soldier tried to pull a ring off her finger. He hit her and she fell down as he wrenched her finger again. A shot rang out and a passenger, an old man, fell to the ground.

"We all need to get out of here," I said. "Hap, can you grab my bag that has the magic boxes in it and do it so no one notices? And get anything else you can carry."

"We aren't going to be able to get very far," Miles said. "Not in the snow and not with the twins. And it's going to be dark soon." A few of the passengers had taken off running, and there were already soldiers in pursuit.

"I've got an idea." Dmitri looked over at the Cossacks' horses, which were hobbled together in a bunch. "I talked to some of those men while you were helping the passengers. They're definitely not Bolsheviks."

I noticed that the Cossacks were gathering together in a group close to their horses and they all had weapons. I knew what Dmitri was thinking.

"You're not the only one who knows how to ride, right?" Dmitri asked me.

"No, we all ride, but the twins only ride ponies."

"That's fine. We'll put them up with two of you."

"Do you really think they're going to sell us some horses?" Miles said. He understood too.

"Dmitri and I will go find out. The rest of you stay here."

Dmitri and I walked over to the Cossacks, who were still in some major discussion. There were fewer of them than there were of the Bolsheviks, but they had the horses, and every single man had a weapon. I didn't see many weapons among the soldiers who had gotten off the train.

Dmitri went over to one man. "Friend, we've got a problem." He pointed over to the children. "We need to get them away from here.

I know you have extra horses, and we'd be willing to pay you quite a bit to borrow them for a few hours."

The man drew back. "Borrow? How would you get them back to us?"

"We'd ride them across the border and then tie them up. You can retrieve them later." Dmitri pulled out a small roll of money and tried to give it to the man. "This is good pay for renting horses. We only need four of them, and just your pack animals, not your best horses, of course."

The man looked over at the children and then back at us. "I don't know. What if someone steals the horses before we can get them back?"

I pulled the bag out from underneath my shirt and took out both a ruby necklace and a diamond one. They glittered in the sunlight.

"These are very valuable," I said, handing them to the man. "They'll buy you supplies and horses for a year."

He held the necklaces up. "I give you my word they are real," I said. "And I really want to get my family to a safe place. My little sisters are only five, and they are very scared."

I held my breath. The soldiers were getting closer to our train car.

The man put the necklaces in his pocket and motioned to someone next to him. "Give them four horses," he said. "You can have them. No borrowing necessary." He turned to Dmitri and began to give him directions on how to get across the border.

I motioned for the others to join us. The captain of the Bolsheviks had gotten about halfway down the train, talking to each person. The ones who had tried to get away were dragged to him, several of them with bleeding mouths and noses from the soldiers hitting them with rifle butts.

"You are attracting some interest, my friend," the Cossack said to

Dmitri. "We may be able to give you some help. We've decided we don't like these men on our territory. As soon as you are ready to ride, we will begin to let them know exactly who we are."

"Thank you," Dmitri said.

I didn't know how Dmitri had become their friend so quickly, and I didn't have time to ask him.

The Cossacks surrounded us to hide us from view as we got organized. "Stepan, you ride with Hap, all right?" Dmitri said. "You two are going to go first. Miles, you put Sophie up with you, and you follow Hap and Stepan. Nika, you're going to ride with Charlotte."

Tears were running down Nika's face. I'd never seen her so scared before. She held out the basket with the kitten to Dmitri. "We don't have to leave her behind, do we?"

"No, of course not. Who do you think is coming with me?" Dmitri put the kitten in his bag and slung it over his shoulder. "I'm going last. No matter what happens, keep going in that direction." He pointed down the tracks. "Ride until you see an abandoned house. That means you've crossed the border."

"Better hurry," the Cossack called. "We can't wait much longer."

We got everyone up. The Cossack called back to us again. "Wait for the first shot, friends." The men around us moved forward until we were behind all of them. Their horses stamped their feet and blew air out their noses as if eager to charge.

When the shot rang out, Hap jerked, but his horse stayed calm. "Now," Dmitri said. "Hap, go!" Hap took off, Stepan behind him, clinging to his waist. Miles followed. Sophie had her face buried in Miles's back.

"Ready, Nika. Hold on," I said as I urged the horse forward. Even the Cossacks' least valuable horses were wonderful. They ran flat out as if they could go on for hours.

I heard shouts of "Stop!" and then more gunfire. The horses kept on. I didn't look back, fearing I'd unbalance Nika. I prayed Dmitri was still behind me. We couldn't have come so far only to be stopped before we reached the border. I was finished with violent, greedy men. They weren't going to win.

As we moved farther away, I began to breathe more easily. The Bolsheviks didn't have horses and they couldn't catch up with us. When I saw the house ahead of me, I slowed down. "Are you all right, Nika?" I said over my shoulder.

A muffled *yes* sounded. "Keep holding on." I looked back. Dmitri was nowhere in sight. I pulled the horse up. "Dmitri!" I yelled. There wasn't any answer.

"Where are they?" Nika cried.

"Hold on. I'm going to let you off at the house and then I'll go look for him."

I dropped her off with the others. Both twins were crying. I thought about telling Hap and Miles what to do if I didn't come back and then I decided I was coming back, no matter what.

I turned the horse around and galloped back toward the train. I came up over a hill and saw Dmitri walking toward me, leading his horse. He didn't look hurt, but I urged the horse to go faster.

When I reached him, I swung down and flung myself at him. "What happened?"

"The horse stepped in a hole and went down. It's lame. You shouldn't have come back."

"Of course I came back. We're not going to leave you behind."

He hugged me and then stepped back. I didn't like the solemn look on his face. I'd hoped I'd been wrong, but I knew what that look meant.

"I know what you are going to say," I told him. "I suppose I've known all along you wouldn't come with us, so you don't have to give me any explanations. You're going back to join up with the Cossacks, aren't you?"

"Yes," he said. "They know where there are some other regiments forming that I can join."

I leaned my head against the horse's neck, feeling the warmth against my face.

Dmitri pulled me away from her, drawing me back into his arms as he whispered, "I'm sorry. I have to do this."

"I know." I felt a tear run down my face.

The horse turned her head and bumped me, blowing out her breath.

"I think she wants a treat," I said, trying to get control of myself, trying to talk about nothing to stretch out the moment.

"She deserves it after that run, but she'll have to wait a bit," Dmitri said.

He took the gold ring off his finger and then placed it in my hand. "I wish I had something else to give you to remember me by," he said. "But at the moment I only have this."

I looked down at it and then at him. I didn't know what he meant by giving it to me. To cover my confusion, I said, "It looks old."

He smiled. "It is old. The bird on it is a falcon, the symbol of the Sokolov name. Someday I will have a ring made just for you, and it will be of a firebird." He twirled a strand of my hair in his fingers. "That should be the symbol of you, Charlotte Danielovna. You bring light where there is darkness." He put his hand on mine and closed my fingers around the ring and kissed me, just once and not for long enough.

"After the war, you'll know where to find me," he said. "Send a message to my house in Petrograd and I will meet you anywhere you say. If you don't want to come back to Russia, I'll meet you in America."

"I'll find you," I said as I put the ring in my pocket. "And I'll keep the ring, but I don't need it to remember you."

He kissed me again. "I know, but it will make me happy to think of you with it."

I took a deep breath and then put my horse's reins in his hands. "You take her. I'll take the lame one."

A squeaking sound came from his bag. Dmitri opened it up and pulled out the kitten. "I'd better leave Musya with you or the twins will come after me."

I took the kitten and held it close, feeling its heart beating.

"Someday we'll ride together again, Charlotte Danielovna," Dmitri said, swinging himself up in the saddle. "And you'll teach me how to juggle."

I smiled, though the tears were still running down my face. "Goodbye, Dmitri Antonovich." I turned and led the horse away. I knew Dmitri was watching me but I didn't look back, not then. I couldn't.

When I joined the others, I put a smile on my face and handed the kitten to Nika. "Let's go," I said. "We'll meet up with Dmitri later." I held up my hand to stop the questions. "And we'll talk later. We need to get somewhere warm."

The others went ahead of me and I let myself look back then. Dmitri had ridden to the top of the hill and was watching us. He raised his hand. I took the ring out of my pocket and put it on my finger, then raised my hand too.

"We'll be back," I whispered. "We'll be back."

Notes

Like all writers of historical fiction, I found it a challenge to decide what to include in this story and what to leave out. Writing a book set during the Russian revolution viewed from the eyes and knowledge of an American girl meant I had to narrow my focus to a short time frame and a small fraction of what was a very turbulent and complicated series of events over a long span of time. Years of oppression of the Russian people preceded the revolution, and many factions were involved, some working for their own interests, and others for the interests of the country. I couldn't include the whole history of these events, but I hope what I did include will give readers an understanding of a tiny part of it. Some of the actual time line is condensed by a few weeks for purpose of the narrative.

I chose to make the main character an American who wants to belong to a place even though she is considered a foreigner there because I had a friend in college who went through a similar experience. He'd lived abroad most of his life, and coming to the United States to attend college had him questioning what the concept of home really meant.

Many of the characters in *Gone by Nightfall* were inspired by actual people.

Dmitri Sokolov, the Russian tutor, was inspired by a man named Nicholas Wreden, who wrote about his experiences in *The Unmaking of a Russian* many years after he escaped from Russia and became the editorial director at a publishing company, E. P. Dutton.

Charlotte Mason was inspired by two different young women, one British and one American. Meriel Buchanan was the daughter of the British ambassador to Russia and lived there for many years, at one point falling in love with a young Russian duke, who eventually broke off the relationship when his father forbade him to marry a girl who was not Russian. The American girl, Miriam Jones Artsimovitch, came to Russia at nine years old when her mother divorced her father to marry a Russian aristocrat. Miriam did end up marrying the Russian baron she fell in love with, eventually reuniting with him in France. Both girls had harrowing escapes from Russia.

Meriel Buchanan wrote several books about her time in Petrograd, including *Petrograd, the City of Trouble, 1914-1918* and *Ambassador's Daughter*.

Unfortunately there is no book written about Miriam Artsimovitch, but I pieced together her story through newspaper articles and mentions of her in other books. I have more information about her on my website.

Charlotte's mother has died by the time the book begins, but she was inspired by an American woman who went by a few different first names, including Lilie and Madeline. I don't think either of those names is on her birth certificate. Lilie/Madeline grew up in rural Iowa, the daughter of a grain-elevator operator. After some earlier marriages that ended in divorce, she married a Russian count and was involved in quite a bit of the intrigue surrounding the Russian imperial court. Part of her story is told in *The Countess from Iowa* by Countess Nostitz (Lilie de Fernandez-Azabal).

Carter Jenkins, the journalist, was inspired by two fearless American journalists, Arno Dosch-Fleurot, of the *New York World,* and photographer Donald Thompson, who worked for *Leslie's Illustrated Weekly.* I learned about both men in *Caught in the Revolution* by Helen Rappaport.

There were many other books I used in my research. Some of the most helpful were:

A Russian Princess Remembers: The Journey from Tsars to Glasnost by Ekaterina Meshcherskaya

Red Princess: A Revolutionary Life by Sofka Zinovieff

An Estonian Childhood: A Memoir by Tania Alexander

The House by the Dvina: A Russian Childhood by Eugenie Fraser

Former People: The Final Days of the Russian Aristocracy by Douglas Smith

The Russian Countess: Escaping Revolutionary Russia by Edith Sollohub

Tattered Banners: A Life in Imperial Russia by Paul Rodzianko

Witness to Revolution: The Russian Revolution Diary and Letters of J. Butler Wright by William Thomas Allison

Acknowledgments

Getting this book out into the world was such a team project, I don't want to forget anyone who contributed. Thanks to readers who offered encouragement in the early stages: Krista Boyle, Tricia Kennedy, and Raye Sifri, and to all the writers at Women Writing for a Change. The group's enthusiasm and support helped me regain the love of writing when I had taken on too many projects at once and was feeling completely overwhelmed.

Many thanks to my Russian reader, Irina Vadimovna Kuznetcova, who guided me in my attempts to get the details right. Any mistakes are of course my own, because they can sneak in without me noticing.

Thanks to Kell Andrews, Ilene Ross Tucker, Donna Mazzoni, and Elliot Spieler, who offered up names of their worthy relatives for me to use as character names.

And of course, thanks to my agent, Moe Ferrara, and my editor, Kat Brzozowski, and the whole team at Swoon Reads. The two-sentence plot idea was the easy part. Actually coming up with the character motivations and a story that held together took quite a group effort.

As always, thanks to my family: Dean, Garret, and Hope, who are involved in every part of the process, from brainstorming to reading early drafts to checking the final version, and who had to put up with a house overflowing with research books for months and months. They came out of this process knowing far more about Russian history than they ever expected to know, but at least they got quite a bit of good Russian chocolate out of it as well.

Finally, thanks to the librarians at the Public Library of Cincinnati and Hamilton County. I can't imagine writing a book without them.

DID YOU KNOW...

readers like you helped to get this book published?

Join our book-obsessed community and help us discover awesome new writing talent.

1

Write it.
Share your original YA manuscript.

2

Read it.
Discover bright new bookish talent.

3

Share it.
Discuss, rate, and share your faves.

4

Love it.
Help us publish the books you love.

Share your own manuscript or dive between the pages at **swoonreads.com** or by downloading the **Swoon Reads app**.